Tina Colt – Role/

## Prologue

The outlines of the house afar, and even with my eyes closed, I could have found my way there because I knew the rough connecting road very well, every stone and pothole, the trees, and bushes along the roadside. I couldn't erase a single moment of leaving this property from my memory. Now, ten years later, I approach stealthily, just as I did back then, hoping no one would notice me. My rusty old car had run out of fuel miles ago. I barely turned onto the small access road when the car gave up and stopped with a groan I clawed, I got out and kicked the door, but it proved to be tougher than I expected, and my foot throbbed from the release of my anger. Typical, I muttered under my breath. I grabbed my two suitcases and quietly, sneakily, made the remaining few meters. The gate was wide open, just as it was back then. Perhaps out of nostalgia, I would have stopped and surveyed the area, checking if the old walnut tree or the weeping willow had changed, how much the paint on the porch had faded, and if my mother's favourite rocking chair was still outside. But now, shame allowed me only a quick glance at my surroundings, and I hurried inside. Upon reaching the veranda, I felt a familiar tightness in my chest: I'm here, I've arrived. I've come home...

Did I make the right decision, or should I turn back? Perhaps no one saw me? Should I continue what I started? But no, it's not possible. I must start over from here, if such a thing exists. With that thought, I closed the heavy entrance door behind me. Almost nothing had changed. It was as if time had stood still. The same familiar scent greeted me inside the house. Carefully, I turned on the lights, and despite the passing years, I instinctively knew where to reach for the switch.

Everything was the same, just as if I were watching an old movie. Vivid images flickered before my eyes. Time stood still. The only difference would be that I knew Beth wouldn't come up to me, asking what she should cook for me and what happened to me that day.

Stepping into the foyer, memories rushed over me: I found it strange that these memories didn't bring sadness, but made me smile. Like when my father used to play with me as a child, or how my mother and I would do homework here. The battleground of sibling fights. Guests always took their seats on the large, flowery couch. Pictures of us lined the fireplace mantel across from it. Mine was from ten years ago. The usual feeling tried to creep back into my heart and soul. I felt a bitter taste welling up inside me, but I pushed it back. I hesitantly turned on the lights in this room too, perhaps afraid that my conscience would appear before me, and I might not bear it. Nothing happened, no one and nothing appeared, only thousands of memories. Yielding to curiosity, I circled the house. The hallway led to the kitchen, the dining room, and at the back, Mary's room, who used to be our nanny and my mother's helper. The upstairs had four rooms: mine, my siblings', and my parents'.

I entered my room and saw, to my misfortune, that everything was just as I left it. Various unbearable rock band posters adorned the walls. Provocative slogans were everywhere, and I had painted my pink sheets black, creating an impression of one big black void. If it hadn't been ten o'clock at night and I hadn't driven hundreds of miles, I would have cleaned everything right away. But I went back to the living room and laid my head down on the couch, drifting off to sleep...

*Five years old. Dad was beating Mom. He cried a lot. Mom was always sad. She wrung her hands. We were poor, barely had enough to eat, yet Dad was always drunk. Became a withdrawn little boy...*

## Chapter one

I woke up to shouting in the morning, with a feeling that I overslept, but I could see that dawn was just breaking. I remembered how much I hated waking up early, but on a farm, there's no Sunday or holiday, every day is the same, and always must wake up early. Just as Dad always said, the animals are hungry; they don't have days off or holidays. I got up, sneaked up the stairs to my room, as if I were still a teenager, and tried to push away the responsibility, just as I did back then. Not successfully. First, it was the rustling, then the sound of the coffeemaker, and finally, the smell of coffee lured me downstairs. To my great surprise, my former nanny, Mary, was bustling behind the gas stove.

"If you came for the funeral, you're a bit late, about a year and a half." She says it without even turning around, just going about her usual motions. Automated movements, as they had become ingrained over thirty years. I regretted many things, if not everything I did back then, but I wasn't the type to admit it. I sat down behind her at the kitchen table, just as before, and observed the former and one of the most important persons in my life from behind. She still wore the same floral dress, of course, perfectly ironed, a white shirt and an apron embodied in her favourite attire.

"I thought I arrived just in time," I say with a hint of mockery in my voice, just like when I was a teenager. Finally, she turned around, holding my favourite mug filled with coffee in her hand, and handed it to me. How did she know I drink coffee in the morning? It will remain a secret, like so many other things...

"You could use a proper meal, it seems," she says. The passage of time was clear on her, but she still appeared the same to me. Perhaps time had been kind to her, or maybe she was still the same for me, unchanged. Her mouth tightened into a thin line, as always, when she pouted about something. It wasn't any different this time. I almost smiled.

"I guess there still aren't any fast-food restaurant around here." I ran my fingers through my hair. This wasn't exactly how I wanted to start the first day of my new life, but just as the leopard cannot change its spots, I won't become a repentant little girl. At least no one sees that in the end... No matter how much I want it, it's not possible. "Let's forget it. Thank you for the coffee." With that, I went upstairs, leaving Mary with her doubts.

The elderly woman couldn't keep this news to herself for long; she knew this girl would eventually come back, although she expected it a bit earlier. This comforted the girl's mother, and now she is here, visibly well. She quickly goes and tells Jack, and from then on, everyone will know...

*Seven years old. They run away with Mom. They travel a lot. By train, by bus, on foot. His mother often looks back. He's a little scared. He had to leave all his toys behind. His mother promised to buy new ones. His mother no longer cries. She works a lot at her new job, but she's no longer sad. He gets new toys too. He feels lonely. His mother is always working. He's alone...*

## Chapter two

Upstairs, after finishing my coffee, I started cleaning my room. How difficult it was to say or even think about it, that this is my room. I haven't had a room in ten years. At first, I only had a bed, which could barely be called that, more like a cot. Then I had an apartment. But this was different. My room. My home. I savoured the word. Three garbage bags filled with ugly pictures hanging on the wall, remnants of my teenage years, and even more darkness. Back then, I reassured myself by thinking that I must have been adopted, that I couldn't be the child of these two perfect people when I was so imperfect. I longed for success, for recognition, while my parents were content with their insignificant lives. That's what I thought back then, and the regret had filled my recent past crept back in and filled me again. Ten years ago, I left just as I arrived last night... sneakily.

I had an argument with my mother for the hundredth time that month, but this one was different because she said that I could finally start thinking about my future and not live in a dream world. Made me so angry because I couldn't understand why they didn't see. All I thought about was my future. That's why I was on a diet, wearing makeup. I couldn't understand why they didn't see, why they didn't hear. Something snapped inside me then. I did it with Daniel. We were together; it was a great love, but I didn't want to let my future slip away. I knew I wasn't meant for Daniel. So, I ran away. I had a few names of where to go and who to contact. I realised my parents would never accept me for who I am. My sister had already made a successful career as an economist, and my younger sister knew she wanted to be a psychologist. And I wanted to be an actress, but no one believed me, no one believed in me, at least that's how I felt. So, I sneaked away and never looked back. No phone calls, no postcards. For ten long years.

I kept in touch with my younger sister just so they would know I was alive and wouldn't send anyone after me. At school excelled and graduated with honours, but so did every other student. Then came the "casting couches," and here I am today. I snuck away from there, too. I'm not proud because I can't be. There's nothing to be proud of. I didn't achieve a shining career. I made a few foolish mistakes, learned a lot of lessons. And here I am again, where it all started. The pride I feel is so far away. Every waking moment is filled with agony. I stay clean despite the difficulties. That's what I promised, at least as long as I can. After clearing out the things I considered trash, there was almost nothing left inside.

"I must go into town; do you need anything? "I asked Mary, who was busy cooking lunch. Some things never change. I didn't know how many workers there were on the Farm now, but in my youth, I thought there were a lot. Mary cooks for them every single day.

"And how are you going to go? With that old clunker you came home with? "

"I thought I'd borrow one of Dad's cars. He doesn't need them anymore."

"Watch your mouth, young lady!" she scolds me, just like she used to. "By the way, we had to sell them."

"What? He sold the only things of value?"

"Times were tough, and your father had to decide either the cars or the Farm."

"It's obvious what he had chosen. My goodness!" I slumped into a chair next to the kitchen table. It must have been a tough time if Dad had to sell his cherished cars. They were his only hobbies, collecting those cursed cars, and he had to sell them. And the birds too. It brought even greater remorse. Maybe if I had been here, if I hadn't left, if I hadn't chased my own dreams. I stormed out onto the terrace in anger and slammed the door shut. A tear doesn't mean much. I don't shed any, not anymore. That wouldn't be me. My mouth tightened into a thin line. Overwhelmed by impotent anger, I kicked the support pillar; unfortunately, it turned out to be solid. Don't kick things when you weigh fifty kilos. You might hurt yourself, right? I sat down, swearing, and stared ahead, trying to gather my thoughts.

"You can take mine. It's in the garage," Mary called out through the mosquito net.

"Thank you." With that, I pulled a baseball cap over my head and set off. Not that I thought anyone would recognise me as an actress, I was much more afraid of being recognised as the destroyer of everyone's youth. I always had an unusual system of judgment, and it wasn't exactly the fairest. For example, I had an unbearable classmate named Samantha, who always teased everyone because she was rich and beautiful with curly blond hair. Well, I made sure she wasn't. I stuck her hair with chewing gum. Or there was a boy, Steve, I think, who mocked me, saying I would never have a boyfriend, so I made sure he wouldn't have a girlfriend either. I put bugs in his pants in front of everyone's eyes, and he had no choice but to get rid of his clothes and run to the boys' bathroom in just his underwear. I could list more of my heroic deeds, but they didn't get me anywhere... Yet here I am again. Head down, wearing a cap, but still here.

"Take that gun and shoot! Don't be such a mommy's boy!" The gun is bigger than the six-year-old boy. The boy is crying. He doesn't want to shoot his favourite dog, but dad says it barks too much and needs to be killed. And he must do it.
"I am not able," the boy cries.
"If you don't shoot it, I'll shoot all the puppies, too. You must be brave!" he yells at him. The boy has known how to shoot for a long time. He learned to shoot even before he learned to walk. He raised the gun, which was almost bigger than him, and shot the dog in the head. The dog had six puppies that will surely miss her. His older brother would have shot it a long time ago, not because he was such a tough boy, but because he feared his father more than he loved the dog or anything else. That's why his father always praised him. He wished his father would praise him too, but he loved that dog...

## Chapter three

The town didn't grow any larger than before, but progress was noticeable. All the shops could be found, serving the needs of the people around here. Not more, not less. The centre of the town was enriched with a fountain and a park. It looked friendly. Surrounding it were benches, small shops, the council, an ice cream parlour, a library, and a pastry shop. The population was only a few thousand when I left, and it was unlikely that many people had moved here since then, so of running into someone I knew. But I hoped that nobody would remember me anymore. I chose the largest shopping centre, which was located further out of the town centre, almost in another city, because people were less attentive to each other there and walked with determination, not looking to the right or left. I just tossed items into my basket and headed straight to the checkout. After paying, I realised that my cash was running low, so I will have to use my savings soon. I can't live from the Farm money; it would be unauthorised. That's how I felt. I was so absorbed in my calculations that I didn't notice I had already crossed the parking lot and was on the road until I heard screeching brakes and a honk. I started apologising for not paying attention, and the driver cursed at me. Then, for a moment, I looked up into those blue eyes that haunted my teenage dreams. I quickly averted my gaze, hastily loaded my car, and drove away as far as the old van would allow. Daniel Jacobs. I hoped the man didn't recognise me.

When I arrived home, I was surprised to see that there were only six workers, and they were eating inside the house. I only knew the older ones who expressed their joy at my return. Jack was on good terms with Mary, but I remembered little else. I didn't want to get in their way, so I went upstairs to start my own tasks. A few hours later, I could finally say that I was done. I had painted the wall white. Three times.

Why didn't my hands break because of the black paint back then? What a terrible teenager I must have been.

Now I just had to wait for the wall to dry enough so I could put the cabinets back in place. The double bed was promised to arrive in the afternoon. If nothing else, I wanted to keep this luxury for myself—to sleep in an enormous bed.

"Jade, come downstairs and eat right now!" Mary called, just like she used to. Long ago, maybe I would have retorted that I couldn't eat that much, or greasy food, or that she couldn't cook well, but now I was grateful that someone cared even a little about me. Besides, I felt starving. The workers had already left, and during these times, we women could eat as well. That was always the way. My mother, my siblings, and I would sit together at the table, having fun. Then I started growing up and began talking back, saying that this wasn't a society of slaveholders anymore, where women were worthless, and so on. It was so typical of me. If I could go back, I would slap myself. We quietly finished the meal, and I enjoyed having cooked food on the table. A car's sound broke the silence, but it meant nothing to me since so many people always came here. Then the sound of footsteps, and finally a voice from the door.

"Guess what, Nana? "Mary was only called that by one person, her grandson. "I almost hit a woman at the supermarket. She was walking on the road, and she looked exactly like Jade." as he finished speaking, he entered the kitchen. My hand had already stopped in mid-air, Mary's eyes scrutinised me, and Daniel paused for a moment. "Oh, hi Jade. I thought it was just a nightmare."

"I'm glad to see you too, Daniel. "I pushed my chair away from the table, considering the meal and the conversation finished.

"How dare you just come back like this?!" he suddenly interrupted with his question.

"I don't even know, Dan.

"Stop, if I'm talking to you! "He called after me from the bottom of the stairs. He had aged, just like me, but he looked good, more masculine in his body and his face had become more mannish, in a good way.
"I thought I was the one living in this house, so maybe you don't have the right to question me. This is a free country, Daniel, read the law. I'm going wherever I want!" With that, I climbed up the stairs and pondered once again whether it was a good idea to come back, but I didn't want to think about that person who was the reason I'm here. About his touch, the smile he rarely showed.

I analysed over this question as many times as my sense of shame and desire to escape allowed me. I no longer had a place in the capital. Why? Was I running away? Yes. Was I made mess? Yes. But does he miss me? Is he looking for me? If he was looking for me or missing me, he would be here by now. But why would he miss me when I gave him everything? What would he use me for if I've already been used for what he was needed for and ultimately discarded? When will the feeling of longing, loneliness, disappointment, and shame after being thrown away fade within me? I know it's only a matter of time, but I want to speed it up, so it doesn't hurt anymore.

A few hours later, after clarifying things within myself, I sat in the dining room again, listening to Mary's stories that always cheered me up. It was probably around seven in the afternoon, and dark clouds were gathering in the sky. The elderly woman glanced outside with a worried look while trying to lift the spirits of the girl she considered her granddaughter.

A young boy rushed in, whom I had seen during lunch; he couldn't have been over twenty, with a hint of hair on his chin.
"Mary, Jack isn't feeling well, but the storm is coming, and the animals are out on the hill!" I didn't need to hear more; I jumped up as if I had been doing this my whole life.

"Call the ambulance and stay with Jack. Leave the rest to me. Who else can come with me? "I turned to the boy.
"Just me. The others have already left," he replies.
"Then let's go! "I quickly grabbed one of my mother's boots and coat, and I was already outside. My heart was pounding wildly as I approached the barn to find a horse for myself. My favourite horse had long since passed away, and I could only survive that loss through a great ordeal.

So, I saddled up the first horse that came my way, four times more skilfully than the boy. I suspected the youngster was still learning the job.

I doubted the boy had never gone out to fetch the animals before because he was still in the learning phase of his training, but he had all the theoretical knowledge. I could see the fear in his eyes, worrying about what would happen if he fell off the horse or if it became wild. If we hadn't been in such a dire situation, I might have even smiled. But I knew time was of the essence because we had little chance of finding any stranded animals in the storm. I encouraged the boy's horse with words, and it responded with loud snorts, as if expressing its agreement. I rode ahead, feeling exhilarated and forgetting how liberating it felt to ride, to become one with nature. The rain poured down as if someone were pouring it from a bucket when we reached the end of the Farm. It seemed significantly smaller than before, and there were only about a hundred lambs in the herd. I would have stopped to chat about the enormous hole at the end of the fence and where the rest of the animals had gone, but the boy was quite frightened. I simply showed the way to the lambs, and off they went and felt relieved that they were not cattle. We herded them into the pen, and by that time, the boy said he would take over. I told him to come into the house when he was done because I needed to talk to him. Then I hurried to check on Jack.
The ambulance was already parked in front of the house.

"Good evening!" I greeted the medical assistant closest to me. "What can you tell me?"

"Unfortunately, it was a heart attack, but a mild one. He will recover; he was lucky we were nearby. We need to take him in for observation. But if everything goes well in a few days, we'll release him. I already told Mary to cook less richly for the old man because it will eventually harm him," he says while filling out paperwork under our eaves. Jack had been with us for about as long as Mary. They were here before I was born. Jack was a kind, soft-spoken old man. He reminded me of a kind, grey-haired grandfather. The paramedic didn't even look at me, and even if I had to know him from the past, I didn't know who he was. And it seemed he didn't know who I was, which was better for everyone.

"Thank you anyway.

"We're just doing our job. Goodbye, under different circumstances.

Jack was already lying inside the ambulance on the stretcher. He showed little sign of life. Mary was angry and sad, and I still had a few questions for her. I couldn't postpone them. We went inside. I rushed upstairs to get dry clothes. Then back down, hoping Mary was still in the kitchen. She was. She was brewing tea. I grabbed a mug for myself.

"I would like to ask a few things, "I tried to start gently, deviating from my usual manner. "How big is the Farm?"

"They took a piece from the end because that's how your father could pay the taxes.

"But who took the end piece? Which is quite an extensive area."

"The neighbour who lived behind us, or rather, doesn't live there anymore. It's just one of their many plots. Remember? They used to live here. They had two sons, Steve and Ben. And a daughter, I can't remember her name. The Starks. But as things got better, they moved to the city. They offered the best price for it."

"How many animals do we have left?"

"There are a few horses, the lambs, a few chickens, ducks, not much else."

"The rest had to be sold. "I didn't intend it as a factual question, more like a resigned statement. Why did this realisation hurt that the Farm was in decline? Why does it matter now when it didn't matter before? What made it different? Or am I just trying to shape out a purpose for myself? Because I have nothing left?

"I will not give a history lesson, but in 2008, the crisis hit us, and no one wanted beef anymore. Your father thought it best to get rid of them."

"Is everyone became vegetarian?"

"Don't pass judgment on your father when you weren't even here. It seemed like the right decision. Then he got sick and couldn't take care of it anymore."

"What do Penelope and the others say? "I referred to my siblings and tried to ignore the offense because it was completely true.

"They say nothing. Both have families and their own lives. They come by sometimes, but they don't know as much about it as you do."

"How much money is in the farm's safe, and who manages it?"

"Jack does. I think it's not in minus right now."

"But where does the income come from?"

"From the lambs' wool and meat, and they sell some things or exchange them for something else.

"Did you know there's a hole gaping in the fence? It seems like someone deliberately cut it."

"The lambs are being stolen, we know that, but we don't have enough people to monitor it. Even with this many people, it's still too much to handle."

"Still, what did Dad say? What does he want with this? Who did he expect to oversee it? And what about Mom?"

"He didn't want to sell it in his lifetime; John said he wouldn't write to sell it or divide it into three parts. He didn't say it, but

he hoped one of your spouses would know how it works and would stay."
"Ah, spouses, of course. "The boy entered, panting, still flushed from the previous run. There was concern in his eyes that truly captivated me, and I felt he was worth keeping. "I'm sorry, but I forgot your name.
"Thomas, ma'am, "he whispered.
"Ma'am is your great-aunt. I'm Jade. So, where do you live?"
"I live here on the farm because Jack allowed it, "he apologised.
"That's great, "I quickly interrupted, "because I'll need you early in the morning. We must mend the fence."
"Alright then... Jade, "he said, squeezing his cap as if hoping for salvation.
"So, tomorrow morning. Goodnight! "I regarded the conversation as concluded. His discomfort frustrated me as well. He said nothing, just silently closed the door behind him. I looked at Mary, who looked back at me. She didn't utter a word, just gazed into my eyes. My childhood shyness was long gone, so I allowed us to lock eyes.
"What do you want to do? Do you want to stay here? For how long?"
"I don't know. But in the meantime, I'll do something while I'm here."
"This is not a play that you can simply exit without consequences when the filming is over."
"At this moment, I'm in charge, even if you don't sympathise with me or my decisions, unless you've been hiding something, and they left it all up to you? "My mouth narrowed into a thin line; I didn't enjoy playing the boss, but now I was forced into it.
"How will you face the people? "She didn't respond to my previous statement.
"You're right, I should be ashamed for leaving, for not becoming famous, for making everyone's life miserable in my youth, for not coming home for the funeral, and we could go

on. You're right, but for now, you'll have to settle for me. "She stared at me with incredulous eyes, while tears welled up in my throat. "I suppose it doesn't matter that I've probably already paid for these mistakes."
"Let it go, Jade. Nothing will ever truly matter to you, will it?"
"I don't know what you mean by that, but I guess you do not know how important playing was to me. But I don't owe you an explanation; I thought you knew. "That's enough for today, and retreated to my room. I took out my worn-out collection of Chandler books and once again escaped into a fictional story, just as I used to do...

I woke up in the morning, not exactly refreshed, but in relatively good spirits. It was still dawn when Thomas and I folded the fence before the others started trickling in. Granted, the average age was sixty, and this was only possible because of me and Thomas. I had decided on a few major changes regarding the farm and was slowly getting ready to implement them. The last time I glanced at my phone, which I strictly kept in my room, deep in a drawer to avoid constant checking, I only received a banking SMS confirming that a certain amount had been deposited into my account, showing the successful sale of my flat; I just needed to collect the money for my car. With that money, perhaps I could restore the farm and then sell it, or I don't even know what else to do with it. I didn't think I wanted to stay here; every memory fills me with pain and shame. However, I owe it to my parents, their memory, to rebuild what was almost lost because of me. Thomas and I met at the pen at three o'clock; that's when he has some time to break away. I tried to teach him every day. He proved to be a good learner and curious, but very shy, so even if he knew something, it had to be drawn out of him, which wasn't ideal. There were situations where decisions had to be made quickly. I was very glad he was attentive and intelligent. I hoped that his shyness would diminish.

As the days went by, I tried to make up for the "lost" time, learning the ins and outs of running the Farm. In the afternoons, I would ride out and hoped to catch the thief.

This day was one of those. I rode out and stopped at a suitable distance with my horse, patting it to keep it from giving us away. I saw a rider approaching the fence from the other farm. From afar, he had an imposing build and figure. He went up to our fence, right where the cut was. But he just looked at it and turned back. Despite us folding it, someone had undone it again that same evening. I couldn't bring myself to spend a single night here or ask Tom to catch the thief. Usually, I just collapsed into bed and fell into a deep sleep; I assumed Tom was the same way. The unknown rider didn't look like a thief at all; his clothes cost more than our farm's monthly income, and his horse seemed well-groomed, as if it was brushed daily.

The fence wasn't too high for a racehorse, but I didn't dare risk chasing after the man with this horse. So, I turned the horse's back. But I thought I should go over to talk about the end of the Farm, about my lambs, and of course, I wanted to get a closer look at the man. That's just how incorrigible I am. I love handsome men, no denying that. Although now I can only look.

Upon returning to the house, I had to conclude that nobody had kept track of where and why the money went on paper. Not a single letter had been written in a year and a half! I wanted to see how much dad sold the Farm for and when. I found it; it was among the last entries. Since then, nothing. Great, it's lucky I know some bookkeeping too, like every actress. I had to learn this skill myself if I didn't want to be exploited by hyenas.

In the evening, Mary and I had our dinner. We talked even less that day. She made chicken pasta for dinner, which I loved, with mushrooms and extra parsley. I didn't think to ask what was bothering her; I suspected she would tell me soon enough. And that's what happened. We were already at our usual cup of tea when she dropped two newspapers in front of me.

"Look and admire your masterpiece! Again," she says, then withdrew to her room and closed the door. I didn't know what could be worse than this. The black sheep who abandoned her parents in trouble didn't amount too much; she didn't even show up for their funeral. How could this be surpassed? Filled with fear, I started flipping through the newspaper. First, the daily newspaper, which was over a month old. I wondered why do they waited until now for me to see it?

In the society section, towards the end, I found it. A picture of me, scantily clad, performing oral sex on Brandon, with his face perfectly visible, and his friend waiting in the line. Well, wasn't that the pleasant surprise in that morning?! The article was about how far the world of celebrities could sink. How true! My casting couch story began like everyone else's... Auditions, I went. I was chosen. I agreed. It was a tough month; I didn't get any roles, bills had to be paid, or I could have gone home in shame. That's when I had been there for two years. So, I would have agreed to anything, because earlier, I was even more vain, thinking I would show them I wouldn't slink back home and admit to my parents that I made a mistake, and they were right. It started with him coming over, and of course, sex was involved, and I got some roles what were enough to cover some expenses. Then I had to do more and more extreme things, but I didn't mind, because I was getting more roles and more money. And now, all I can notice is one of my legs sprawled across an armchair, while the other is spread wide on the floor...

*His mother is very ill. Although he studies well and behaves well. His stepfather is very kind to him, but it hurts him a lot. His mother is sick. He does everything he can, but still loses his mother. He doesn't talk to anyone...*

## Chapter four

My body lies on the cold floor. My attire is far from formal. Black gloves. Reaching up to my elbows, the strap of my bra slipped off my shoulder. From below, a boot and lace lingerie what appropriately revealing in the right place. That's all. Brandon's tongue is inside me, rough and wet, but it might just be my imagination because the amount of drug consumed doesn't let me feel anything.

I'm not even sure about the cold. It's just as I gather my thoughts the next day at the airport, these trivial details come to mind. The essence is still that I'm lying here, Brandon playing a tune on me with his mouth, his friend watching, and when he reaches an appropriate state of arousal, he pushes his friend aside. Throughout the night, they both enjoy every inch of my body, making love to me, or rather, I allow them to do whatever they want. This is my "casting couch". That's what I thought and did this for eight years.

Brandon would show up once a week or even more frequently, bringing along one of his dear or less dear friends. I became completely accustomed to these encounters, the special attention I received that my fellow actresses did not. This guy had been here before. He wasn't bad, had a sense of humour, quickly dispelling my fears before the first line; he wasn't rough even when he reached the end. Brandon didn't let himself be overshadowed. He wouldn't yield for a long time, and there were things he wouldn't allow anyone else to do. The sequence was always the same.

I would arrive at his place, or they would come to mine. We would drink, smoke weed, then the stronger drugs would come, and I would put on a sexy outfit. He never asked, always by my choice. When everything took effect, depending on his mood, it would happen on a bed, a couch, or on the floor. He would start licking, with his friend always watching. Then the friend would play with me, either anally or in the usual way, but no one else could touch me elsewhere. Then, after he ejaculated inside me, I had to perform oral sex on Brandon, but he never finished in my mouth. I could always sense when he was close, but it never happened. In those moments, he would lead me into his room, or we would go to my room, perhaps so his friends wouldn't see how tender he could be. He would completely undress me, wipe me down with disinfectant wipes, and kiss every inch of my body. Then, depending on his mood, he would either ejaculate anally or normally inside me, but he preferred the traditional way. Why did I do all this? Why do all girls do? I can't speak for the others, but I can speak for myself. It wasn't just for the roles, although that was dominant at the beginning. I didn't have the courage to become a waitress like many others did, and end up aging behind the bar, waiting for the big break. Strangers would grab their buttocks, enduring any kind of rudeness for a small tip. Or at least I did it for a short term... Looking back, maybe this was a less poor decision than mine. When I thought about all this, it was already too late... I fell in love with the owner of the casting couch. Irrevocably, I loved this morally questionable man. But what made it different?

That morning, around eight, he shook me awake after one of these encounters and told me I had to leave. He walked in from the kitchen, didn't look at me, just told me to get up. My head was a little fuzzy, but I sensed his anger. I didn't say a word; I started gathering my things. Usually, his friend would leave, and I would stay. Then we would have coffee together, but we never touched each other anymore. He was already dressed, wearing jeans and a tight white shirt.

When I went into the living room, his friend was still there. Half dazed, he lifted his gaze to me and asked if I wanted another round. Brandon told him I had to go. I looked at him from the doorway, hoping he would say something encouraging, craving every kind word, but his look held only pity, something I never wanted to see. That woke me up. It felt like a slap in the face. It was worse. I had to realise how much I humiliated myself. Again. And again. Why? For nothing. But I lost myself when I stood there trembling at the audition and he came over, reached out his hand towards me, and introduced himself.

From that moment on, he guided me, protected me, or so I felt. When I got my first role after a year of knowing him, that's when these encounters began. I still remember the first one very well... He didn't say it, but I knew I owed that role to him. Sometimes we would bump into each other on weekdays for a coffee or lunch. It was good for me to be seen with him, but I don't know what his intentions were. He probably did the same thing with someone else every day, the other event as well, but I didn't want to think about him doing this with someone else because even the thought of it made a knot in my stomach. This went on for almost seven years. I became a middle-tier actress because of him and probably not on giant posters in teenage boys' rooms, and teenage girls don't want to resemble me, but occasionally I get recognised, and that feels good. I have a car, an apartment, and a few valuable possessions, but must be careful with my wardrobe, so I can't wear the same thing twice, but I tried to solve it cleverly, selling it once I wore it, and so on and saved enough money to leave.

But do I have enough strength too? Can I stand my ground, no longer letting others dictate what I wear, where I go, what I do? Is there enough strength in me to run away and never see Brandon again? These thoughts rushed through my mind as I walked past the receptionist, who had seen worse, seen me in even more revealing attire. He smiled friendly, as always. The face of the man from moments ago, filled with pity, came to my mind again, and I felt determined. Gathering all my strength, I smiled back, gathering the last crumbs of my dignity, hailed a taxi, and took myself home. Standing at the airport, I didn't end up buying a ticket anywhere, spoke to my lawyer and, using the mannerisms of a hysterical actress; I pretended I wanted to sell everything I owned, and if that succeeded, I would buy a new house, a car; made up everything, and he believed that my current possessions were too small and not trendy enough and didn't want anyone to know where I was going or why and told him to transfer the money to my account, and I would call him once found a new place. I went back to where it all began. Home... And that's where I am now.

In the gossip magazine, the picture was the same, just as much bigger, and the article extensively described how I was just one among many who passed through Brandon's bed, and wondered what his wife and daughter would think of it. What?! How could I be so stupid? I could have easily found out. I just had to ask someone. But I probably didn't want to know. I still had hopes he loved me! A picture of his wife and daughter, barely visible, and she was a lady, not some third-rate actress. I was ashamed, not just because I was seen, well, also because of that, but Brandon... Was it true, and me...?

I stormed into my room and put on a coat. I had to go anywhere, everywhere. Away. The pouring rain didn't bother me. There was a storm. I ran, I ran as fast as I could, tears streaming down my face along with the rain. I ran towards the garden, just like I used to when felt hurt in my youth. Over the years; we don't give up our ingrained habits. My favourite tree at the edge of the garden was still standing there, just the same. It was a weeping willow, with such dense branches that even a grown person could crawl under it in complete tranquillity, knowing that it would protect from the rain and from the rest of the world. I huddled down at the base of the tree and continued sobbing. There was no better

place to hide, no deeper pit to sink into in a person's life. I always found someone or something to blame, but in the end, I was the only one responsible for what happened. I chased a foolish dream and gave up everything had value for it. And was the one who fell in love with this man and gave him everything. It is me, and me alone, who is to blame. "I put that rabbit in the hat, even if I deny it to myself..." What should I do? I felt like had no more strength to get up, was exhausted, and there was no "starting over" here. If I don't play this well – and I didn't play it well – it will have irreversible consequences for my future. I don't know how long I sat there, soaked in the rain, but I heard some movement, and the rain let up. I pulled my coat tightly around myself, feeling cold. The footsteps stopped near the tree, and Daniel crawled in beside me.
"I thought you would be here. "He placed a lantern between us. Until then, I hadn't even noticed that I was sitting in pitch darkness. He said nothing for a while, just gazed at the flame of the candle. I braced myself to receive his scolding, even if it was justified. I didn't have the strength to object.
"So, you saw," he finally spoke.
"Yes," that's all I say.
"Do you want to talk about it?"
"What should I talk about, Daniel? How have I messed everything up? How anything I touch turns to ruins, deteriorates, becomes a shame that I must leave behind? You know what happened. There was a girl who chased big dreams but achieved nothing. She left, abandoning everything, and ended up in a few shows through a casting couch, but she was foolish because she fell in love with the owner of the couch and believed that one day, when she had given up everything, this man would awaken and confess his love to her. And of course, it turned out that the man was married, and the entire world laughed at this foolish girl. Even without that information, I felt miserable and ashamed, and I regret not coming to the funeral, not being there in times of

trouble, and so much more. "I unloaded everything on him all at once because I knew him. How many times did we hide here back then? How much did we talk, and when it turned into love, we even kissed, of course!

"I have a story too, Jade, "he mumbled. "Once upon a time, there was a boy who didn't weave grand dreams. He was happy wherever he was, and he had a best friend, whom he fell in love with as they grew older. This girl had a big mouth and big desires. However, this boy loved no one else more than her. Then, one night, this girl gave herself to this boy. The next day, this boy became uncatchable. He even bought an engagement ring, hoping that despite the girl's restlessness, she would find peace with him, and everything will be fine. On that day, he visited the girl's house to ask her father for her hand in marriage, but he was met with the news that the girl, without just a single letter, had left without leaving much behind and went out into the world. Over the years, the man hated the girl, her memory, and even all women and everything else. He went through hell and vowed that if he ever saw the girl again, he would make her life a living hell." I listened to the end of the story with disbelief. Oh, yes, it's me again. Suddenly, I felt quite uncomfortable in his presence. The silence he left behind was eerie. I stood up. He stood up. He blew out the candle and squeezed his hand around my neck, not hurting me, but filling me with fear.

"Just pick a number, Daniel, but it's pointless for you to do anything because I'll ruin it myself, as you can see. I'm sorry, that's all I can say. I didn't run away because of you."

"It doesn't matter anymore. You shattered a boy's dream, his love."

"Let me go! "I pleaded.

"If I were to rape you now, there wouldn't be anyone who would believe you."

"Do you think that's what I want? Do you think I would tell anyone? After this, you can't show me anything new."

"We'll see, Jade! "With that, he pushed me out into the yard.

Summing up the past days, weeks, I could easily compete in the "how to make everyone hate us" competition, if such a thing existed. And there, in the mud, I had no strength left except to laugh at this, or rather, at myself. A hearty laugh, and when I finally stopped, I brushed myself off and went into the house, then upstairs, laid my head down to sleep. The next day, I knew that if I didn't do something, I would go insane. I had to divert my attention and knew what I had done, and I knew what happened. I wasn't chasing illusions. That it was in the newspaper only strengthened my resolve that I had made the right decision. This couldn't go on any longer. It gave an end to it. It was good this way. But I had to do something. Anything. It had always been like this, trying to fix the unfixable the next day. After the usual chores, I went to the owner of the neighbouring plot.

He was beaten at school, and he couldn't hide it because the class teacher called his parents and told them. When he got home, his father foamed with anger and beat him so badly that he couldn't get up for two days. He yelled he didn't raise a mama's boy, but a tough man. He kept hitting him until he said to him he would never let himself be beaten again.

## Chapter five

First, I went upstairs and changed my clothes so that if I faced a pompous owner, he wouldn't feel so superior. I put on jeans, slip-on boots, and a blue knitted sweater that stressed my pale skin and enormous eyes. Mary was downstairs in the kitchen, but I didn't talk to her. Instead, I asked one worker where I could find the man whose land was next to ours. He explained he likely only had his workers here, so I would have to go to the nearest town and look for the nicest house on the main road. No name, no house number, just the nicest house. I humbly thanked him, and off I went. Someone had filled up the beat-up old car that I bought when I returned home, and with a flick, it started. I pressed on the gas pedal as much as I could, eager to get this over with, marvelled at my small village, seeing it now with completely fresh eyes than before.

I found it remarkable that people, like little bees, worked with their two hands, not chasing foolish desires, but being happy and content, helping each other where it was needed, for those they found worthy. It was truly an impressive impulse. The town was ten kilometres away from our village, and as high school students, we could go there once a month, when one of our parents brought us and took care of their business while we girls stared at shop windows or occasionally went to a movie or had a hot chocolate. Amazing changes had taken place in this town. It got a university, its main square was completely renovated, and all kinds of shops could be found in the downtown area, even the ones I used to visit. I was in awe. But I couldn't stare for too long; I had to find the nicest house on the main road. Ridiculous. Then, fifty meters from the centre, I saw it... Even if I hadn't been looking for it, I would have at least slowed down to look. I won't say that you can't find anything nicer in the capital, or that I have seen nothing nicer, but here it stood out from the rest and was so different that it was worth visiting the town just for this sight.

    The front yard wasn't overly large, and I couldn't see the back of the house, but from what I could see, it was already magnificent. Behind the electric gate, in the middle, at the end of the driveway, there was a fountain. Colourful flowers surrounded it. Then there was a grassy area, followed by the curved-shaped house. At one end, there was a terrace-like structure, and at the other end, a wall extended with a roof. The middle of the house was taller than the rest, emphasising its importance. Scattered benches could be found in the yard and the driveway. It must have been stunning when lightened at night. I didn't linger, parked by the side of the road, and rang the doorbell. A mechanical voice asked who I was and what I wanted. I politely introduced myself and waited for a response. The gate silently opened before me, and as I took those thirty meters, I could admire the eternal work of a person. This masterpiece was created with both comfort and ostentation in mind.

    A butler-kind man greeted me at the door, and it felt like I had been transported back at least a century. He wore a black and white butler's suit, a frock coat. Inside the house, there were Persian rugs, paintings on the walls, carved and lacquered wooden surfaces, and everything was impeccably organised. Stepping inside, I found myself in a foyer-like area. Such high ceilings are no longer used nowadays; it's simply wasteful to heat. But as I had already noticed, this place was meant for showmanship, and whoever lived here probably didn't have to worry about paying the gas bill. To the right and left, heavy doors with gilded handles closed off my view. Then the butler led me through the door on the right, revealing a living room. A fire crackled in the fireplace opposite the door, although it was only for show and didn't emit any heat. Near to it was a sofa adorned with many cushions. A bar cabinet and additional seating completed the furnishings. The man assured me that his boss would be here shortly and asked if I would like some tea. I declined and eagerly awaited the chance to be alone by the panoramic window and gaze outside. In the meantime, I looked at my watch, which was one of my bad habits. The thought that time is money solidified in the depths of my mind, even though around here, if nothing, but time was abundant. I had been gazing at the garden for ten minutes when a well-built man, whom I estimated to be around my age, tore open the door, or at least, as much as one can tear open such a massive door.

"Sorry, Jade, for making you wait," he says. My eyes widened in astonishment. This was the man who rode out almost every day to inspect our fence, but beyond that. Who was this man, and do we know each other? I didn't remember at all. His brown locks fell into his eyes, and his shirt clung to his sculpted body. His green eyes seemed to shine.

"I don't mean to be rude from the very first moment, but do we know each other?" (And why do you stare at our fence every blessed day?) Of course, I didn't say the latter out loud.

"Ahem. You don't remember me, which is not surprising considering your past..." Do I have to defend myself again? Isn't the best defence a good offense?

"Maybe you'd like to contribute to the ride?"

"You misunderstood," he says, looking up from arranging the papers in his hand. "I assume as an actress, you know many people, and it's no wonder that your personal life is exposed, which I deeply regret." I listened in amazement. It's incredible the depths and heights I experience in a single day. "We went to the same class. I'm Steve Stark. "He came closer and extended his freshly manicured hand, while mine was calloused, dry, and the least cared for in the past month. Mary even mentioned that they bought it, but I didn't connect the dots, that he was my classmate, among other things...

"Oh!" I slumped onto the couch after we shook hands. "I'm sorry about the quirky incident, I..."

"It was a good prank. Forget about it. You want to buy back the end of the old farm, don't you? Am I guessing correctly? I noticed the fence had been cut the other day."
"Yes, how much did you buy it for?" We'll get back to the cutting later. How did that kid turn into this handsome, commanding man? So, he just got on my nerves terribly. And he seemed so strange before.
"Not for as much as it would have been worth ten years ago."
"Heard you still offered the fairest price for it."
"Liked your father." stared out the window. I liked him too; I was just too flawed to tell him. And now I'm left here, carrying this burden myself, knowing I should have been there and everything else.
"How much do you want for it?"
"As much as I bought it for."
"You don't have to be charitable."
"I'm asking for as much as I paid for it." I looked back at him again. He was looking at me, but there was no pity in his eyes. Maybe understanding.
"Great, then it's a deal." I stood up and waited for him to say something, like when and how. But he said nothing, just scrutinised me with his gaze. I was standing, and this wasn't the first, nor the last, time someone put me under a microscope.
"I still have some things to take care of, but we'll meet in the afternoon and sort it out."
"Perfect. They're stealing the lambs," I say.
"My people don't steal; you can bet on it."
"Did I say that? I don't think so."
"My people don't steal, "he repeated, with a hint of annoyance in his voice.
"Fine, let's drop it. So, see you in the afternoon," I declare. The conversation finished, and so did he, as he resumed organising his papers.
"Goodbye, Jade."

I dedicated most of the afternoon to training Thomas, as I did every single day. Even if I keep Jack, it's solely for maintaining the farm, not for any serious work, as his condition no longer allows for it. But, not out of disrespect, I wouldn't want them to stay here. This is a new chapter - mine. They were all past retirement age. They were experienced, and that would have been good, but I wouldn't have the heart to make them work. However, to get the farm back on its feet, it required hard work and perseverance. Thomas learned quickly, and he was interested in what I explained. Most of the things were already in theory in his mind; he was just too shy to put them into practice. His slender, tall figure, messy brown hair, and barely stubbled chin truly reflected his age. We talked a little about personal matters. My life was accessible to everyone anyway, and he didn't seem too talkative. I asked if he had friends who also wanted to work in a similar place or if he knew anyone looking for a job. The answer was not what I hoped for, which saddened me a bit because I was hoping it would relieve me of the burden of finding new people. Currently, I had six employees, excluding Thomas, all well over sixty, but what could I do? They had all spent half their lives here; I couldn't just send them away.

Supposedly, Jack would return in the morning, so I called everyone for a little meeting. I was still pondering what I should do. As promised, Steve arrived with a two-hour delay, and the handover of the farm went quickly. Six workers came into a van. He had changed his gentleman's attire for worn-out boots, jeans, and a t-shirt, but he still looked great. My shabbiness was not worth mentioning. I was wearing similar clothes, my hair sticking to my head from sweat, and I hadn't ironed my shirt, but it didn't matter that much. He glanced at the hole we had patched up again, but said nothing. His workers quickly and silently worked. They all seemed around thirty and skilled in their field. I was surprised how well things were going for him, while my father, who knew it best, could have ended up bankrupt like this?! I didn't understand, and there were many other things I didn't understand either, but didn't plan on asking. The paid workers and younger ones will do. They don't have to be experts. At least as a start.

As the days and weeks went by, I became more and more afraid that Brandon would blame me for everything that had happened. I didn't understand why it bothered me, why I should care about his life of wealth, surrounded by his family, what he thought about all of this, while my daily routine involved cleaning the stables, feeding the animals, and taking care of the farm. And, of course, keeping myself clean, which is not such a minor task either. In the morning, after reclaiming the farm, I called everyone together. Unfortunately, they still didn't allow Jack out because his condition wasn't good enough. So, there were five workers, me, and Mary, present. The event didn't end happily, unfortunately. I had to part ways with Mary because she said she couldn't continue this with me anymore. The older workers also left, but I gave them a nice compensation package. Thomas and I clarified the terms, and I offered him a decent salary, but I asked him not to live on the Farm. He said he needed to save money to move out, but I had become so accustomed to having him there that I didn't want to let him go.

It turned out that Thomas had chosen this job out of necessity because his parents died in an accident. To support himself, he dropped out of college, where he was studying law; the accident happened in his first semester. He was eighteen at the time and did not know how to play this whole adult game—earning a living, paying bills, and all that. Unfortunately, he had to realise that he couldn't even pay the mortgage on their house alone, and the bank took it away from him. He wasn't from around here either; he just bumped into Jack by chance, who was going to town for fodder, and saw the boy giving away his resume. I also called my siblings, and they gave me their permission to do whatever I wanted, or rather, they didn't care about the place and were glad to have one less to worry.

So I had a new purpose again, a reason to get up in the morning. And it had nothing to do with what makeup I use or how is my appearance. I enjoyed that part the least, at the beginning. Since then, I have hired three more young boys and a girl who was also interested in this field because she will start studying it at university next September. We had a great time, meeting once a week, having drinks (of course, I only had tea), and talking. The farm didn't experience rapid development as I had hoped; instead, it remained stagnant. I was considering going to Steve for advice, although it would have been quite difficult for me. My phone calls were going unanswered, and I knew I couldn't postpone sorting them out any longer. I expanded our livestock, bringing in cattle and pigs again. I didn't dare to take bolder steps until now. But this spring, I plan to plant an apple orchard in one parcel. It shouldn't be too much trouble, and it can be profitable. It was feeling like I would break if I didn't lower my expectations of myself. I woke up at four in the morning to feed, clean, and let the animals out. Then I dealt with the bills until the others arrived, and around noon, I rode out to check if everything was fine. In the afternoon, before it got dark and after the others had left, I went out again to gather the animals. Finally, it was back to the bills, and I contacted the buyers. If I had to go into town for something, Thomas took over from me. But the bills and the buyers were my responsibility, either in the evening or at night, and this routine continued day after day.

Today was also one of those days when I had to go to the feed store, where I had previously negotiated a small discount because of the large quantity. I entrusted everything to Thomas and instructed him to lock the gate after me because no one could enter. It was the day when I felt strong enough to have my phone with me and answer it too if someone called. It had been almost two months since I left. Thought the dust had settled and no one would look for me. I was right in the middle of the shopping centre when my little smart device suddenly rang, and I hesitated for just a few seconds before deciding whether to answer it. I didn't recognise the caller's number but didn't give in to the temptation of cowardice. And picked up the call.

"Yes," I interjected with a mild sense of resignation, - the freedom, the secrecy, and the hiding are over.

"Hi, Jade!" It was the voice that still made my heart skip a beat, made my blood rush, something I thought it could no longer do to me. And yet it did.

"Hello, Brandon," I let out a soft sigh. Neither of us spoke; I could hear him sigh, too.

"When are you coming back?"

"I'm not going back."

"Where are you?"

"Why does it matter? Far away." Everything came back up to the surface when I thought I was strong enough. I had to realise that I wasn't. All the walls I had built around my heart seemed to crumble.

"I miss you..." he wanted to continue, but he stopped, leaving that statement hanging in the air, and I... I don't even know why.

"You can find a thousand and one replacements if your wife isn't enough. And if you were to forgive me, I wouldn't have the time." With that, I hung up, but would have preferred to slam it shut like the old phones, but the progress of technology doesn't even let you vent your anger anymore for those girls who fell in love with a morally corrupt man who also has a wife and put away the phone and just stared ahead. I wanted to go out, run away, but then I gathered my strength. I couldn't be the same as before; couldn't run away now. I was still stunned by that call and absentmindedly put the items in my basket. Then I noticed someone calling my name. Great, couldn't have come at a better time, I thought bitterly. I could bet my life that this person didn't want an autograph. I was still reeling from Brandon's call.

"Who did the wind blow in? Jade, really, Jade Donovan? "Full of mockery in her voice, but I didn't turn around. I didn't know who it was. "Jade Donovan. Quite something to have such a big star among us!" I still didn't turn around until I mustered up the courage and forced myself to act casual. "Well, don't you even recognise people anymore? "It was Samantha, the one whose hair I shaved off in high school. Oh, no, wait! I didn't! I covered it in gum, and it had to be cut off. We were classmates, and we hated each other. I didn't like how she acted as a superior to everyone. Steve was walking alongside her, but I could tell he wasn't really part of the game. He tugged at Samantha's shirt, signalling her to move on, but it didn't make me hate him any less in that moment. I didn't know they were together. Well, they made a delightful couple. Both were rich and beautiful. How would I have known? I didn't know anyone in town, and the few people I knew either hated me or were over sixty.

"Sorry, I forgot your name, and you've gained a few pounds. "That wasn't true. She still looked stunning, but she was vain even back then, so I thought it would hit the mark. Her blonde hair cascaded beautifully over her magnificent figure. Perfectly round breasts and hips, while I resembled rather of a board. More like a thorn... in their side.

"Of course. You know, when you left, the town breathed a sigh of relief. Unfortunately, you achieved nothing there either. You disgraced your parents, and that wasn't enough. You came back and now you're ruining everything here, too. Everything you touch turns to ruin."

"As I can see, you have achieved little yourself. If you would excuse me, I don't have time for this!" With that, I gracefully hurried away, or as much as the tank-sized shopping cart would allow. I rushed to the self-checkout counter, paid, and raced back home and just prayed I would make it to the car without crying, but then I was just angry. I didn't want to cry, just smash something or someone. Especially because of Brandon, not Samantha. Or maybe a little because of both.

Then I let the feeling take over at home. I smashed like a maniac, threw glasses against the wall, then plates, and eventually the chair, kicked James and Tom out with such force that they left as soon as they came in. I released all the built-up tension at once, releasing stress I didn't even know I was carrying within me. Everything because of my career, because of Brandon, because of my parents and the farm, because of the workers, because of Mary, and I could go on. Then I heard the doorbell, but I paid little attention to it. To my surprise, Brandon showed up at the door.

"What are you doing here?" I yell and throw a glass at him, but he skilfully dodged it. He still looked heart-breaking.

"I came for you. Stop this!"

"I'm not going anywhere, just disappear! "Slowly stopped throwing things, started paying attention to him, observing every movement and myself, trying to understand what I was feeling. I felt ashamed, but it took time to analyse the rest.

"You're coming with me! "He commanded.

"Bet you I won't, "I raged, even though I tried to control myself.

"I have a fantastic role for you, "he changed his tone. I could never say no to that. Neither could any other woman. But now, I can.

"I don't care. I won't be your mistress anymore! "Shouted.

"But of course, you care. I know it well. "He stepped closer and closer, almost within reach. I could smell his familiar scent, which brought back a flood of memories. "This is not your life, that is. Come with me, baby!"

"I'm not going, Brandon, not now, never! "He touched my arm. I tried to pull away, but he wouldn't let go, his grip getting stronger.

"You're coming with me now, willingly, or I'll take you by force, "he whispered, but I could feel the threatening edge in his voice, or rather, that's how I truly felt it. Over the years, I had seen him truly angry once, and I knew it was better not to provoke him, but I had no intention of going with him.

"Let go of me. You know there's someone better, someone else for you."

"I need you. Come with me. It'll be good, I promise, "he started, pulling me out of the house. And I tried to break free. I didn't want the young ones to see me struggling with him. I trusted them, but here the question was rather how much they trusted me.

"Let go, I'm not going with you! "It was too late. He was already dragging me across the yard. It didn't hurt as much as it was humiliating to be yanked around like that. Such a fancy vehicle, a brand-new Mercedes parked in front of the entrance, which seemed out of place. James, Thomas, Tony, and Katie were gaping and watching the scene with fear. I signalled them not to even think about intervening. "Please, let go. Leave! "I whispered. We were already close to the gate, which was closed, only the small gate was open. He still gripped my right arm and suddenly pulled me towards him.

"You're coming with me, and that's final! "With that, he shoved me into the iron gate as if I were a doll. I crashed into it and every part of me ached. I slowly slumped to the ground. Screeching tires showed another car had stopped nearby, but I couldn't pay attention. Brandon lifted me up from the ground as if I were a baby, and then let go and pushed me ahead of him.

"Sit nicely in the car, Jade! "He had never been violent like this before. I couldn't understand what suddenly came over him. Why did he want me so badly? I could barely take my eyes off him. The past eight years of my life. The man I loved.

"Let her go! "Steve's voice cut through sharply, like a knife. I turned my head and hoped that Samantha didn't come with him because that wouldn't end well.

"What's the matter, sweetheart? Did you replace me? Are you his mistress now? And how does he pay you? With cows? "But finally, he let me go. "I'll be back! "He whispered in my ear, then got into his car and drove away with screeching tires. And as fast as I could, I rushed back into the house, not even sparing a glance for Steve.

Once inside, I locked myself in the bathroom, wanting to wash away the dirt I felt, the dirt that came back with Brandon, but no matter how hard I scrubbed myself until I turned red, I still felt it on me: the hands of men on my body, their tongues inside me, and them in my mouth. I made myself vomit, haven't done it since I'm here. Since I'm clean. I washed myself until I bled, wherever I could, and sobbed while doing it, but the feeling didn't go away. I still felt just as filthy. Like a rag being used and thrown away. He does not love me; he just uses me until he gets bored. Now he sees money in me, that's why he came back. He doesn't want me. I don't understand why he came. He only sees an opportunity for me. I need a fix, just one, have one in the drawer; I need it, otherwise, I can't stand it. Everything seems to fall apart. The entire wall, the building, it's all going to collapse on me, wrapped myself in a robe, didn't bother closing it, didn't count on anyone. I rushed through broken glasses, broken plates, into the room, to my salvation, my saviour, searched, threw everything out of the drawer. I saw nothing else, felt nothing else, just the need. But I couldn't find it, even though I knew very well it was there. My hand trembled, and I sobbed. I continued searching.

"Perhaps you're looking for this? "Steve stood at the door, waving the bag in his hand.

"Don't play the saviour, give it to me and leave!"

"Close your robe."

"Give it to me!"

"Close it! "I complied, hoping he would give it to me sooner this way. I didn't look at him, knew what I would see, and I didn't want to see it. Blood flowed from my leg in streams as I glanced down, but I felt nothing, just the urge.

"Don't play the saviour! It's enough that you pamper the likes of Samantha. Just give it to me and get lost!"

"It's lucky I was here today."

"What do you want? Would have managed without you. "
"I saw... just calm down. "I knew I would regret it tomorrow, but it's my compulsion to do things I'll regret the next day. But I didn't care, I was only interested in the present moment. I took off the robe. He wasn't waving the bag anymore and was looking at me, and I approached him. He looked at me with disbelief and could see the desire in his eyes. I know that look of men. Especially these kinds of looks. My breasts brushed against his chest. He touched my waist. At first, he wanted to push me away, but with a brief resistance, he gave in. He touched my breasts with his tongue and then began sucking. His hand moved frantically up and down on me. A deep sigh escaped his mouth, and I felt that I had gained control; I snatched from his hand what I needed, and I was gone. "I knew you were aiming for the same thing, "I said back before slamming the bathroom door shut. He didn't knock, I didn't hear a sound. Then I snorted my little dose, and afterwards, nothing hurt and nothing bothered me.

The next day, I woke up in my bed, covered with my blanket, naked except for my bound feet. I didn't care how I ended up there or what happened during the lost time; I didn't know. It was ten o'clock, and I woke up with the terror I experience every blessed morning that I overslept: but this time it was real. I rushed to the kitchen as much as my painful feet allowed, and there was a cup of coffee on the table with a note next to it saying it was cold. Half-dressed and wearing boots, I hurried to the others with the coffee in my hand. If there were still others, if they hadn't left after what happened. But no... the usual sounds greeted me in the yard. Corn grinder, lawnmower, Katie was arguing on the phone when I entered. She stopped talking when she saw me. James also stopped sorting papers, and they all looked at me, waiting for me to say something. In situations like this, I'm not good with words.

Tony and Thomas were probably responsible for the noises I heard. I still couldn't utter a word, but eventually, they came in as well.

"I'm sorry about yesterday. You shouldn't have witnessed that and thank you for still being here."

"We're sorry for letting him in and not intervening. We could have protected you. "This was Katie speaking, who may weigh fifty kilograms soaking wet, but I could sense in her voice that she would genuinely do it.

"I'm glad you didn't intervene. This is my business; I just don't want... don't want the Farm to suffer because of this. I know I have talked a little about my past, but I assume you know everything about who he was, who I am.

"Of course, "Katie said again. The guys didn't dare to look at me.

"I just want everything to go back to normal, like before. Is that possible? "I blurted out. I always feared that if I did something stupid, everything would change, but I loved the monotony.

"Yes, but we need another person in your place. You can't do everything. You're the boss, and you have a life of your own. There must be something beyond this. Because if not, I'm sorry to say this, but it will end up like with your parents. "Katie was a straightforward and adorable girl and really liked her. She was one of the first I hired, and she proved herself capable. Because of her parents' involvement in this field, she aspired to work in it too. However, she preferred to gain knowledge elsewhere and had plans to study agriculture in September. She just needed some money and practice beforehand. With black hair, brown eyes, and a slender figure, she was a pretty girl. She didn't enjoy drawing attention to her appearance, but she certainly did with her personality.

"I know, and I've been thinking about it. If you know anyone, please let me know."

"Alright, boss."

"Don't call me that, just call me Jade."
"Who was the second man?"
"Just a former classmate."
"He sat in the car all night and only left at dawn. He was guarding you."
"I'll be inside the house. Just let me know if you need me.
"What else should I have said? Steve stayed here out of guilt, even though he didn't need to feel that way. He seemed to have everything under control, unlike me, so I'd better retreat and tidy up the house and my mind as well, won't have much washing-up to do, that's for sure. I have broken everything. I could clean up the entire house, play to rearrange it to my taste, but of course, alongside that thought, there was also the lingering doubt that Samantha might be right, and it wouldn't be successful because I started it. However, I didn't want to leave; I had grown attached to the farm, or maybe it had grown attached to me.

The neighbour's little boy had an electric car that a kid could sit in and drive anywhere. He loved it very much. It was cool, blue, and white, looking just like a real sports car. Somehow, word got to his father, and he beat him again. He brought out the belt or a wood stick, and he was already terrified. He didn't understand what he had done wrong in this case.
"My son, if you want something, either take it or destroy it so that no one else can have it. I didn't raise a mama's boy.

He received many lessons like this from his father, but he mostly remembered the beatings rather than the teachings. There were etched into his mind or beaten under his skin. One of them was that family comes first. Right after that came the lesson that if you want something, take it, or destroy it. And, of course, never let yourself be taken advantage of.

## Chapter six

Days passed with nothing noteworthy happening. Perhaps the only significant events were I set up a corner of the kitchen as an office. Mary's room became mine, and I didn't use the upper floor at all. Hired a chef who also did the cleaning when needed, while I continued to handle invoicing and the commercial side of things, also hired Linda, a recent university graduate who had just moved back home. I didn't know her, and she didn't know me. She became my substitute when I wasn't around, as this was her profession. The rest of the team quickly accepted her, even though she spoke little. She was a beautiful young woman, full of ambitions and eagerness to work. I immediately liked her attitude. Despite her slender, almost boyish figure, her thick, curly brown hair reached her waist, making her attractive. Her almond-shaped eyes and full lips could arouse passionate desires in men. I couldn't understand why she chose this profession; she had the looks and the intelligence for anything. Maybe she wanted to prove something, but it was hard to know to whom and what. But it didn't matter; I was grateful to have a professional on board. All my knowledge came from my father and his employees, and sometimes it proved to be insufficient, so I also learned from Linda.

Steve didn't hire women, but I didn't discriminate against anyone, so she approached me and felt thrilled to discover a job in her field of expertise, which was quite rare these days. And I was delighted to have a professional on board. Her salary wasn't sky high, but she still signed a one-year contract. I made it clear to everyone that until the farm started generating income, I couldn't offer more than minimum wage. At least I could provide a single meal with Suzy, the chef. She cooked very well, and even I enjoyed her meals, despite being quite picky. She was in her mid-fifties but had a youthful spirit and always had a smile for everyone. Her children had flown the nest, and she wanted to supplement her retirement income while well using her time, so we understood each other well. Fortunately, Linda was also from the next town over, not a local, so I didn't have to go through the delicate process with her. She didn't know who I was, and I didn't know who she was.

Brandon bombarded me with apologetic messages, to which I didn't respond.

On that day, I sat at the computer, organising expenses and income. I sold cattle and pigs once a week, although the number of pigs was currently limited, but it was something. I generated some income, but far from enough from paying the employees' wages from it. However, there were plans to have them come twice a week in the future, and I was really hoping for that. My mobile phone rang.
"Hello? "I answered hesitantly.
"Hi, Jade! "It was Jessica, whom I occasionally spoke to. We started together in auditions, and she also had a similar career to mine, but she always found someone to support her. She was foolish but beautiful, and I liked her.
"What's up, Jess?"
"I can't believe I finally reached you. What's the deal with you? They're saying you don't want to come back. Is it true? You won't believe what's happening here?! These little brats think everything is theirs just because they're the fresh meat. Each new generation is worse than the previous one! "This is true; the young ones no longer needed outstanding acting school certificates, they didn't memorise poems, prose, or songs, if they even went to acting school at all. They just had

to use their bodies, especially their mouths. That's the truth. My generation was a bit more restrained at the beginning.

"I really don't want to go back. I've quit. "She was glad to hear that, and I didn't blame her. One less rival.

"Well, maybe in another life, if I were smarter, I'd do the same."

"Who is Brandon dating? "I don't know why I asked, although I could take it back. Why did I even ask?

"He met a cute blonde at the audition, as he does every year, and he picked her. Why do you ask? Did I mention the guy will be your downfall? But these new outfits we must wear, we look like aging prostitutes, and I'm only 28. It's not worth talking about it anymore. I must rush now. I'm going for a photoshoot, you know, I must make some extra money somehow. Well, take care, darling."

"Goodbye, Jess, take care of yourself!"

Just as I hung up, the landline phone started ringing.

"Yes?! "I answered. Maybe I should say "Donovan Farm," but it does not come to my mouth just yet.

"Hi, Jade!"

"Hi, Steve! "I wonder what he wants, to finish what he started? I'm being wicked. He wanted to protect me from myself... Should I thank him? Or apologise?

"Would you like to have dinner with me? At my place... "It always starts like this. An offer that I either accept or decline. But he's not like the others, or is he? Do I want him?

"Yes, Steve... I'm sorry about last time."

"No problem. "What does that mean? "So, come over at 8 p.m."

Am I falling into the same mistake again? Really?

*His stepfather sends him to a live-in school. He misses his mother. His stepfather can't cope with the pain and commit suicide. He is all alone and doesn't have any relatives. Ends up in a foster home. He is often mistreated.*

## Chapter seven

After a longer preparation, I stood in full splendour at half past seven in the evening. The guys admired me and went home. I wore a tight-fitting purple silk dress with a single strap that connected from the top to my hips. Ankle boots completed the outfit, along with a suitable handbag, applied for my favourite perfume and wore my most flattering makeup, tied my hair into a simple bun with a few loose strands cascading down my neck. I won't do the same as always. I will never again demean myself in front of a man. Just a dinner, and then I'll come home, won't drink. I won't stress, don't want to please. These were the words I repeated to myself like a mantra, and perhaps for the first time in my life, I truly meant them. That's not entirely true; there were other times when I meant them, but back then, the desire to please was much stronger. Today, I know I am who I am, and those who don't like it can take it or leave it.

Today, I could accept myself. Or maybe I felt stronger and hoped it would remain the same in any situation. Perhaps it was the country air. Or turned the corner to maturity. Or maybe it was the responsibility I took one day after day. The animals' lives depended on me and my care for them. For them, it didn't matter what appearances I presented, but how well I attended to them. Maybe that was the reason behind it. Or maybe I was just imagining too much. But it reassured me to think that even if I said no to Steve, they would still be there for me tomorrow. They don't care. And it's still better to be alone than to wear a mask forever. I pondered these thoughts throughout the journey, and I already felt sweaty. The gate was open and there were many cars in the parking lot. I didn't know what the situation was or what was happening anymore. Did he invite a bunch of Samantha's type to confront me? I will go in; I won't back down. The house looked beautiful even in the darkness, with the lightened garden. At the entrance, the same butler-looking guy greeted me, flipping through a list and without asking questions, he crossed out my name from it. But this time, I didn't have to turn right or left; instead, I went behind the stairs and found myself in an enormous ballroom where many men in suits and women in evening gowns were enjoying themselves, chatting and laughing.

Steve was in conversation with an older gentleman when he spotted me. I tried to exude indifference through my eyes and face. I had to take a glass of champagne from the tray offered by a waiter. The room was made even more spacious by large windows, and in the centre, there was a terrace from which a gentle breeze blew in from the April night. On the left side of the room, there was a buffet table, and the women mostly gathered around it, chatting in cliques. The men, on the other side, conversed in groups along the wall, occasionally glancing at their women or their potential prey. It was mainly the women who reacted to my arrival. Steve stood at the other end of the room with the older gentleman, engaged in a secretive conversation. Then the older man looked at me, said something to Steve, and went over to the others. Steve just looked at me, and my legs trembled. I could read every thought on his face, and I was a little disappointed to find myself in this situation again, but of course, I caused it. No one else. He looked incredibly handsome in his expensive suit, with his boyish face and muscular body. His green eyes devoured the sight, and there was something else in his gaze that I couldn't quite place. Then he grew tired of observing and started walking towards me.

"Good evening, Jade! You look great," he says, while his gaze pierced into mine, not turning right or left.

"You can't complain either, "I said. My mouth was dry, I was nervous, and I wanted to be over with it. With everything. The evening.

"I would like to introduce you to a few people. If they leave, we can have dinner in peace," he whispers into my ear, leading me towards a dark-skinned beautiful woman. Her skin was so amazing that it immediately caught my attention. She had no foundation or makeup on, yet she stood out from the crowd, even though her attire was quite modest, which is why I hadn't noticed her before. She turned towards us with a curious gaze, and I couldn't tell if it directed at me or the charming man standing next to me. "Kyra, let me introduce you to Jade Donovan, who...

"I know who she is, don't worry," she says with an angelic smile on her face; I couldn't determine if she was being sarcastic.

"You can leave us alone, handsome. We'll be fine. Don't worry, I'll take care of her."

"Then I'll slip away and get through the formalities. Enjoy yourselves!" With that, he left, leaving me in the hands of a stranger. Of course, I didn't know him either, just slightly better. In my world, where people come and go, this counted as acquaintance. You can't exchange two words with someone, and they disappear from the stage. We stared at each other for a while and said nothing. There was no malice in her gaze.

"Let's go to the ladies' restroom!" What does she want from me? I ask myself, of course, I didn't say it out loud. My face showed nothing. I just followed her. It felt like we weren't in a restroom of a house. There were at least four stalls next to each other. Events like this must be frequent here.

"How long have you known Steve?" I ask Kyra, who was adjusting her invisible makeup. Personally, I was never a fan of fixing makeup. If I put it on in the morning, it stayed on until I washed it off. I couldn't understand those women who always excused themselves to fix their makeup in the restroom.

"It's been about seven years. Our relationship hasn't always been smooth. But that's not the topic now."

"What is, then?"

"I want to manage you."

"I'm not acting anymore."

"It's not about that. Your business. The Farm."

"Why, though?"

"Steve believes it would be good for the place if we did some advertising."

"It's not just about that. I'm actually hiding."

"You shouldn't be. You have no reason to be ashamed.

"Oh, but I do! "My eyes widened at her statement. Where has she been all this time? In some private cell? "Don't you read the news or something?"

"Others do similar things. They're just not in the newspapers."

"That's precisely it, and don't convince me that this is insignificant, or something similar!"

"So, you're not involved?"

"I don't know if I am. What does it even entail?"

"You just have to lend your face; I'll take care of everything else."

"How many does it cost me?"

"Only in the sense that if I'm good, you'll recommend me to your acquaintances."

"If you're not good, then I'll fail."

"Not much depends on that, right? I mean, the Farm isn't flourishing now either, so you're not losing anything."

"True. Can I have some time to think it over?"

"Of course, I also need some time if your answer is yes. I'll be with you day and night for a while. I want to know everything from Samantha to Brandon. Everything, consider if you're willing to let someone back into your life. And now, let me introduce you to a few people. Let this be a warm-up. "I wonder if Steve told her everything. Are they best friends?

The whole evening was spent meeting various women and men of different shapes, nationalities, and temperaments. The women were mostly wives, but there were also high-end escorts for the men who came alone. I knew their type: they chose the "easier" path, which is quite difficult and rough. Steve withdrew with one of them, which bothered me more than I will admit. Most of them knew who I was: they recognised me as an actor. However, Kyra introduced me to everyone as Steve's competitor, which made the women even less sympathetic towards me. The girls looked at me with caution, wondering if I posed a threat; I tried to make it clear to them I had no such intentions. It was much easier with the men because they were only interested in cleavage; a woman posed no threat in any regard.

Everyone liked Kyra, both men and women. She effortlessly navigated through conversations and knew what to say to each person. When she mentioned I would be Steve's competitor, everyone paid attention to her, and no one laughed. I think they knew she would keep her promises. Although they didn't see me as an enemy in a professional sense, I was already dizzy from all the names. Hours later, only a few people were getting ready to leave. I was also preparing to leave because I had to wake up early in the morning, like every blessed morning, regardless of the day... Steve was standing by the door, bidding farewell to everyone like a proper host. It was my turn, but he didn't want to greet me. He always pushed me back and shook hands with someone else.

"I'm leaving too," I say to him.

"Wait a little longer, please. We still need to talk!" He didn't look at me while saying this, so I waited. I went back to the room where no one was left. I went out to the balcony. The backyard was huge, but it couldn't be seen from the front. I couldn't see what was behind it, either. It was entirely covered in grass, bordered by hedges on the sides, and there were candles stuck in the ground. I don't know how long I waited, but it got chilly. When I turned around, he was there, looking at me. I don't know for how long.

"I'm sleepy, and I must wake up early in the morning. What do we need to talk about?"

"Did you enjoy yourself?"

"It was interesting. I met many people, but I can't even remember their names, and they probably don't remember mine either. Kyra?"

"She's wonderful, isn't she? I really like her."

"I noticed. Why did you invite me after what happened?"

"Afterwards, many things went through my mind. At first, I was angry with myself, then with you, and then with myself again, until I spoke to someone and knew that this was an excellent opportunity for you."

"Thank you. What do I owe for this? And Kyra?"

"Everything has a price, right?"

"Absolutely."

"Then let it be that you have dinner with me now, as that was the goal. You haven't eaten or drunk anything all evening. Am I right?"

"Yes, you are. It's just that in places like these..."

"I can't eat either," he smiles, but I could see that he was also tired.

We ended up in the kitchen, where he moved around comfortably. He asked me what I wanted, and I just asked for a slice of bread with some cold cuts and cheese. He ate something similar but five times the amount of what I had. I also received a fruit juice on the side and couldn't complain. And would have expected the kitchen to be all chrome, not a scratch in sight, everything perfectly tidy and the least bit homely. But it was a pleasant surprise; everything was made of wood, with notes scattered everywhere, glasses and mugs on the dining counter. There was a drying rack for dishes.

Could see the wealth, but it still felt like a place that was being used.

"Next time we gather for a meal, I must take you to my favourite pizzeria. You've never tasted such divine pizza in your life."

"Most likely, since I couldn't eat something like that before, and now I'm very busy."

"You're overworking yourself. Will you be able to drive home?"

"Not today, maybe at the beginning, but now it's much easier. Of course."

"How long have you been clean? "This question shocked me because I didn't understand how it was relevant or why it mattered. My hand stopped with the food. Just when I was rebuilding myself and believe that I'm just as deserving as anyone else, someone comes along and tears it down by bringing up my past mistakes. It would have been so easy to just forget about the past.

"Since I left the city, I only stumbled that one night."

"Are you proud?"

"Should I be?"

"Can you answer properly?"

"No, I'm not. I'm not capable of it, "I finished, losing my appetite. I gathered my bag, stood up, he stood up too. We didn't speak, we just looked at each other, and then he escorted me to the door.

"I suspected. Drive safely, Jade. Goodnight!" His lips touched my face, but that was it, nothing more.

At home, I noticed myself lying in bed, utterly exhausted, thinking about him. His charm, kindness, thoughtfulness. And that's when I realised I had felt something for him. There was something dangerous in his sight, lurking there no matter what he did, whether he was organising documents, talking, eating, or drinking. Like a hunter always pursuing its prey, be it in business, women, or anything else. I couldn't remember if he had siblings, a family, or anyone else. He didn't mention it, and I didn't ask. Amidst the mental gymnastics, I just fell asleep.

I woke up to my alarm clock in the morning, and everything continued as usual. I pondered Kyra's offer for days, weighing it thoroughly, and finally decided that I had nothing to lose. My relationship with the guys kept improving; sometimes Katie stayed overnight just so we could chat about guys and everything else. Katie and Thomas didn't get along too well, or rather, the girl was annoyed by the boy's introverted nature because she couldn't fathom someone being like that. There were also times when everyone stayed over, and we watched movies until we all fell asleep wherever we were: on the couch, on the carpet. The house underwent a complete transformation. The kitchen and dining room remained as they were, more youthful. Old furniture was removed from the living room, and I thought about selling it at a flea market. Only the big-screen TV, the couch, and a coffee table remained. Mary's old room became mine, complete with a bathroom, and I set up my office in one corner of the kitchen, where I had a view of the farm during the day while I stare at the monitor. I had many quiet evenings, which didn't bother me at first after my city lifestyle, where I always had to be present at some party. Steve didn't reach out, and I didn't either. Brandon's messages became scarce, and my pain seemed to fade away. Kyra happily welcomed my positive response, promising to occupy my living room by the weekend. Until then, I had two days left to enjoy being alone. Then Steve's call interrupted.
"Hi, Jade!"
"Steve!"
"I heard you said yes. I'm happy about that. We still have two days until the weekend. Would you like to join a sleepover party and then a day of hiking? "I listened and weighed my options. Of course, I couldn't deny that I desired him and missed sex itself, but it was so difficult to go back to my old self, who just threw herself to others, expecting nothing in

return. The silence dragged on, and I couldn't bring myself to speak. Instead, I hung up the phone.

"Stupid idiot! "Said to myself.

I glanced at the others and told them I was going to take off for a bit. I left, but why? To explain the hung-up phone call or why I wanted to make a fool of myself again? Halfway there, I stopped, stepped aside, and kicked the car. It didn't help. What do I even want? What do I want from him? From my life? Why don't I have a concrete plan? Am I going to make a sport out of kicking hard objects now? Luckily, I wasn't a ballet dancer. Everyone else knows they'll get married, have children. Or pursue a career as an accountant or something. I had that too; it was rock-solid, but now I have nothing. No plans, no goals to achieve. Well, there's the farm, but that wasn't my goal. I just inherited it from my parents out of guilt.

The sun was shining beautifully, radiating light on the car hood. My parents always said that health is the most important thing. If you have that, things can't go too wrong. Yet, I collapse day after day, like a decaying building, and I try to pull myself back together. I patch up a reason, interests that I must pursue, but it's not the meaning of this existence that I create myself, it's something I inherited from someone else. Here, my ancestors. Several cars, mostly trucks, rushed past me, going about their business, while I had no destination. Should I run into the arms of a man again?

I don't think so, can't use someone else as a refuge again, headed towards the beach; I've wanted to visit there for a very long time. We used to come here in the summers with my mother and siblings, and we enjoyed it so much. The water has always had a great impact on me. It attracted me and terrified me at the same time. Since I always push my limits, I learned how to swim and spent as much time near water as I could. I loved just watching it, how it washes everything away. How the light plays on its surface. How it embraces the shore like a secret lover. I sat down on the sandy beach and enjoyed the water tickling my feet. With my eyes closed, I savoured the caress of the sun. Suddenly, there were no problems.

"Somehow, I always know where to find you. "Daniel's voice cut through the silence like a knife and lost my temper straight away.

"What do you want now? To rape me? Please, go ahead. Did you come because of Mary? I don't care. She got paid well, and she couldn't work with me. What do you want?" stood ready to fight, prepared to defend myself if necessary.

"I wanted to apologise. I was stupid the other time. You know I would never hurt you, right?" I looked at him sceptically upon hearing his words.

"I used to know, but these days I know little... "I slumped back into the sand and continued to gaze at the sea.

"You're right. It was a poor start from me after all these years. I saw that picture, and anger overwhelmed me. Thought you loved me too, and... I don't even know."

"I loved you so much. That's what gave me the initial push to leave. Couldn't give you what you deserved. I'm not the motherly type and can't sit still for long. I didn't want you to suffer more because of me. Just throw myself at men and then run away because I'm afraid of what comes next, I think... but even I haven't fully figured it out yet."

"I know very well what you're like. You don't need to introduce yourself. You were everything to me, so I hold every tiny piece of information about you deep within myself. I wasn't fair the other time. And I didn't tell the truth either. I have a family. I love them, but you stirred me up. You appeared, and I felt eighteen again. "He continued, surprised by my expression.

"It's Liza if you still remember her. We were classmates, then she went to university in the capital, and when she came back, we ran into each other, went on dates; eventually, that's how Lucy, our daughter, came into the world, my pride and joy, who is already in nursery. "I listened in awe and envy

as he spoke about his wife and their child. We talked some more, catching up on lost time. It was already getting dark. He told me he became an IT specialist, which he loves and has never left the county, and he's perfectly happy this way. He also admitted that he eventually realised it was better for me to leave, exactly for the reasons he knows and understands - I would have gone crazy if I didn't leave the village and didn't see something else. And maybe this way I see the Farm and the city differently. As we were about to leave, I said to him,
"See, Daniel Jacobs, what a good I did for you by leaving back then."
"Maybe, maybe not. You must get to know them. Come over for dinner on Saturday."
"You mean, should I bring all the residents of the Farm?"
"No, I mean bring Steve."
"Oh, sure. Can't I come alone?"
"Yes, of course."
"Bye, Dan!"
"Bye, Jade!"

    I got back into my car and drove home. There was no one and nothing waiting for me there. Everyone had already left, and darkness ruled at Tom's place. They left a message saying everything went well with the delivery. The little buddy had come into the world, not to worry, and we'll meet tomorrow. I rushed out to see them. The birth of a new life is always wonderful. The mother was panting, and the little one was sucking on a pacifier. It was a rare case for a summer birth. They usually happen in the fall, which makes it even more special for us. The first newcomer in our little family! I turned off the light in their room and went back into the house, missed lunch by a long shot, but I knew Suzy had prepared something for me. I wasn't disappointed; the food was in the fridge. I heated a portion and while surfing the internet; I enjoyed my meal, did little, yet I felt completely exhausted, had already started getting dressed in the kitchen when I saw light filtering out of my room. Instantly, all dreams disappeared from my eyes. I went back to the kitchen and grabbed a knife out of necessity.

The thought of having to gain some self-defence weapon occupied my mind, although it seemed ridiculous that I was afraid, me, who had experienced the big city... and yet. Fear crept into my life, like lice in hair, or like a tick latching onto a person, difficult to remove and can only be dealt with carefully. Then I became angry. Was I going to be the one to be afraid? Me, who had survived so much? Me, who had seen and experienced so many things? Someone wants my life. Well, let them take it. I tossed the knife back onto the table. I walked in wearing an unbuttoned blouse and waited to see who would surprise me. It was Steve. He had fallen asleep. I don't know how long he had been waiting here. There was a bouquet next to him on the bed. Should I wake him up? I won't. I'll just go about doing everything as I normally would. Of course, more quietly. I went to take a shower, and when I came out, he was still asleep. I hesitated for a moment. Should I lie down next to him?

Eventually, drowsiness took over me again. I took off my slippers and climbed into bed, then covered both of us. Don't know when the last time was. I slept so peacefully next to a man, feeling completely safe. Never. We woke up to my alarm clock in the morning. He was startled by me, or rather, because he didn't know where he was and what I was doing there. These thoughts probably flashed through his mind in an instant. I was just scared because there was a man next to me, which was unusual in this situation, in this house. Then, true to my habit, my blood pressure dropped, and half-awake, I went to get my coffee. No one can say that I bombard a man with stupid questions right after waking up when he himself doesn't even know what kind of event he's attending. Because usually, I don't know either.
"Good morning! "He joined me in the kitchen, without a tie and jacket. He looked dishevelled, but in the best shape. His

gaze was already alert while I was still blinking the dream out of my eyes.

"Good morning! "I didn't want to ask him with questions. If he wants to share something, he will; if not, then not.

"I'm sorry for falling asleep in your bed."

"I'm sorry for hang up the phone. Then I wanted to go over, but something came up."

"Daniel Jacobs came up if I'm not mistaken. "My eyes widened immediately.

"It's none of your business who I spend my time with. Or are you already following me? How dare you?"

"Jade, Dan is my best friend, "he interrupted my torrent of words, which was for the best because I would have made an even bigger fool of myself. "Why do you always assume the worst and always attack me?"

"Great, so you two had a discussion? Did he give you information about what I'm like in bed, and do you want to try it out too? Shall we go back? Do you want to test it? "As soon it, I regretted it, but by the time he finished speaking, I had already started because I can hardly take back what comes out. That's the sad truth.

"Why do you always jump to such conclusions? Why do you think every man just wants that from you?"

"Experience, Steve, "I said and went back to the room to get dressed. When I came out, he was still sitting in the kitchen, sipping on the remaining coffee. He said nothing, and neither did I. Went out to the guys. Half an hour later, a car came to pick him up. He didn't say goodbye, and I didn't say goodbye. I figured I probably wouldn't hear from him for a while, or maybe never again. I tried not to think about it, but it was quite difficult because Katie kept pestering me.

"What did you do last night? Where did you go? To him?"

"Katie, aren't you afraid of getting old quickly? Anyway, nothing happened. How are things going with Thomas?"

"What kind of question is that? "She got angry immediately. "Even if he were the last guy on Earth, I still wouldn't be interested. No one could excite him. Even a whole harem wouldn't be enough."

"Well, good luck with that, "I continued to tease her. Because hate and love are closely related.

"Stop messing around, Jade. I don't care about Thomas!"

"Of course, of course. Are you trying to convince me or yourself? Because it's difficult to fool me. I see what I see. "I had just finished the sentence when Katie seemed about to explode, and that's when the mentioned entered the shed.

"Guys, I thought we could use one outbuilding for these gatherings because, as I can see, you don't really like coming to the house, and it's strange that we gather in the shed where it's dark, smelly, and full of tools."

"I want to resign, Jade, "James said this as he walked in. I tried not to show anything to my face. He was the team's sexy joker. With his creole skin, well-sculpted body, and always cheerful nature, he had won everyone's heart. I felt sorry, though, because from the beginning, I could see that he needed more money and was more ambitious than this little place could offer.

"Alright. Tomorrow we'll fill out the paperwork, and if we find someone to replace you by the end of the month, then you can leave."

"Traitor! "Katie said this. I really liked her outspoken nature. Linda still hadn't fit in properly, so she usually kept quiet. She didn't even come to the last pyjama party and excused herself with some made-up reason. She was from another town. And Tony, he is so kind, smart, considerate, not overly handsome, but he had a heart of gold. He was a great team player. He was quiet enough, but always up for some fun.

"I forgot to mention, from tomorrow evening onwards, a girl named Kyra will be here for a while, and she'll be observing our every move. I think they call it a marketing manager, but as you know, actresses don't have big brains. "Everyone laughed at this. I was happy when they were in a good mood.

Currently, they were my family. "And now, let's get to work a bit!"

I couldn't say that everyone understood everything perfectly, except for Linda, who studied this. James could learn anything if he wanted, so he was also knowledgeable as a worker. Tony, Thomas, and Katie were dedicated to the cause or the money, which was irrelevant because they did their job well, forgot nothing, and were honest. And personally, they were perfect, just the way God created them. Even if I couldn't trust my life to them, I could trust the Farm to them anytime. Perhaps not my life, because I didn't even fully trust myself. I had assembled a good team. True, now I had to find someone to replace James, but we were still in good shape. The Farm was already producing a bit. Not much, but something. I still had some saved money. It would be enough for half a year. But I really wanted to renovate the outbuildings. There were three of them. One of them could be turned into a workers' dining area. But before I started on that, I had to finish my own affairs. Once Kyra was done, I would go back to the capital for a few days. If it's going to be as big as she promises, it's better if I'm there when it explodes, and I'll try to be at my best. But until then, I still had some time to gather strength. To prepare for the unprepared.

"Steve?! "I dialled his number.

"Yes, Jade?"

"I'm sorry for being so unbearable this morning, I apologise."

"It's alright."

"Is the sleepover party still on?"

"If you're in, of course. If you're available, then we'll go far away tomorrow."

"I'm in."

"Fancy dresses are out of the question."

"Understood. I'll be there tonight. "There's no need to overthink or imagine too much into it.

Two adults, a man, and a woman, spending some time together and having fun. Yet, I was getting ready for the evening with pure stress. I tried to appear completely relaxed. I wore a light dress, flat sandals, light makeup, nothing excessive. Of course, he looked like he could go to the opera even in his khaki pants and simple black shirt, while I felt totally underdressed. We didn't even go inside the house; we immediately got into his MG coupe, reserved for such occasions. It was a pleasant evening, with a gentle breeze caressing my hair. We drove along the bay for about thirty kilometres and stopped at a secluded place, a lovely little restaurant filled with guests. Grapevines covered the total area. It was built with adobe, at least as much as was visible through the abundance of plants. Lanterns lit up the place romantically. I thought there wouldn't be any space or we would have to wait, but when they saw Steve, the owner came out to greet us and led us to the terrace on the rooftop, where there was only one table: ours. If this were our first encounter, it wouldn't take much more for us to end up in bed. He knows how to set the stage for everything, as I suspect.

"How do you like it? "He asked. These were his first words since we got in the car.

"It's beautiful, "I smiled at him. "I love it. I've never heard of it before, and I haven't seen it yet. How long has it been here?

"It was built four years ago. The owner came from Italy, and I supported his idea of bringing their fantastic flavours here."

"Do you have a hand in it? "I felt like he was involved with the restaurant.

"Not anymore, but I crave nothing more than it. "I could see that he regretted saying that. The wine paused halfway to my mouth, and I smiled.

"You don't have to rush into things headlong; everything has its time, "I said.

"In the beginning, I was involved. He needed some capital to get it started, but then he paid me back after half a year because it was going so well. Crisis or no crisis, people need to eat."

"That's true. I'm angry about this whole crisis thing because..."
"The world of film?"
"What? No way, because my father worked his entire life, and what did he become? Dead. Along with my mother. Let's leave it at that."
"Do you miss acting? The big city? "He asked instead. Perhaps he intended it as a diversion.
"I miss acting, but I wouldn't want to act in movies anymore, only in theatre. If I could. Well, I have moments when I feel like that. I don't miss the city; I don't miss my life there. I love living here. That's how I feel at this moment."
"Did you make the Farm your own? Isn't it difficult after everything you've done? Because it's the complete opposite."
"Let's not forget that I left from here. This came first, not the other way around."
"I remember when you started taking this thing seriously. We were in seventh grade, and we went back to school after summer break; everyone met a completely different Jade. The girls started disliking you, most of them out of jealousy, and the boys started looking at you completely differently. I remember your grades dropped. You only studied what you noted down during class. Except for literature and sports, of course. The teachers were disappointed in you, but you were determined. I remember you only hung out with Daniel, and the boys really ostracised him for it, but he didn't seem to care. At least he didn't show it. You attended extra literature and grammar classes, and of course, sport. I admired your determination. Maybe that's what set me off, too."
"I don't see that time so beautifully, unfortunately. Maybe the memories will become beautiful someday. Samantha doesn't make it easy for me to see it that way. Anyway, I can't always blame others for something that was mainly my fault."
"You're too fond of attributing too many mistakes to yourself. Maybe that's why you became who you are."

"A nobody? "I laughed at that. The wine had got to my head, but it was so heavenly that it drank itself. Slightly muscatel and sweet, exactly how a wine should be. For me... of course. I couldn't even imagine how someone could drink dry, acidic wine.

We talked a lot; the pizza was divine. While we sat there, I could even imagine that if we went down the serpentine road, the street would be cobblestoned, the sea would kiss our feet, and the houses would be squeezed together, as if we were in the good old boot. He entertained me, and I laughed. Then we prepared to go home, and the fear crept back into my stomach. When we arrived at the counter, there was still a line waiting for a table. The owner stopped us. "Are you not Jade Donovan? "I glanced slyly at Steve, who raised his hand in confusion.
"Si, "I said in Italian. That came to my lips because of his accent.
"Perfavore, mi potresti firmare il libro degli ospiti?"
"Molto volentieri."
"Grazia, signorina."
"Ok. "So, I wrote in the guest book that I had enjoyed the hospitality tremendously. It was perfect, and I would recommend it to everyone. "Grazie, Giovanni."
"Arrivederci."
"I didn't even know you spoke Italian, "Steve says in the car.
"I don't really, I just play it well."
"You're being modest."
"Not me. I know many languages, but they wouldn't save my life. "I smiled at him. "We had to know so much that nobody even suspects when watching movies. Knowing languages is a basic requirement. Torturing your body is almost mandatory. Endurance is not the least important. Knowing the capital of almost every country, the celebrities, and the list goes on. So, if someone thinks that we just play a role and then go home, they're mistaken. Our work is 24/7, every day of the week. We must know everything about the scripts, who wrote them,

what's in them, who gets the role and why. Coaches, who to be seen with, and who's worth their money. We sell the American dream to the viewers in front of the TV, even though it doesn't exist. The real American dream is when the mother finishes her eight-hour shift and goes home to her happy family; luxury or loneliness doesn't define the American dream. The real American dream is built on family, on work; the sick media have twisted it and instilled in teenage girls the idea that they must torture themselves and forced young boys to desire fancy cars and trophy girlfriends. It drives them to treat women like rags. It's a filthy world, and yet I wanted to be so much a part of it, I almost sacrificed my life for it. Once. I don't want to act in movies anymore, I want to act in theatre, where real art is created."
"You articulated that beautifully, and every word is true. I believed in it too, "he said as we turned into the garage.
"In what?"
"The American dream. And did you live it?"
"I thought I did, but I had to realise that my current life resembles it much more."
"Are you disappointed?"
"A little, because I fought for something my whole life that is false, something that doesn't even exist. "Silence filled the house as we turned on the lights. We entered his study, where he asked what I wanted to drink. "Whatever you're having. How often do you drink?"
"Not very often, usually just a little at events. I have little time for leisure."
"What about your parents?"
"My parents and my sister don't live far away. We bump into each other sometimes."
"It sounds like your relationship isn't very good. I forgot; you have a sister. What does she do? "He smiled at this, and I didn't understand what was funny about it.
"Our relationship isn't that good. Well, there's no anger or anything. We're just distant from each other. "I didn't quite

understand. I didn't have a great relationship with my parents either, but that was because I was hot-headed; still, they loved me no matter what.
"Why?"
"It's a long and complicated story."
"I understand. "If he didn't want to tell me, then he didn't have to. I couldn't force him. "And your sister? "Why didn't he want to talk about it? What's wrong with this question?
"They are doing great. The younger recently started working."

Nothing else was on my mind except that I was going to make love with him, and I wanted it. I wanted it so badly. Every fibre of me being burned with desire. Perhaps my gaze had changed because he put down his glass, took my hand, and gently pulled me up from the couch. He placed his hands under my chin, looking deep into my eyes.
"Do you want this? Do you really want it?"
"Yes, I do."
"I hope you're completely sure because there will be a point of no return for me if I'm not over it already. I desire you. "He kissed me gently. I could feel his it as he pressed against me. "Let's go upstairs! "Urged by desire, we hurried up to the first floor, where there was no escape, where both of us got lost. I could barely register the surroundings. I only felt his body, the urgency inside me, needing him to penetrate me because living with the absence of it was painful. He had to fill the void within me. He started gently, but then he too lost control of his will and sucked on my breasts while his hands greedily explored every corner of my body, and finally, unable to wait any longer, he penetrated me. We danced a wild dance in which we both got lost. I was beside myself with pleasure, but even in this moment, he had enough presence of mind to take care of me. He didn't waste time and skilfully finished within moments, and we continued where we left off. We both reached that place where all pleasure originates from a single point and then explodes throughout the body.

Finally, we slept in each other's arms, and in the morning, we woke up almost in the same position. I got scared for a moment, and that was enough to wake him up.
"I'm sorry for waking you up, "I apologised, jumped out of bed, and started searching for my clothes.
"Where are you rushing off to? "He looked at me, and his smile was gone. In fact, I was acting like a mad person.
"I, um... must go, it just occurred to me that need to take care of something before Kyra comes. I'm sorry "lied; think he knew it. But he said nothing.
"We'll meet in the afternoon, right?"
"Of course. In the afternoon. Bye! "I rushed out the door and hurried down the stairs. The butler was already waiting in the foyer; I mumbled a goodbye to him and was on my way. I drove as if I were being chased. Of course, I didn't have any urgent business. I just needed to disappear. I had to analyse the situation. This is me, the little analysing crazy person.

What can I say? Here I am again. Entangled in a man, clinging to a life that may not even be mine, just observing, hesitating. Am I overcomplicating things? It's possible. I'm not the first one to accuse myself of this. I was so terrified of making the same mistake as with Brandon, of getting trapped once again, without properly untangling myself. There's nothing to think about here. I don't want to humiliate myself and submit again.

Then I slowly turned onto the side road, deciding that as soon as I got home, I would call Steve, meet him, and discuss what's next or what he wants, when I noticed the guys were trying to scrape something off the gate. As I got closer, I saw the "whore" inscription screaming in my face, along with "go back where you came from" and other similar delicacies.

I told them to leave and mind their own business. Ultimately, I decided not to call Steve because of this impact on me. It was probably because of what happened last night that I spent the night with him. I tried to look beyond my initial reaction of "just to prove a point" and figure out what this whole situation triggered in me and what I really wanted to do. I love the farm; feel it's important to me. Sometimes, the feeling of shame overwhelms me. Even though I know what I should do, I still don't do it. That's why I didn't come to the funeral. I was ashamed to leave them here. Of course, I'm still a shitty person since if they judge me based on my actions, I'm a jerk for not attending my own parents' funeral or for not putting a stop to Brandon, and so on. Even if I did it out of cowardice or overflowing emotions.

After all, it's time for me to take responsibility for my own actions, not blame others, and react smarter to the punches life throws at me. This is a small town. Whoever vandalised my gate probably expressed their opinion about me to everyone, which is worthless if I don't react to it. They wanted to provoke me and thought I would react the same way I did in my teenage years. And they wouldn't have been far off if I had succumbed to my first impression, giving them a reason to gossip.

I'd like to believe that I'm wiser now, or just sneakier. While contemplating these thoughts, I checked if everything was working fine on the Farm, went through the mail, and replied to a few messages. Then I finally called Steve, as if nothing had happened, but he already knew.

"Hi," I started after a brief pause. "I'm sorry for just leaving earlier. Could we meet somewhere?"

"Well, the hike I planned for today is still on, if you're interested. Should I send someone for the fence issue?"

"We can go. No, thank you, it's perfect this way."

"Alright, I'll be there soon."

"Okay, see you later than."

I quickly took a shower and put on comfortable clothes, comprising a snug tracksuit, a t-shirt, and sneakers. No makeup. Just a sweater. I talked to Kyra, who only wants to meet with me today, so she promised to be there around eight in the evening.

Tina Colt – Role/Play

*Fifteen years old. Falls in love. They plan their future together. Happy once again... The girl disappears. He is suspected. Loses faith and hope...*

## Chapter eight

Once I finished all my tasks, the chauffeur arrived. It wasn't him who came. I sat in the backseat. I engaged in conversation with the driver, or at least tried to, yelling from the back to overcome the noise of the engine. He said little about Steve, just that he had been working for him for five years and he is a wonderful person who helped him get back on his feet. Now he lives happily with a woman, which was strange to him because he used to be a big womaniser. They even have a child together. His wife is Spanish, with a fiery temperament, and he loves that about her. She is the woman who could never predict, which made it exciting. I couldn't help but smile at his candid confession.

We didn't go to Steve's place, but to a private airport. Steve was already waiting there, talking on the phone. The

plane was roaring, and I couldn't understand how either of them could hear anything they were saying, but they didn't seem bothered. Steve gestured as if the other person could see him. Men! Then he finished the call, seemed grumpy, but didn't waste time. He greeted me, and we boarded the plane. It was designed for about four to six passengers. I had been on such planes before, but I would never invest my money in one. First, because I'm afraid of flying—it gives me a feeling of being out of control—and second, because I considered it a display of arrogance. After all, there are commercial airlines for those who want to get from point A to point B quickly. Or what's the use of Uber??? We sat facing each other. I didn't ask for anything, just fastened my seatbelt tightly, and prayed that the pilot knew what he was doing. Steve didn't tell me what to wear, so I felt silly in my sweatpants while he was dressed in suit trousers and a shirt. I mentioned this to him.
"You said we were going on a hike, and I dressed and here you are?"
"I had a meeting before I came, but don't worry, I have a change of clothes. I'll put them on once we're on board."
"And where are we going?"
"To my second home," he says with a hint of sadness in his voice. I observed his face. Perhaps to an average onlooker, his expression wouldn't have given anything away as he stared out the window. He pursed his lips. Not enough for anyone else to notice, but for someone who constantly analyses its surroundings and scrutinises everything, it was clear. As much as he tried to exude ease, I could sense the flood of memories that surged within him at the mention of his second home.
"I can't wait. My life is already boring. I know it inside out."
"I know little about your life, I mean, I'm up to date until you left, and the next news was the movie where I first saw you, but I didn't have the chance or the time to delve too deep into the world of celebrities. Somehow, gossip and famous people didn't attract me. I was happy about your success. I was mad at you for making Daniel so sad, but in the end,

that's what brought us together. And I'm grateful for our friendship."

"Well, not much happened in the meantime. I tried my hardest to break into the big ones, but unfortunately, didn't get a good hand. I didn't become famous or extraordinarily rich; made a bunch of mistakes, plus one more. There's no sugar-coating it. I thought I was smart enough or had enough courage, but wasn't."

"Why? "He asked as he changed his clothes.

"Why do I feel like I didn't make it? "I kept staring out the window. I didn't want to look at him. Not because I'm a shy traditionalist, but because I didn't want to interrupt the conversation.

"Why do you feel that way? Why do you think you didn't succeed?"

"It's not a feeling, it's the truth. Where do I stand among the real big shots? It doesn't mean I'm a poor actor; it simply means I was in the wrong place at the wrong time. Or I chose the wrong couch."

"Have you moved on from it?"

"No."

"Me neither. "I had to look at him at that point.

"You mean you haven't got over about my casting couch?"

"I'd be lying if I said yes."

"Then why are we here? I will prove nothing to you, just so you know. Or explain myself."

"Honestly, I can say that we're attracted to each other, and in time, it will become clear if this whole thing means anything or if it's worth everything. We shouldn't label it."

"I understand, "I said, and his previous statement echoed in my mind. I found it intriguing. It might be foolish of me, but I never even dreamed that someone would be filled with jealousy or hesitation about my casting couch. Maybe the latter is more accurate. And what does it mean for something to be worth everything? I didn't ask him to sell his property and shack up together.

"So, you're not saying anything, Jade? I was expecting you to come at me now. You're always ready for a fight."
"I'm tired, Steve, but I won't do anything that I don't feel is appropriate: you should know that. It's nice to start a day out in nature with such a conversation."
"What do you expect from me? If I were to ask or say these things in the city, you would already be long gone. This is the only way to talk to you when you're locked in, "he said as we started descending.

To some extent, he was right. I always ran away when I felt like I didn't know how to handle a situation or when I was proven wrong. It didn't feel good to hear what he said. But that's adulthood, and it only felt so bad because of my life story. We meet, we talk, we get to know each other, and then we decide how to proceed. How much we give up on ourselves, or what each of us does for the other, is up to us. I can't blame him for saying that. Meanwhile, we landed and got into a taxi. The noise of the big city crept unmistakably into my mind, and I had to realise that I missed it. This wasn't my city. Of course, I had been here before, but the sounds were the same everywhere. Nervous honking, screeching brakes, shouting, the noise of restaurants. The smells were just as distinctive: gasoline, grease, and steam.

I tried to lock the previous conversation away in the back corner of my mind and enjoy every moment. The taxi stopped at a rundown building, which surprised me, not because I'm picky, but because Steve seemed like someone who wouldn't choose this. It was an artist's loft from the 80s. It felt like everything was frozen in that era, just renovated. Even the elevator required manual pulling down the gate. Upon reaching the floor, the sight behind the heavy door didn't surprise me at all. Everything was in one space: the kitchen, the living room, the bedroom, the architect's desk with architectural plans and more. A window facing the street covered one wall, with a ledge to curl up on during winter evenings. I instantly fell in love with the apartment. The tasteful stack of pallets adorned the wall next to the door. There was black silk bedding, something I didn't expect. Vintage pictures and signed vinyl records decorated the walls. On the other side of the door was a bookshelf filled with many books. And there was the writing desk. Parallel to the door was a dining counter and a small kitchen.

"It's beautiful," I remarked, and I wasn't exaggerating. It won my favour. Steve went to the desk, looking for where he left off the last time he was here.

"I moved here after college when I was testing my luck. I studied architecture, among other things. Then things didn't work out as planned, but later I bought the building. Too many things tied me to this place," he says, as I sat on the ledge, listening to what he says and, of course, observing what his body language conveyed, as well as peering out the window.

"What didn't work out?"

"It's a complicated story," he says, handing me a glass of wine. "Let's toast to the first. I don't even know what."

"To us. Because we deserve it," I reply. The drink shimmered golden and clear in the glass. I had to run my finger along the edge of the glass, which made that distinctive clinking sound. When I tasted it, I detected a sweet muscat flavour in my mouth. I rarely drank alcohol, mainly because I had a high tolerance for it, so if I wanted to get drunk, would have to consume a considerable amount, and the intoxicated state was never entertained. Stupid giggly girls always drove me crazy.

"A friend of mine is coming up soon, and I want to introduce you to her. If Kyra wasn't going today and it wasn't so damn important, we could have stayed for another day, but I know we must go."

"Okay." - Who is this friend? I asked myself silently.

"She'll be here in just an hour. Shall we go for a walk until then?"

"Sure."

We strolled through the smelly streets, and I savoured every moment. How could I have thought that I could leave the city completely behind? How foolish of me with this constant escapism. I, who examines everything, cannot see the obvious, didn't see that I love the city and need its pulse. Of course, I also need tranquillity, a retreat, but I can only find fulfilment by embracing both from time to time. We talked a lot and laughed. We went to the university; he showed me the dorm where he lived. The places he ate at instead of the cafeteria, although he considered those to be below average, and eventually, we had lunch in an upscale restaurant, although given the time, it was more like an early dinner. I asked if he wanted me to pay, but he took offense at that and refused to speak to me until we returned to the apartment.

"It wouldn't be appropriate right now to ask you to make love to me because you would associate it with paying for the meal. I know that's how you would think, but it's not about that. It's because you feel good with me, and you desire me, so I would like you to do it if that's the case, of course, only if you want to," he says. A knock on the door interrupted my hesitation, and I felt a bit relieved to be saved from this situation. Of course, I enjoyed being with him, and only a fool wouldn't desire him, but later, I would really bring it up; how transparent I am, if he knows it, too. He took a deep breath, called out through the door to hold on, and went to open it.

"Hi, Christine!" he exclaims excitedly. A blonde, very attractive woman walked in and planted two kisses on Steve's cheek. She looked stunning in her blue summer dress that matched her eyes, with her voluptuous body and light makeup. And what did I see when I looked down at myself? A woman in sweatpants, pale, thin, probably dishevelled after the walk. Fantastic. – "How are you?"

"Thank you, Steve, I am fine! You look fabulous," she says, still smiling. They liked each other. It wasn't an act.

"Let me introduce you to a dear friend of mine," he pointed at me and guided us towards each other. "Jade Donovan.

"Oh, my god! You're Jade Donovan? The Jade Donovan?" I hesitated, wondering if this was some kind of prank.
"Yes, I am. Nice to meet you," I finally uttered.
"I'm Christine Stewart. I'm sorry for bombarding you like this. My little brother and sister are constantly watching your movies. And I must admit, I watched them too back in the day."
"You're kidding me," I gasp.
"No, I'm not," she says, her smile and kindness infectious. It was impossible not to like her, and, of course, envied people like her. Me, I can be quite unpleasant, which didn't endear me to anyone.
"Well, I'm glad," I reply.
"Steve, you knew her all along, and you never introduced us?" she says, outraged.
"Well, we're getting reacquainted now. We were classmates."
"What? I can't believe this. Nobody will believe me. Seriously, Steve, and you forgot to mention this to me in the past years?" She says this while sitting with another glass of wine. I was sitting by the window, and they were on the sofa at the end of the bed, but it didn't hinder our conversation. We weren't far from each other. I learned they met at the university, tried dating, but it turned out to be a disaster, so they remained friends. I felt that this friendship was mutual; both spoke openly about their own lives, their problems, and concerns. Christine found her place in the fashion industry. She was during a divorce from her second 'asshole,' as she called him. She asked me questions too, and I spoke to her as I had learned how I had to act with a fan. The actress poses the illusion we show everything is good and beautiful. No emotion, no truth. We had to leave soon if I wanted to be home by eight. I nervously glanced at my watch, which I always explained as a bad habit because I sometimes checked the time every minute.
"How did you feel? I'm sorry we could only spend such a short time," he says, scrutinising my face.

"I felt good. Thank you for the invitation." We discussed this on the plane back, where we continue drinking wine. He seemed contemplative. "Christine is a likable woman. Why didn't it work out between you two?"
"She was too good for me. I don't say this with the cliché that people throw around. She's an angel, something I was far from being back then."
"I understand what you mean, and that was my impression of her, too. I've never been like that, and I never will be," I say. We started descending slowly, so we said our goodbyes. The evening had fallen, although the weather was still young.
"We'll see how things go with Kyra, and then we'll know how we can meet again."
"Ok."
A car is coming for you."
"Ok. Thank you, Steve." I lightly kissed him on the lips and got into the car. It was the same guy as in the morning. I even asked for his name. He was called Bobby, which suited his Afro-American identity well. His gold tooth was glowing. He looked like a cool dude. He asked how our trip was, how the journey went, the weather, and such. But I was completely lost in my thoughts, unable to respond sensibly to anything. By the time I returned to the Farm, silence prevailed; the sign was still there, but it didn't bother me anymore. It hadn't crossed my mind all day, which was already a big step for me. There were still ten minutes left until eight. I sifted through the mail, and my eyes caught a typed envelope and put the rest into its own box, thinking that I would deal with them in the distant future. I tore open the envelope, feeling no pleasant sensation, and as soon as I saw its contents, the awful premonition was understandable. Pictures of Steve having sex with a woman. In his own bed, recently. The woman was unidentifiable, only Steve was visible. And the message read: "Are you always aiming for someone else's? Go back to where you came from." The world spun around

me. Was this for real? What had I got myself into again? Before I could overcome the nausea, the doorbell rang.

"Hi, Kyra!" I say as I opened the door.

"Was the sign at the gate supposed to be some poorly executed advertisement?"

"You're funny. It's my fans, nothing I can do about it. Were you prepared for this?" I ask and hand her the letter.

"Oh, my god! Well, I don't know. I've had more challenging cases before, but it was a man. It was different. Let's sit down. Let's talk and please think of me as a confessor. Nothing will leak from here. I won't disclose anything. You must trust me. Completely. Will you be able to do that?"

"I think so."

His father often mentioned the neighbouring farm, says it should belong to them. Because John was just a halfwit and knew nothing about it. Of course, Donovan's family was doing much better than theirs, and his father resented it greatly. He constantly went over there to spy on them, to see what they were doing and how. At night, he would go out and cut holes in their fence. They lived there too, behind Jade's family. The same Jade who was in her class. He often daydreamed about the girl but didn't dare to say a word because his father would immediately disown, he, or maybe even kill him. He told him to gather information from Jade, to find out what they were doing, but he couldn't bring himself to approach Jade, who was always with Daniel and treated everyone else rudely. Because of this, his father constantly humiliated him in front of everyone. He would say things like he was born as a girl but worthless. Pathetic and useless. When the time for his high school graduation came, he left home. But the knowledge that family comes first, and you take what you need or destroy it, had burned itself into his consciousness...

## Chapter nine

Then we talked all night. And I told her everything. Really everything. I didn't care about the consequences anymore if she used it against me. It felt so good to say things out loud. To cry, to be angry, disappointed, and vulnerable. Just once. She would inquire if she didn't understand something. We searched for reasons. Why's. Answers. Then we got to Steve, and I also asked her about her relationship with him.

"He was my hard case. We had sex once, but that was it. There was nothing more, and we wanted nothing more. And it was a long time ago. Since then, we've been friends. Very good friends. He was a big womaniser back then. A different woman every week. But that's not relevant now. I must tell you; you're giving me a challenge. Because believe me, it's not about whether you can raise cattle well anymore, it's about how well you can sell yourself. Of course, do it well, but trust me, there are those who sell crap with good management."

"Why do you want to do it for free?"

"It's a real challenge for me, too. And if it goes well, I'll have so many orders through you I won't be able to handle it, and besides, I have other sources of income."

"Do I seem like such a hopeless case?"

"Something has changed since I last saw you," she ignored my question. "Something beneficial for the business. I mean, I liked that fiery chick, and I hope she hasn't disappeared forever. But for now, I can say it's going to be great. We have good chances. But if you don't mind, I'll go to sleep now. What time do you wake up?"

"At six o'clock."

"Oh, damn, it is almost here."

"I set up a room for you upstairs. There's internet, TV, chargers, everything you might need. We'll meet in the morning. Goodnight! It's the first room on the left by the stairs. The bathroom is right across."

"Thank you. Goodnight!

Then, in my solitude at two in the morning, what would I have done with myself if I hadn't sent the pictures to Steve? Of course, I regretted it afterwards, but I still sent them, and there was no way to undo it. There was no reply. Not surprising. He must be damn busy, I thought angrily. Then I also went to bed.

Morning came quickly, and I was very sleepy and difficult to handle. I tried to moderate myself. But Kyra's presence annoyed me. She got to know the guys, except for Linda, who was on holiday for a week, but everything went smoothly. She had trained everyone well. I had little to do with the animals or the property anymore, unless two people were absent. They usually had weekends offed, but I asked them not to this time. Everything went smoothly with the inn and our deliveries. I felt like we were already past the worst. In the house, I checked the mail, but since it was Sunday, there wasn't much I could do. I thought it was time for a big shopping trip. I hoped Kyra wouldn't come, but of course, she did. She inquired about my financial situation. Reluctantly, I confided in her. On our way back home, Suzy was already bustling in the kitchen. Someone had cleaned the sign off the gate. I think it was her. I relaxed a bit and talked to Kyra as if she were my friend. She asked if I had any intention of buying a new car instead of that piece of junk. I told her, of course, I just didn't want to spend in advance when there's a chance I might fail in managing the entire farm.

"We're doing well, "she said as we packed up the stuff, and Suzy was cooking. "I thought you would have a harder sharing your things with me. Steve didn't say a word to me for a week. Christine recommended him to me when he moved back home, and he only accepted it because of that, but he was unbearable. I followed him around like a dog for a week, and he didn't say a word." "Surprise. He's easy for any woman to open," I say in a sarcastic tone.

"I'm not willing to delve into that topic. Let's continue. So, I think I know everything, and I've noted down what I needed. On Wednesday, I'll organise an interview with the local newspaper. On Thursday, with the local TV, and on Friday, with the county ones. Since you're quite familiar with these things, I don't see any obstacles or difficulties for you. What you need to prepare for is that there will probably be people working there who don't like you. But the media is owned by people who like Steve, which is also not good in this case. I won't give you, specifically you, a lesson in media since you know exactly what to do. We'll be together tomorrow and the day after, so I think until Friday, but then everything will go its own way."

"I wanted to go to L.A. before that, but it may not matter. Maybe I can go afterwards. Do you have any idea what they will make out of this? And what will you get out of it?"

"I think have an idea."

"I don't think so, Kyra. Don't think you have a clue, and I'm not saying this because I underestimate you, but because you're not aware of the power of the wrong people. You'll face such terrible things that I just outlined to you yesterday. It's hard to endure them with a clear, sane mind. Are you prepared for this?"

"Financially, I can live for about five years doing nothing, and by then, everyone will forget," she says, laughing, but I saw the shock on her face.

"How quickly do you think the news will reach L.A.?"

"A week, I don't know. It depends on how focused they are on you."

"Not at all. They would be here by now if that were the case. Although I always made sure they didn't know where I came from. Then I'll go next week. It's not that important."

I was afraid that I had too many enemies. If I thought about the gate and the messages, or what Samantha threw at me, I wouldn't worry unnecessarily. And I didn't know what Brandon was planning to do; I felt like there would be a big fuss. Wherever I go, that's what happens, but at least people around me aren't bored.

Contrary to missing my privacy, Wednesday came quickly, and I was more nervous than bothered by Kyra's presence because I wasn't as prepared as someone who graduated from this. I knew what I knew from my father. So, if the journalist wanted to mess with me, could easily do it, and I still didn't know who it would be. I prayed it wouldn't be someone I had a deep grudge against.

They wanted to conduct the interview at my place. I wore simple jeans and a T-shirt, with light makeup. My hair was tied back, as always. But in a magazine, that obviously wouldn't show, so I didn't see the importance of dressing up.

Kyra was more nervous than me. She fluttered around me, which annoyed me even more. Memories rushed into my mind. They weren't pleasant. I tried to push them away. Screeching brakes, and a Jeep turned into the yard. The guys promised not to come forward accidentally. Suzy was nowhere to be found today, either. Footsteps. A man. We held our breaths. Knocking. I went to open the door, and Kyra went to the kitchen. I had never seen the guy in my life, and an enormous weight lifted off my heart.

"Good morning! "I greeted him with a shy smile.

"Good morning. I'm Robert Gregor, the responsible editor of the local newspaper."

"Jade Donovan. Please have a seat."

"Can we use the informal form?"

"Of course.

"Then let's get started. "He took out the recorder and placed it on the table between us. "How did you go from Hollywood to animal farming?"

"Actually, I came here from there, so this came before that."

"Do you regret coming back home?"

"No."

"Do you feel you failed in the world of acting?"

"No. I feel like I can't accept the rules they play by these days."

"You mean you're not willing to try out another casting couch?"

I could have known this topic would come up, and I should have been prepared for it, but I wasn't. Of course, my face gave nothing away.

"How would you describe yourself as an actor?"

"I would say I'm a middle-range actor. I was young and naïve."

"What do you derive from your performance or achievements?"

"Both, actually."

"How does it affect you that your comeback is not seen in a positive light?"

"How does it affect me? Everyone may decide whether they're happy about it. It doesn't affect me."

"It doesn't bother you if others like you or not?"

"How often do you investigate where the meat at the butcher's counter comes from?"

"But to buy something from someone, you need a certain level of sympathy."

"Hopefully, the quality is more important than the person behind it."

"Do you feel knowledgeable about what you're doing?"

"I learned everything I know from my father, so I trust in his expertise."

"But he also failed in the end, if I'm not mistaken."

"That could only happen because he resisted modernisation. It wasn't a lack of expertise."

"I heard you employ people for minimum wage, including a minor. Is that true?"

"Until the property is restored, I can't offer them more, but I made that clear to them in advance. And the minor is aware of what he is doing. Besides, he is not really a minor, almost twenty years old."

"And if the property never gets restored?"

"That's always a possibility. It's always there."

"Do you have any long-term plans? Or will you get bored with this, too?"

"I can't predict what the future holds, but currently, this is the first and only thing I consider in my life. You could call it a purpose."

"Thank you for taking the time for me."

"I thank you for listening."

As soon as he left, Kyra burst into the living room amidst shouts of joy.

"You were so professional. He was such a jerk, but you handled the obstacles so well."

together with those who were shallow and greedy, or complete opposites, so-called angels. They weren't his type. But Jade completely captivated him. Of course, he couldn't tell her many things because he didn't want to scare her away. Not about how he fantasised about her back then or who Linda was. And the list could go on.

His insatiable desire wouldn't let him sleep that night. Her eyes wandered in his mind when she looked at him, when he offered sex, or when he kissed her goodbye. Oh, what that mouth could do? He didn't think he could sleep that night, so he went to the gym. When he returned, there was a message waiting for him from her. His heart skipped a beat, as it was a picture file. Well, it wasn't what he expected. It really made him angry. Then he didn't know how he should react. He knew who was in the picture and when the opportunity to take the picture arose. She believed she could keep him in check with that picture. And she did. So far. Harming Jade wouldn't be a smart move.

He didn't know how to approach Jade again; her trust was fragile. He said nothing and didn't reach out. He knew what was going on inside her, so he let it be. The next day, his first task was to confront the responsible person. Without sugar-coating, he threatened her for life not to do such a thing again. But he was tiring of it all. Maybe it would be better to go public, then they wouldn't have anything to blackmail him with. Meanwhile, Kyra bombarded him with messages. He didn't respond because they were together. He was waiting for the right moment. Then today, Kyra just pounced on him unexpectedly.

"Don't you usually respond? "That's how the usually calm Kyra started, raising his eyebrow.

"I thought you were very busy with Jade, "the man said.

"You're hilarious. What did you do to her? "She asked, looking quite angry.

"She got what she deserved. "He chuckled to himself, sounding as if he assumed he was buried in the backyard.

"I know everything about you, Steve, and that's why I'm asking. "She was fiery.
"Nothing. I'm thinking."
"You must tell Jade the truth. Or what do you want from her?"
"I'm playing."
"With whom, Steve? With her? Specifically, with Jade?"
"Does it matter to you? "He was tired of women interrogating him.
"I thought you cared. I thought she was important to you."
"She wasn't, "he lied.
"You can't be serious. I believed you wanted her to be happy. And that journalist today? I can't believe this. She prepared me for it. It was a mistake for me to come here. "She stormed out of the office, slamming the door as much as a fragile girl like her could with a solid two-meter-high wooden door. She was right. But he was also a coward. He knew what he should do, but he didn't dare. Why? Because he could lose everything. Does he have everything if he cared about everyone's feelings? Then he wouldn't have the wealth to support her drug-addicted brother or provide for her father in prison. And the list could go on. He couldn't give up all of that for a woman, not even for Jade. He had to put an end to this affair. Either this way or that way...

*Eighteen years old. Gets out of the institution. He is alone, with nowhere to go. He is homeless. Goes to work. The street gangs are constantly robbing him...*

## Chapter ten

Kyra sent a message saying that she might not sleep elsewhere after all. She needs to take care of a few things and might come back in the evening. I told her that Steve just informed me he wants to take me out for dinner and talk, so I'll meet him at seven. She acknowledged everything was fine and that she'll be here at eight in the morning.

There was nothing specific in Steve's message, just that he's coming to pick me up at seven and we need to talk. I replied, saying it's fine. I was already prepared for everything because I was getting ready for the interview the next day. Since he mentioned dinner and the weather was nice, I chose a black strapless dress that gently hugged my figure. My back was completely bare. Black net stockings and black sparkling high heels, along with a matching small purse, completed the outfit. I applied makeup suitable for dinner and styled my hair in a bun. I looked good and felt satisfied as I glanced at myself in the mirror. The doorbell rang exactly at seven. I didn't know if it was him or if he sent someone. I draped a stole over my shoulders and headed out and locked the door and then the gate. Silence reigned behind me.

Bobby came to pick me up and whistled loudly. He seemed even more relaxed than the first two times, which I attributed to us knowing each other somewhat, talked about his daughter recently walking and his wife going to the gym: his whole life was an open book. He parked near an elegant hotel-restaurant in the city centre and mentioned that he didn't know how we would get back because he was instructed to return to the garage once he dropped me off. I shrugged, showing that I didn't know either. I thanked him and gracefully, as much as my dress allowed, stepped out of the car. They were already waiting for me at the reception, and they escorted me to our table where Steve was already seated. He stood up when I approached and pulled out the chair for me, just as a gentleman should. He touched his lips against my cheek.

"Hi, Jade," he greeted me. He seemed serious. He was wearing a blue silk shirt that complemented his eyes.

"Steve?" I responded. He had already poured himself a glass of wine and poured one for me without asking.

"I'm sorry I haven't been in touch. I've been busy. How is everything with Kyra?"

"It's going slowly," I smile. "I mean, I love her. She's very kind and sweet, but it was difficult to let someone in again after months of solitude."

"I can imagine what you mean. And what does she say? What are the prospects?"

"She's hopeful. I'm going for a TV interview tomorrow."

"You're not slacking off, that's for sure."

"And how about you? Have you spoken to Christine since then?"

"Yes. She was so thrilled to meet you she keeps nagging me about forgetting to ask for an autograph."

"Don't even try to embarrass me. It won't work."

"You're beautiful," he says, and I looked up from the menu to see if he was referring to my previous statement. But no, he was staring straight at me. Every thought was written on his face. We didn't mention the pictures. I didn't want to delve into that.

"We can go," he called the waiter, instructing him to call a taxi for us. The waiter promised the car would be here in two minutes. He handed him a wad of money. And the car was already here. We didn't even have to mention the address; the driver knew where we were going. Either Steve did the same thing with a different woman every week, or he really had a big reputation. I didn't care, I wanted him too. I could think about the rest tomorrow. As we turned onto the ramp, Steve opened the gate and asked the driver to take us to the house. He paid for everything properly. Just as he closed the

door, he was all over me. I tried to look around to see if anyone was there, but I didn't see anyone.
"Don't worry, no one is here. Or rather, no one will come here, "he reassured me. It didn't calm me down. I only relaxed when we reached the bedroom. We undressed each other wildly, grabbing each other wherever we could. "I want you," he gasps in my ear. I felt the same way. Urgent desire and pain exploded within me. I couldn't wait for him to enter me, but he had completely unique plans.

He hustled me onto the bed and attacked my mouth. I struggled with his tongue. After a while, I pleasured him orally. But he couldn't last long and finally penetrated me. It was intense, but it didn't hurt, at least not as much as last time. This was different. It was savage lovemaking, and I enjoyed it just as much. We ended quickly and lay panting in each other's arms. "I'm sorry for coming on to you like this. And I'm sorry about the dinner. We can order something."
"It's fine. There's no problem."
"You're so beautiful, I can't get enough of you," he says. He ordered food while naked, and I could peacefully rest my eyes on him. Then he returned to bed and kissed wherever he pleased. We talked a little. I was given a gown, and he put one on as well. We went downstairs to get the food. We ate in silence in the kitchen. He ordered pizza, and I had no objections. I also received a glass of wine. It seemed like a mandatory element for our encounters, at least that's what I observed. Insignificant bits of information. Later, I lay in his arms in bed. We had deep conversations, and he caressed me until I eventually fell asleep. It was a peaceful slumber. Traces of satisfaction were still within me. It felt as if I could sense his touch on me all night long. I woke up to the sound of his phone ringing. He was already dressed, staring at me as if waiting for me to wake up. His gaze unsettled me. It felt like I had seen that look before. Suddenly, fear gripped me. I had seen this same gaze a few months ago, which is why I ran away. It's why I left my dream behind.

"What's wrong?" I ask with a groggy voice, still tangled in the remnants of my dream, felt like we could handle anything together; I thought the same last night, that it couldn't be a big deal if we're here for each other. That's how I felt. But why does he look like this? Does he too? What the hell is going on?

"I'm marrying Samantha this weekend, "he said. That's it. No introduction. No discussion. Just a conclusion. What I should have expected. I should have known, won't create a scene. I won't give him that satisfaction. He must have already known. He knew a long time ago. When he said on the plane, "We'll see how much this all means or if it's worth it," "he already knew. I got up. I started getting dressed, gathering my dignity once again. When I was ready, I left the room without a word. He stared the whole time. The taxi was waiting outside, of course. When I got home, I just got into my car, feeling the need to go somewhere. Anywhere. I sobbed, cried, drove, stomped my feet like a mad person. Then I tried calling Kyra, but I had to pull over if I didn't want to die. I wanted to cancel the whole interview, the program, everything. But a woman answered, and I couldn't even comprehend what she was saying.

"Excuse me?" I ask in response.

"Kyra Smith is in the hospital. Are you a family member?"

"I'm her friend," I say.

"She's in the accident ward, in critical condition."

"I'm coming." That sobered me up a bit. Now I drove with purpose, like a mad person. What happened? I wondered? I burst into the accident ward with cuts and bruises. She was already in the room, surrounded by many friends and family members. But they didn't let anyone in yet. She had just come out of surgery. Her injuries are quite serious. They said she was beaten up. I couldn't believe my ears. The doctor was still with her. That's why they didn't let anyone in, but afterwards, they would allow people in one by one. Children are not allowed, but there are still so many people ahead of me. It was already nine o'clock.

"Is there a Jade Donovan here?" asks the doctor, who had just stepped out of the room.

"That's me" I showed.

"She wants to speak to you, but please don't upset her."

"I have no intention to. Thank you. "The doctor looked at me with surprise, taking in my smudged makeup and the wrinkled state of the beautiful dress I thought was perfect yesterday.

Inside, her room looked like something out of a movie. Machines, tubes everywhere. I had never been in a hospital before, and for that, I was grateful. I only know what it looks like from the ER, and it was exactly like that. Kyra was covered in bruises, shades of blue and green. Her eyes were closed and swollen. A nurse monitored the fluctuations on the monitors. They both looked up when the door closed. Kyra did so with difficulty. She tried to smile, then saw my face. I held her hand. I said nothing, waiting for her to speak. She gathered her strength. It was a struggle for her to breathe. Everything hurt, that's what I thought.

"Go there today," she says with difficulty" nothing else matters" Her gaze contained everything. That she knew and regretted, but also encouragement.

"I'll go, promise. I'll come afterwards," I say, and meant it. In that moment, it became my solemn determination that no one would mess with me. I'll show them who I am. Like an enraged beast, I stormed out of the building. No one even tried to talk to me. It wouldn't have been advisable. All my anger surged from my core. At home, I put on a short skirt, something that should be banned on the streets, and a similar top, or rather, I'd call it a rag: it barely covered my nipple. Plaid stockings and high heels completed the outfit. I didn't want to cause a massive car crash. My makeup wasn't ideal either, everything was excessive here. In the big city, no one would pay attention to me, but here? If there was nothing to gossip about before, there will be now. I'll make sure of it. But before heading to the TV station, I called Samantha. What do I care about responsible thinking? What do I care about regrets?

"Hi, Samantha, I'm Jade Donovan. I wanted to congratulate you on your wedding with Steve on Saturday. I tried him out in bed last night so you wouldn't have to. You can have him. He's good at licking and fucking," and then I hung up. I didn't calm down, and even if it was stupid, I didn't regret it one bit. Then I started walking. I just had to endure the path from the car to the entrance on foot, in the presence of onlookers, but it was nothing compared to the red carpet, so it went smoothly, didn't let anyone change my appearance. I prayed for a male interviewer, and then would tear him apart. It didn't matter what questions he tried to corner me with. And way. An aging jerk. The set was a studio set up like a living room. Red chairs. A white coffee table is between us.

His mouth dried up as soon as I sat down across from him. But he's been in the business for a while, so I couldn't shock him as much as I wanted to. Anyway.

"Dear viewers, we have a real Hollywood star among us. Jade Donovan. Here with Jeremy Collins on Channel 5 in Our World."

"Greetings, everyone."

"How come you left the golden goose?"

"Had enough. It's much more peaceful here, you know."

"Interesting that you say that, considering we just received news that your manager was beaten up."

"Yes, unfortunately, that's true. But the perpetrator will pay for it."

"Is that a threat?"

"Not at all. I trust our fantastic police force and the justice system."

"Your career came to an ugly end. What do you think about that?"

"I was a stupid girl, that's what I think."

"Do you think you'll have more success here?"

"We'll see, but I'll do everything in my power."
"So, does that mean you'll sleep with Steve Stark?"
"What can I say, Jeremy?" I ask in that annoyingly whiny voice that only kittens can do. "I fall for morally corrupt men."
"And yet you still employed his sister?"
"I don't differentiate between people. If someone does a good job, they can be anyone to me." I knew it! No one said it, but I suspected. Only since yesterday. Linda's peculiar holiday, the wedding, and the other pieces I put together in the puzzle.
"That's very kind of you. If my information is correct, you also employ a minor."
"Yes, well. He's not a minor anymore, just young and came to work of his own accord, and he knows what he's doing and why. He can understand the contract too, as he studied law before his parents died in a car accident. But he's starting again in September, and I'll support him however I can."
"You're a beautiful young woman. I can't understand why you want to work with animals."
"This was first, not acting. I've been away a lot, but I feel like this has always been my life."
"And the funerals? Please don't take offense."
"Jeremy, dear, I deeply regret not being there at my parents' funeral, but I'm sure they knew I loved them, even if I didn't always express it fully."
"You seem very fragile. Are you sure you can handle such a hard task?"
"Anything, Jeremy, "I said again in that whiny voice.
"And the professional expertise?
"I learned everything from my father, and he was very good, and yes, his stubbornness against innovations was his downfall, but he was still the best."
"You convinced me. Ladies and gentlemen, here she was, the new cowgirl, Jade Donovan. A truly kind and remarkable young lady. "I stood up, we shook hands, and I left. I didn't feel like I was at my best during that conversation, but not

that bad. And in the end, everyone takes away what is meaningful to them. Afterwards, I drove home to change into something more comfortable, but Linda was already there. I was angry that she didn't tell me. But should I be angry at her? When her wonderful brother doesn't hire women, and maybe if I had known she was his sister, I wouldn't have hired her either.

"Hi, Linda. Thank you for letting me know Steve is your brother. I almost embarrassed myself on TV if I hadn't put the puzzle together yesterday. Anyway, I need to hurry. What's going on?"

"My brother wants to make an offer for the entire farm."

"It's not for sale. Is that why you came? Are you a postman now? Until now, it was such a big secret that you knew each other."

"No, I came to apologise for not telling you. If you don't want to employ me anymore, I understand that, too."

"Why wouldn't I want to employ you? I accept your apology. Things don't seem to go well for you two, I see. Let's leave it at that. Can you work for me knowing that your bother is our competitor?"

"Of course."

"I don't want any family drama. I have enough of that already."

"Alright and thank you."

"Is everything going well otherwise? Lately, I have had little time to focus on the place, just..."

"I know. The article turned out great. Yes, everything is fine." Meanwhile, I grabbed a T-shirt and jeans, and I was ready to head to the hospital to see Kyra.

"We'll meet in the evening."

"Goodbye."

Tina Colt – Role/Play

Then Jade appeared, and it was as if every wet dream of his teenage years had come true as he looked into her large blue eyes. But he couldn't let this fleeting desire grip him in the groin. Yet she was so sexy, with her slim figure, black hair, symmetrical face, big blue eyes, and those full lips. He knew they were real, as even in his teenage years, those lips had got him into precarious situations more than once.

But it was all in vain because his father had taught him well how to take what he wanted. Maybe he didn't agree with him, which is why he fled to a distant city for university, but subconsciously he absorbed all the lessons of upbringing that his father had instilled in him. And as soon as he saw the broken Jade, the puzzle came together in his mind. The girl who was rejected by her parents, not accepting her, not helping her achieve her dreams, and then a man also took advantage of her hideously. It would be quite easy to lure in the wounded girl. He thought. Finally, his father would be proud of him. He would take what he wanted most.

## Chapter eleven

The days passed by slowly. Kyra was healing nicely, but she couldn't identify her attacker. She kept repeating that they had got out of a dark car, or rather a van, and beat her in the parking lot. They had sent a message for me to go back where I came from, or they would continue. But she somehow forgot to mention that her pink SUV had been vandalised days before. I was preparing for the county interview, and Linda helped me with a few things. The resulting article wasn't as terrible as I had expected, but the TV coverage didn't have the impact I had prepared for.

As the days went by, the dust settled. After the interview, I was getting ready for the airport. I felt strong enough to go to L.A., talk to Brandon, and settle things there. I still cursed myself for the Steve incident, but I had told no one anything. Kyra wasn't in a condition to discuss it, so I struggled with it internally. The last evening was so good, it made me believe everything would be wonderful, and I could finally be happy with a man. I didn't feel the same crazy love as I did for Brandon. Perhaps that only comes once in a lifetime. I sympathised with him, found him interesting, and on some level, he captivated me. I thought maybe this would be a mature, responsible relationship for me, even without the insane longing I felt for Brandon. I thought it might be better this way to avoid pain.

And what happened? The slap in the face came. And it wasn't just any slap. In our conversations, I got to know a sensitive man who respected where he came from and what he achieved and didn't look down on people who were below him on the social ladder. The farm was successful, and it depended on him. Before, it belonged to his father, but there was some complication. I don't remember exactly what. His father often went to my father, seeking advice and help for his own farm, but it never flourished like ours did. But I don't remember the reasons or what my father said about him back then. They were friends, and my parents always helped everyone. I always saw it as others stealing our time or taking advantage of us, and no one ever helped us with anything. They only came to us to ask for things, neighbours, and relatives alike. They never came bearing gifts. And my parents always went out of their own capacity to help them instead of dedicating that time to us. That's how I always experienced it. Maybe that's why I became a bit withdrawn, so that no one could take advantage of me. And yet, it happened to me too, just differently. But mistakes can be corrected. Well, I haven't done so yet, but surely, it's possible.

    The time for the county TV interview came, which had been rescheduled for a week later. Until then, I had time to prepare the youngsters for my absence from the place for a week. Linda had everything under control, and from what I saw, she was dedicated to my farm; thought I could trust her. I set up a bank account for her to make purchases for the Farm if needed, and it was all in order with receipts. I entrusted the house to Suzy, who cooked for them and kept the house in order. Katie took care of the mail. I felt like everything would be perfectly fine. I only stumbled upon the wedding photo of Steve and Samantha once, and even that was purely accidental. That's what I kept telling myself, but it didn't quite reflect the truth because I searched for the photo. They were an adorable couple, but they made me sick to my stomach. Although I didn't read the article about their wedding, I'm sure it would have made me vomit. It was good this way. Everything went back to normal. I was alone in the evenings with a book, my thoughts, or managing the affairs of the Farm. However, I regretted how I appeared in the TV interview. It brought out a side of me I didn't want to revert to.

    For this interview, I wore a suit, black pants and jacket, white top, and shoes. Afterward, I headed straight to the airport. It was faster this way than driving. Besides, I couldn't bear to make that journey again with the vehicle I came back with. As soon as I entered the TV headquarters, this was a county-level station, not a small-town studio. Professional makeup artists, dressing rooms, and many people rushing around with headphones on their heads. I hoped that Samantha or Steve's influence wouldn't reach this far, and I would deal with a completely independent person. Here, it was a female interviewer. She didn't want to talk to me before the interview. I didn't mind. I didn't have to wait long before they led me in. It was like the previous setup, a room arranged like a living room. Cameras from every angle, but it wasn't new to me. When I was a beginner, I used to get nervous. But since then, as soon as I walk onto a set, I focus on my role, and the outside world ceases to exist. Here, my role was to answer questions. The interviewer was a likable, beautiful woman with a warm smile. She had shiny brown, long hair, and a fit figure. She wore a sparkling top with black pants. You can tell a lot about a person just by looking at them, although maybe it's just me. But she seemed very kind to me.

"Now, dear viewers, we have a genuine star celebrating among us. Let's welcome Jade Donovan with great love, "she announced as I walked in. We shook hands, and she introduced herself. "Katie Simons," I smile, and offered me a seat on the red couch. I sat down. There was a glass of water in front of me on a small coffee table. She sat across from me, and the cameras were to my right. I had to look over there from time to time, obviously.

"Well, where should I start? What is it like to walk on the red carpet? Tell us, simple housewives, what it's like there?"

"When I bake something, which doesn't happen often since I'm not the kitchen wizard type, but if I decide to make something like that," she didn't understand what I was getting at, "and I take out the baked cake from the oven, then slowly, carefully, but with great pride, I bring it to the kitchen table, balancing it perfectly so as not to drop it, well, that's

exactly the feeling and sequence of movements," she smiles, understanding. Oh, thank goodness.
"That seems like a good analogy. But perhaps not as grandiose."
"The cake is much more grandiose. Believe me."
"Casting Couch? Does it really exist? "I've heard about the show, all emotional and soul-searching. But I didn't care anymore; everyone saw it in the newspapers.
"Nobody would believe it if I told them all. Let's just say it's even better than before."
"Is it harder to succeed as a woman? "Uh" oh! The alarm bell rang in my head.
"I wouldn't state it that way, and I wouldn't deny it either. A lot depends on timing. If someone is in the right place at the right time, gender doesn't matter. However, I think it's a bit more challenging for women in all areas, and it's not some feminist rhetoric, it's just how I see it. But since we're talking about the Casting Couch, women still have a second chance that men can't claim for themselves."
"Haven't you found your life partner?"
"No. I'm still searching."
"What should a guy be like?"
"Handsome, funny, kind. Educated."
"Brandon or Steve?"
"Neither."
"How is the farm going?"
"Well.
"We have some questions coming in from viewers. If you don't mind, I would ask those too," she says, and I didn't object.
"What advice would you give to a woman with a broken heart? A certain lady asks that her boyfriend just broke up with her, and she truly doesn't know how to process it. She has even contemplated throwing her life away."
"She should never do something like that. First, nobody deserves it, and second, if he caused her that much pain, it's

better if he's gone. There should be something meaningful in her life, and if there isn't, she should find it. And she should strengthen herself. It's crucial to stand on her own."

"Do you feel, Jade, that you're strong enough? Alone?"

"There was a time when I thought I needed a man, needed validation from someone else. But it was probably just an outdated ideology. Since then, I've realised that I'm accountable only to myself, and I don't need validation from any man." After that, a series of questions came, probing into my life there, how many clothes I had, who I met, what it was like to be famous. I answered kindly and with a smile. Katie was truly kind, with no ill intent. She asked nothing that could be hurtful. It lasted for an hour, and I felt a bit drained afterwards. I went to the airport from there, and two hours later, was back in the city. I messaged Brandon that I was here and wanted to talk to him. Obviously, we couldn't go to a public place, but I really didn't feel like going up to his place. He immediately called me as soon as I sent the message.

"Yes? "I asked. More angry than fearful.

"So, you've come back?"

"Just for a few days."

"Come up to my place. Where else would you go? To the castle?"

"I wanted to go there, "I said, sticking to the truth. The castle. Even if I just thought about it, the sense of hopelessness that one feels when they still live there after two years came back. There are the aspiring actors who came out of drama school but haven't got their big role yet. It was like a dormitory, but everyone called it a castle mockingly. Because a successful actor renovated it, but it still hosted many shady characters. And there was more cocaine than detergent. And the renovation was ages ago. "Alright, "I reluctantly agreed.

I hailed a taxi and took myself there, where I fled from that last morning. I hoped I was different now. Months had passed. In the meantime, I strengthened my soul. Hoped that it was true. Granted, I still felt different when it crossed my mind, but I reassured myself that I was over it. The Farm was mine. Brandon didn't matter anymore. That's what I kept telling myself. I needed to talk to him and find out what his actions meant last time. And why did he even do it? The house hadn't changed a bit, still with its marble floor and red carpet, and unfortunately, the porter was the same as that morning. He smiled encouragingly at me. And I proudly smiled back, knowing that I was no longer the person who left that day. He couldn't touch me anymore...

He was a likable older man, with grey hair that always reminded me of a kind grandfather or Santa Claus. I don't know if he was truly kind because I never spoke to him, but his smile certainly was, went upstairs, wish him good night, and the door was already open. I thought this was Brandon's apartment, but after the article from last time, I had to realise that this was just his place for entertainment. It had two rooms, a large living room, and a small kitchen that he didn't use. The living room had a magnificent view of the city. There was even a balcony. He was standing outside on the balcony when I entered. I closed the door behind me. I poured myself a drink and went out to join him.

"Hello, Brandon! "I greeted him, observing my own reactions. He looked at me but said nothing. He hadn't changed a bit. Unfortunately. He stylishly wore his blonde hair, his muscular upper body covered by a tight shirt, and he was wearing black trousers. He looked good, no denying that.

"Jade "he pronounced my name the way only he could, usually sending shivers down my spine. But this time, I tried to ignore it. "I missed you, "he said, and it seemed sincere, but I didn't fall for it.

"Why did you come last time?"

"I told you why. I just told you "He stepped closer, and I weakened.

"Stay there. Don't come closer, "I said, although my voice wasn't very strong, eight years. Eight long years. My heart

was his prisoner. "Why did you come? How's your wife and daughter? "I tried to divert the conversation.
"It's just business, baby. She was a wealthy hen when I married her, and I needed the money. Then Lilly came along. I can't get a divorce. But you... "he sighed and stepped even closer. I couldn't back away anymore. He grabbed the back of my neck and pulled me closer. He placed a kiss on the top of my head while whispering in my ear. "I want you, "and I knew I wasn't over him. But I didn't want to give in. I weakened. Too easily. I was angry at myself for it.
"That's your problem, Brandon. I came here just to tell you I don't want to come back. I'm done with this circus. That life left behind."
"I don't believe you. Your life was to play, to perform. You were capable of anything for it."
"It's true, and that's exactly it, Brandon. I did too much for it, and I got nothing in return."
"Baby, I have a role now. I want you. You're the most suitable for it. The shooting is here, and your part will only last a few weeks. You can make the biggest profit from it. It could be the movie of your life. Afterward, you can quit if that's really what you want. You need the money for the Farm as well. Come with me on Monday, let's talk to the writer. Or you talk to him."
"Why? Tell me the truth, Brandon. "I hated being lied to, so I took the wrong path because lying seems to be the norm here. If an average person encounters two hundred lies in some form every day, then in this profession, it's a thousand or two thousand per day, of course. So, I didn't expect the truth from him.
"Why what?"
"Why me?"
"Because you're the most suitable for it. I told you."
"Did you hurt Kyra?"
"Who? "He did not know about anything, and he wasn't just pretending. He really didn't know. And I didn't know him as

someone who would do such a thing. Not because of any moral reservations, but it would have required too much effort. "Just come on Monday, talk to him, see what it is, and decide if you're interested or not. Get someone to substitute for you until then. A few weeks. Of course, if you agree."
"I wanted to know why you came last time. But never mind. "I didn't get an answer, although I really wanted to know, maybe subconsciously hoping for nonsense.
"Do you want a strip, baby? "He asked. The temptation was enormous.
"No. I'm clean now. "The thought of coming back to play, like a last act, excited me, and I would have said yes almost immediately. But on one hand, I didn't want to slip back. I couldn't just abandon the Farm once I got bored with it. As Mary had pointed out to me. And finally, just because he wanted me didn't mean that the writer or the director would want me to. One should never rejoice in advance; I've learned that many times, but I could wait to see what Monday brings.
He finished the rest of his drink and didn't hold back, snorting a line of cocaine. I was terrified that it would make him aggressive, and I wanted to leave. I anxiously watched to see what it would trigger in him. Well, he had never been aggressive before, except that one time when he came to the Farm. Before that, I hadn't seen him angry. Now, however, I was afraid that he would be. But he wasn't. I didn't understand why that thought crossed my mind.
"I desire you, Jade. The longing for you is tearing me apart. Do you understand? "He didn't seem like he was lying, and I don't think anyone can lie while under the influence of cocaine. He seemed almost vulnerable. "Jade, go away because soon I won't be able to control myself, "he said. "Go! "He pleaded. "Go quickly. I'll call you. He ushered me out of the house, but I hesitated. Who would I give myself to if not to someone who admitted that he genuinely desired me?
"I'll stay, Brandon "I said. He froze, looked at me, and his eyes revealed both doubt and gratitude. I tasted the familiar

flavour in my mouth. His kiss was passionate. He greedily devoured my lips while already stripping me of my clothes. And I helped him. His hands caressed wherever they touched, leaving me with a deep sigh escaping his mouth. As soon as my breasts were freed, he almost pounced on them. He apologised if he caused any pain. We ended up in his bed, completely naked. He gently laid me down and pleasured me with his tongue. Then I returned the favour, giving him the same pleasure. But he wanted to penetrate me soon. It was as if he couldn't control himself. He pushed deep into me. He was almost in a frenzy of pleasure, and we quickly reached the point of no return. And perhaps for the first time, I regretted nothing. Because I knew everything about him. And I knew he desired me. Not someone else. He held me close to him and caressed my back.

"Thank you, Jade. I'm sorry if I caused any pain."

"It was so much better than before, Brandon. It was just fantastic."

"I messed up before and can't fix it anymore. Sorry. I pushed you away from myself and pushed you away from what you loved the most."

"It doesn't matter anymore, Brandon. I was also at fault, shouldn't have been so stubborn. I should have realised that it wasn't working and gone home."

"Now you think there are only dirty agents and dirty love, right?"

"It doesn't matter what I think, Brandon, loved you."

"I know, and took advantage of that. I'm sorry. But you're still a good person."

"I'm a confused person, slept with a guy..., and then he announced that he's marrying someone else. "I don't know why I told him this, but it just came out of me since he opened to me like that. "And with you, it happened more than once, and you already have a wife and a child. Maybe I don't deserve..."

"Sssh... Don't say that, "he hushed me with a kiss. "You're fantastic, "he whispered in my ear. He was ready to become one with me again. But this time, it was gentler. He enjoyed it leisurely, slowly, as if he wanted to etch every moment into his memory. I heard my phone ringing in the distance, but it was already night. Nothing important could be happening. At least that's what I thought.

Then, hours later, the urge to smoke a cigarette overcame me. Brandon peacefully slept next to me, got out of bed, and went to the living room. I took a cigarette from the coffee table, grabbed a robe and my phone, and went out to the balcony to smoke. I inhaled the first drag with such pleasure as if I had smoked yesterday. Once you've smoked, you never fully quit. After savouring the first puff, I finally looked at my phone. Tom called me twenty times, and Steve called me another twenty times. Five messages. The Farm is on fire. Oh, my god. How can I get there now? There are no flights until morning. Taking a taxi would take at least three hours. I quickly put on my clothes. Brandon also came out when he heard my movements.
"Where are you going, Jade? "He asked desperately.
"I have to go home; the Farm is on fire."
"But how will you go home now? It's night-time."
"I know. By taxi."
"That's a three-hour drive. I'll take you."
"I can't just sit here idle. It's a three-hour drive, Brandon.
"I know. But it's three hours with you. And it's the fastest option. "He was right. I hesitated. Months ago, I would have given anything for him to talk to me like this, to do these things for me. I didn't want to do it again. Like before, chasing after roles.
"Fine, but I'll pay."
"Don't mess around, Jade! "He quickly grabbed a hoodie.
 I didn't understand his sudden change towards me. I didn't understand his behaviour to begin with. Why now? Why me? What happened to the new girl? We were already

covering the miles in his new Mercedes. He drove confidently. Concentration suited him well. I admired his perfect facial features, which had meant so much to me recently, for which I had done so much foolishness.

"Brandon, would you tell me what happened earlier?"

"We made love. "He asked. But of course, he knew I wasn't referring to that. "When you left, or rather, when that article came out, all I could think about was what Amanda would say when she finds out she's taking Lilly. But she said nothing, just made me sign a prenuptial agreement that if we divorce, she will take everything from me, even my underwear, and take Lilly away forever. I can't allow that. I mean, Lilly. When I got married, I was burned out. It seemed like a good deal. I'm sorry to say this, but it wasn't great love, it was an investment. And she knew it. Then I became successful as an agent, and I didn't depend on her anymore. She depended on me. And here we are. Or rather, when I became successful, I started living, taking advantage of the young girls who would do anything for a role, and again, I must apologise. That's how it was, how it is. I exploited that. And then you came along, and you did what they did, but it was different. It pierced through so much, contradicting your principles, as if you were always testing yourself. It excited me even more. To break you. "A tear rolled down my cheek as he summed up how I had lowered myself. It was sad, but was the truth. "I'm sorry, Jade. "He slowed down and glanced at me. "Don't cry, baby."

"Please continue. I want to hear it."

"You see, that's it. That's who you are, what excites me. You push your boundaries to the limit. And then you walk away. I saw it in your eyes that day that you had enough. And in that moment, I knew I messed up. I lost you. Of course, I tried to fill the void, but I couldn't. I missed you."

"It's hard to believe."

"I understand. "We fell into silence. He focused on driving, and I contemplated what I had heard. "Tell me your story,

Jade. If you're not afraid that I'll expose you. If you're afraid, I understand that too."

"It doesn't matter anymore. We are three siblings. They don't live on the Farm. I have a sister who lives far away. She already has two children. She's an economist. I haven't seen them since I left here. My younger sister is studying psychology, working on her doctorate. I haven't met her either. But I talk to her sometimes. Our parents died two years ago. "He lifted his head at that but didn't interrupt. "I left here ten years ago. I was a terrible kid. My parents were constantly frustrated because of me, that's for sure. They always tried to talk me out of acting, told me to grow up already. And I ran away. I didn't write or call them. They died, and I didn't even come home for the funeral. And then I messed up everything there too, and I came back. But no one was waiting for me, only enemies. I started rebuilding what meant so much to my father. Steve introduced me to a woman who became my manager, or she was, until someone beat her up so badly, she ended up in the hospital, and she's still there. Everyone wants me to disappear from there as well. They painted the fence with messages like "whore, go back where you came from," things like that: well, these are the things happening to me. I slept with the guy, and in return, I received a picture of him in bed with someone else, telling me to get lost, and then he himself announced that he's marrying someone. What can I say? I love the Farm. I always have. It's not for you, it's probably hard for you to understand. Animals and manual labour, but it was my first. It's like it's in my blood. And now someone is setting it on fire. Steve wants to buy it. Maybe I really should consider it. That's it, in a nutshell."

"Jade, my life also started in the dirt, somewhere deep down. There's no point in sugar-coating it. I don't even know who my father is. He exploited my mother, treated her like a slave. And we lived in the countryside. I know very well what manual labour is, even though I always went to bed and woke up with the determination that I never wanted to have the same fate as my mother. I mean, being poor.

"That explains a lot, but not why, if you're so averse to it, you force young women into the role of a whore? "He pondered my words for a moment.

"It's because of power, but you're right. It was a despicable thing for me to do."

"I was missed, and…? That would have faded away."

"It didn't fade away. I tried everything. Women, more women. Alcohol, drugs, work, and even more work. I even took my family on holiday, hoping it would help, but I felt even worse. And then the other day, when I went down and saw you raging, I wanted you even more. I'm in love with you, Jade. Of course, I know what happened and I understand."

"I don't know, can't do it. Sorry. I can't even believe it."

"I know. It hurts, but I understand. I was stupid, deeply regret it."

How much would I have given for this confession before? What wouldn't I have done for it? I would have given everything. What I felt for him was an unparalleled crazy love, the kind that makes your stomach twist, that takes away your appetite and comes with many tearful nights. It brings a sense of euphoria from a message, a greeting, a word. Why didn't this come earlier? He's in love with me. I wouldn't say that it doesn't fill me with joy now, but somehow, I felt I would have been happier with this information back then and there. Now I had to consider what I truly felt.

We arrived slowly at the farm, or what was left of it. The firefighters were still there. Steve and Thomas as well. Both are covered in soot and dust. I almost jumped out of the car to talk to Thomas. Brandon parked neatly to the side, not obstructing the path of the firefighters. The house and the Farm were reduced to ashes. In the courtyard, my father's neatly collected pile of bricks and stones remained unharmed. He always collected everything. He didn't want to build anymore, but he kept everything like that and stored it in tidy order. There was nothing left of the rest of the property. I wanted to go in, but I was held back. Not by Thomas, who was still very timid, but by Steve. I wanted to scream. I wanted to stomp my feet. Why were they taking away everything I loved from me?

"Are you happy? "I asked him.

"Stop it, Jade! "Steve replied with patience in his voice.

"Wasn't it you who wanted to buy the whole thing?"

"Cut it out, Jade, "he said threateningly. At that moment, Brandon arrived and stood behind me, and I was very grateful to him.

"What happened? The animals? "I asked.

"All the animals were saved. I released them in time."

"What happened, Thomas?! You were here! "I confronted him, even though I didn't want to, because I knew him.

"I don't know, Jade. It was just like any other evening. The others left. I was still packing up a bit, then I went to bed. But I wasn't asleep yet. I just saw the flames. My ears were covered with headphones, so heard nothing. My door was locked, too. I felt nothing. I just saw it, but it was already too late, called the firefighters, called you too.

"By the way, where were you, Jade? When have we called? Did you retreat to your casting couch? "Steve asked, but before he finished, Brandon intervened and punched him. Steve's mouth cracked, but he didn't hesitate and tried to strike back, but Brandon was in good shape and was used to this kind of thing. If nothing else, bar fights were always happening in L.A.

"It's none of your business, Steve, but if you're so curious, yes, I was there, twice in a row. "I stroked Brandon's arm and tried to calm him down. We didn't need a fight for this. The firefighters were already part of the show, anyway. At least we brightened up their day. They were already getting ready to leave. They handed over the paperwork and expressed their regret that they couldn't save anything. "Just go home to your dear wife. You didn't need to come here."

"What are you going to do with the animals? The foxes will take them all. And the horses will go wild and trample everything in their path."

"I don't need a lesson in nature. I know very well. Just go away. I'll handle it."

"I'll help, Jade "he said. I didn't want to hear that, was angry, but if I thought soberly, I knew I couldn't solve this alone. That made me even angrier.

"No need. Just go. "He shrugged, got into his SUV, and left.

"Brandon, I can't accommodate you. "I turned to him, but I would have done something, taken care of it. "There's a hotel in town. Go there, don't turn back now. You're tired."

"And you? Are you staying here? What will you do at night?"

"I'll go get them. Don't worry! Just get some sleep. Thank you for bringing me here."

"Should I stay?"

"No!"

"I knew you would say that. I'm so sorry about what happened. Baby, everything can be replaced, except people. Remember that we'll meet later. "He kissed my lips and was already gone.

Thomas didn't say a word, he just followed me. I had nothing left. I should have been in black pants, a white shirt, and high heels, but I set off barefoot. My anger propelled me. I didn't feel the stubble under my feet. I just kept going and raging. My parents and I invested so much energy into this. Especially them. They worked their whole lives for this, and now everything fell victim to the fire, and although I think insurance will cover it, it will take a lot of time to rebuild everything. You can't erect the work of a lifetime overnight.

And all my memories of them. About them. Everything was gone. I scolded myself for not focusing on it, just one thing at a time. Usually, the horses are in the stable or the paddock. Now, they are running wild somewhere on the Farm, or if they have had enough courage, they have gone beyond fences and boundaries. The lambs and cows also have their separate grazing areas, but now all the animals are crowded together, trampling each other to death. We could hardly see anything.

Thomas got some flashlights from somewhere, but they didn't illuminate a great distance. At least we didn't stumble upon the trampled animals. It must have been around three in the morning, and I felt like giving up and crying. But in the next moment, I was so angry that I felt like running. We kept going. Thomas still didn't say a word. He didn't have a place to stay, either.

Finally, we spotted the lambs. But we needed the horses, and they were likely at the far end of the Farm. It was difficult to navigate in the darkness. I didn't trip without shoes, but Thomas did several times. Even if something hurt my feet, I couldn't feel it. I estimated we would reach the end soon. There should be two hundred sheep. Fifty cows and ten horses, which, apart from horseback riding, I did not know why we kept them - crossed my mind. Everything was mechanised nowadays. Well, we needed a few horses to herd the animals, but not ten. I spotted a couple of horses and immediately headed towards them. Bella neighed to show its presence. My favourite. Knows me. We didn't have saddles or anything else. It wasn't a problem for me, but I assumed it was for Thomas. Anyway, he climbed on one. Once we were both up, one of us went towards one end of the property, and the other towards the opposite end. That's how we herded the animals uphill. Well, the ones that were left. We saw quite a few carcasses on our way up. We had no whip, no lasso, nothing.

Our voices and the height advantage from the horses were our tools. The lambs followed skilfully wherever we herded them. The cows were much more difficult to handle. We made slow progress. We tried to cover as much area as possible and not let any animal go back. It was already dawn by the time we reached the top. Both of us were exhausted.

We tried to separate the animals in the upper area and tied the horses to the gate.

We found seven. The cows were on one side; the lambs were on the other, and we gathered a few beams from the burnt ruins to construct a makeshift fence. Linda was the first to show up. Then, slowly, the others arrived. They stood there in shock, just as bewildered as I was. My feet were bleeding from countless wounds, but that was the least of my concerns.

"Did you notice anything strange yesterday? "I asked. They shook their heads, unable to speak. They all stood there above us while we sat on rocks.

"Did everyone leave at the usual time?" I continue.

"Yes, everything happened as usual. It's a good thing Tom was still awake. What would have happened if he were inside when it caught fire?" Katie cries, which was surprising coming from her.

"And did Suzy do everything the same as usual?"

"Why are you asking these questions now?" Linda was taken aback. It was difficult for me to determine if any of them were lying or involved. They all seemed sincere to me.

"Because the police will ask you the same questions, and I want to know what happened. Especially if it turns out to be intentional arson. Then I'll be the first suspect, followed by all of you, one by one."

"But you have an alibi," Linda says.

"That's true. Anyway, never mind. Stay here today and help keep the animals inside. I'm going to take a shower and come back. If someone comes, call me, or wait for me. Starting tomorrow, take a holiday. I'll pay you as if you were working. Then I'll figure out what I can do." I was exhausted and dirty, but I couldn't sleep. I borrowed Tony's car, and despite it being his love, he gladly let me use it. A Porsche Carrera turbocharged... of course. One day, when this is all over, I'll have it cleaned for him. I was sweaty and dirty. I reluctantly put my shoes back on, which made me want to scream in

pain, but I needed to buy clothes first so I could shower and not have to put them back on. Stopped at the first clothing store and quickly grabbed what needed. I didn't want to give people a reason to talk, though now they wouldn't talk about me every five minutes, but only every ten. And in the next ten minutes, something much more exciting than might happen. But of course, I wouldn't be myself if I didn't clumsily run into Samantha, looking her best as she swayed towards me, while I balanced the shopping bags on my way out. Honestly, I hadn't seen her since the incident. I didn't want any trouble. I hoped she wouldn't approach me. But of course, I couldn't be that lucky. I put on my calmest demeanour and forced myself not to let her get under my skin.
"Hey, Jade!"
"Samantha!" I almost reached the car when she stopped me there. "Congratulations on your wedding!" I say, to which she raised an eyebrow.
"I'm sorry about what happened to the Farm," she says.
"We'll rebuild it" I tried to sound indifferent.
"You could have accepted Steve's help, "she said, and I didn't quite understand where she was going with this game. But I didn't want her to see through me.
"I'll handle it on my own. Everything is fine."
"Your foot is bleeding. Oh my god! It's already seeping out of your shoe." I looked down, and it was true.
"It's not that bad. But I must go now."
"If you need anything, just let me know."
"Sure. Thanks," I hope I was 'fake' enough for her to believe that my 'sure' was a well-intentioned 'sure' and not a 'maybe, if it freezes.' "Bye." I got into the car and went to the hotel. So, I had to reschedule that car wash for Tony. At the only hotel in our town, I hesitated whether to go to Brandon's or rent another room. And if I don't go to him, will he be mad at me? I asked at the front desk for his room number, but they solved this problem for me because they couldn't give it to me. They had to ask if they could let me up. I looked quite

shabby, so I wasn't surprised that a decent hotel wouldn't allow me to wander around like this. Brandon said to let me up.

"I'm sorry for waking you up. I just didn't know if... well, I came to take a shower," I tell him as I stepped out of the elevator, and he was waiting in the hallway in his robe. It wasn't a Hilton, that's for sure, but it was the best in town, or rather the only one. Apart from that, there are rundown motels, but if I had to compare it to the thousand hotels I've been to, not that bad. Purple was the dominant colour, but I liked it. I had no problem with it, especially not now.

"Jade, what happened to your foot? Oh, my god. Come, sit down! "He pushed me onto the bed in the room and started carefully taking off my shoe and was hesitant to touch it, but it wasn't because of the blood. He didn't want to cause any pain. "We should go to a doctor."

"No, we don't need to. I just want to take a shower and change clothes. I must go back."

"Don't be ridiculous! "It looked awful. But I walked here on this foot, so it can't be that serious.

"Brandon, stop it. I just want to take a shower. "I could see that he had something to say, but he didn't utter a word, just raised his hands in resignation. He stepped back, but as the adrenaline left my body, it became quite difficult for me to stay standing. He rushed over and tried to help, but that's when the tension snapped. "I don't need help, can go alone, don't need you or anyone else. Leave me alone! "But he didn't leave. He held me even tighter.

"Come on, sweetheart. Let's shower together. Come on, baby. I love you. "Oh, my god, he said it. Even in this miserable state, it melted my heart. But I couldn't react. I hoped the shower would refresh me because the world was spinning, and I wasn't sure if it was because of the blood loss or exhaustion. He quickly took off his robe and was already next to me in the shower. We fit in comfortably together.

Showering turned into him, washing me and kissing wherever he could reach.

"You're beautiful, "he whispered in my ear. Even though I couldn't believe in my current state, I saw it in his eyes, which revealed everything. It crossed my mind that he truly loved me. Just the way I am. He knows every part of me, every dark side. Of course, it also occurred to me he couldn't get a divorce. He led me to the bed, a question, or rather a plea, in his eyes. I reached out my hand to him. He kissed me passionately, as if he was afraid of parting. He quickly positioned himself inside me and loved me swiftly. Maybe he didn't want to hold me back, maybe he couldn't control himself. His muscular body towered over me, moving rapidly, bringing both of us to the end. "I'm sorry if I caused you pain, "he said, his voice filled with remorse.

"You didn't. Not at all. I would gladly stay here in your arms. All day long. And tonight, but it's not possible. "The ringing of his phone interrupted our intimate moment. He glanced at the screen and his eyes widened. I thought it must be bad news since he answered the call, which was unusual for him on a weekend. He listened to the caller and said,

"I'll leave right away, but it will take at least two hours for me to get there. Call Dr Jackson. 'Then he hung up. Disappointment crossed his face, followed by shame.

"I must go home. Lilly is ill. I'll take a flight; it's faster. I'll leave the car here. "He handed me the keys.

"As it's easier for you, "that's all I said, even though I wanted to ask him what was said on the phone and where the car was. But now the previous expressions made sense.

"I'll bring it back on Monday."

"Will you come? "He asked, his face brightening. 'I'm happy. Then we'll meet on Monday. At two o'clock. I'll send you the address. "He was already prepared to leave. "I booked the room for the whole day, just in case you don't want to go back with this foot."

"I brought bandages, shoes, don't worry about me. "He kissed my lips and then he was gone.

*He is twenty-two years old. His path is slowly taking shape. He learns self-defence and works as a security at a bar. He builds connections. A wealthy elderly actress takes him under her wing. She sends him to school, dresses him up, and teaches him the ins and outs of life. Especially how to take money from people and exploit them. He quickly pairs up with a rich and untalented actress. Although he is searching for the love he once felt for the girl, it just doesn't come. In the meantime, he takes from each girl whatever he can, just as his mother was taken from him. Hatred burns within him towards people, especially happiness and wealth, as he lacked both. He couldn't accept that someone could have them effortlessly. He despised them all and wanted to take everything from them...*

## Chapter twelve

Felt lonely as he left, but I didn't have time to dwell on it. I ordered a coffee and an energy drink, and it arrived just as I finished getting dressed. I rented the room for another two days. At least I had somewhere to come back to. I drank the coffee and was on my way. I went back with Tony's car, apologising for getting it dirty and promising to have it cleaned once I have the opportunity. Everyone was picking up debris in the yard, but there wasn't much to do. By the time I arrived, the police had also arrived. They questioned everyone. It was determined to be arson, so I can only receive the insurance money if it's proven that I wasn't responsible. I received the reports: an investigation will be launched. Despite having an alibi, I could have asked someone to vouch for me.

Supposedly, they found a homemade incendiary device among the ruins. When the police left, I sent everyone away since there was nothing more to be done. I asked Thomas to come by on Monday and feed the animals because I wouldn't be there. Had to take on the role if I got it because I didn't have enough money to rebuild the farm again. I was angry and disappointed, but I waited until everyone left before crying. Fortunately, Katie could take in Thomas. I promised them I would pay for their forced holiday. I hoped they could come back soon. Of course, I still was sobbing when Kyra showed up. She still didn't look perfect, but was much better.

"How are you? "She asked. Since we became good friends, she changed her style towards me. I liked this much better than the well-mannered, always polite Kyra. She was friendlier with me.

"Shit always hits the fan."

"One of my friends always says that even if shit is up to your neck, at least it's not waving."

"Optimistic.

"Tell me everything, "she said. Her creole skin was still beautiful, and she was still very attractive, but she had lost a tremendous amount of weight.

"Why didn't you tell me that your car was vandalised?"

"I didn't think it would escalate. If I had told you, you wouldn't have continued."

"Maybe, but then we would have known that someone is capable of such things."

"Who do you think it was?"

"I do not know, "I said, telling the truth. Many things crossed my mind, but I didn't want to share them, fearing it would only get her into more trouble.

"And is it one person or two? 'I shrugged at the question, not wanting to discuss it with her either.

"I think your work here is done. Find a less troublesome client."

"What are you going to do? 'She asked. She settled down next to me on the ground.

"I'm figuring that out. Almost nothing is salvageable. A bunch of animals died."

"What about Steve?"

"What about him? He was here last night, helped put out the fire, but I think he was more interested in fuelling it than extinguishing it. Let's leave it at that. Seriously."

"Ok. I must go. I'll come back. Jade doesn't give up. If you need me, let me know and I'll come."

As she left, Suzy came in too, bringing me some food. I almost cried from her kindness. She said she wouldn't go anywhere else until this place was restored. Her loyalty touched me deeply. Of course, I couldn't eat, but I appreciated it. I started calling carpenters, masons, and plumbers. Setting up appointments, requesting quotes. Thomas and Katie came back and brought feed for the animals from the store. Steve also sent them a couple of bags. I didn't want to accept them, but I didn't want to send them back either; it would be too Jade-like. I let it go. Since I didn't need to be here for the phone calls, I asked Katie to take me to the hotel. It wasn't too far, but I didn't feel like walking in the distance now. In the room, I ate a little. I took care of the calls I could and then calculated the finances. In the meantime, I fell asleep and didn't wake until the next morning.

My phone was filled with messages and missed calls. Mostly from Brandon. I wrote to him I was staying at the hotel, and everything was fine, just fell asleep. I also inquired about his daughter, but he didn't respond. Quickly got up and went shopping. I had to pull myself together by the next day, didn't tell anyone why I wouldn't be around. I only bought clothes for the following day because if I stayed there, I could replace what I desperately needed. And if not, then I would have them here. Given the circumstances, I really hoped I would get the role. I also went to the Farm. There was a lot of feed leaning against the gate, and the three lost horses were tied to the fence too. Maybe not everyone in town hated me after all. I quickly brought everything inside and tied the horses with the others. I called Tom and asked if he could be here from tomorrow because the workers were coming. He asked if Katie could come too. I had no problem with that.

Brandon sent me the address, and the script, which seemed like it was about my life. A woman who always falls in love with the wrong man. The male lead was in a much higher category than me. Thousands of women swooned over him. I felt hopeless. Even though I liked the role, it was so fitting. Anyway, I wanted to be in my best shape for the meeting tomorrow with the writer; writers are quite quirky for the actors, and in every other aspect as well. But Brandon knew how to handle them. He could charm them all. The offer was included too. With all the films I had done so far, I hadn't earned as much as I could with this one. Not to mention the boost it would give to my career. But I didn't want to think about that. It would only paralyse me. I took a long, relaxing bath, applied various creams to my legs, although I didn't expect the wounds to heal by tomorrow, but it helped a little. I left them uncovered to dry. The shoes I bought were going to torture my feet, but I couldn't go into slippers either.

In the afternoon, I received various offers, and it seemed like they could start the work. It made sense to prioritise the accommodation for the animals. The house could wait. They could finish the stable and the paddock in a week, horses settled. I presented a plan, not deviating much from the previous state. They accepted it. The lambs' area wasn't such an enormous investment either. They said they could start that tomorrow and finish it in a week. The cattle were a tougher nut to crack. It required a lot of machinery and a larger building. I had a plan for that as well, and they accepted it, thought to myself, it's now or never, and left the end of the farm for the apple orchard. I divided the remaining part into sections for the lambs and the cattle. But now it was getting closer to the house. I wanted to have more poultry and pigs in the front. Eggs, milk, apples, and pork. These might be bold steps, but if not now, then I'll never do it. And there was plenty of space.

A one-bedroom house would be enough for me. Across from it, a dining area for the workers, and accommodation for Tom or anyone else who might need it later. After that, the poultry yard could begin, followed by pig pens and goat enclosures. Then the horses, lambs, and cattle. They could also change the fences. I wanted to plant the apple orchard myself. Or rather, I wanted to help. Maybe I'll be back home tomorrow evening, and then I can take part in everything. But that would require taking a loan, which may not pay off. I might fail. But that's always a possibility. I quickly went to bed to be fresh and vibrant the next day. I looked up the writer and the other principal actor. I didn't know who the other competitors were. It would be revealed tomorrow. I thought about Brandon. And his wife and daughter. Why didn't he say it earlier?

Or did it take this for him to realise? If so, what should I do now? Or what does he want from me? What should I do? I asked myself these questions a thousand times and pondered over things. He was so kind to me, and we knew each other well. We knew everything about each other. I wasn't indifferent to him yet. Despite the bad things, he still held a special place in my heart. Then I fell asleep. I woke up to the alarm clock at eight in the morning. I ordered a coffee while I showered and got dressed. For the long drive ahead, I wore jeans and a simple t-shirt. My leg was much better now, but still not perfect, far from it. However, I didn't want to drive for three hours in slippers, nor would I be capable of it. Brandon wrote to go to his apartment with no worries. It didn't seem appropriate, yet it felt logical to me. Maybe his wife didn't even know about this apartment. I chose my favourite songs for the road to make the highway less monotonous. If I didn't have a destination, I would choose the country road instead of the highway, but I couldn't afford to get stuck in traffic. And there was still a chance, albeit smaller.

Then I didn't encounter any traffic jams, and I arrived there in three hours. The doorman just waved. He didn't say a word. I parked the car in its place, of course. I refuelled it and had it washed. There was no one in the apartment. I felt like an intruder. Even though I had been here many times before, Brandon wasn't with me this time. He left a cigarette on the table, and once again, I let myself be tempted. Then I changed my clothes. I chose a blue dress that stressed my nicely tanned skin. It wasn't flashy, yet it was feminine. Black stocking, black high heels, black purse. A subtle necklace. My watch, which I got from my mother in year seven. True, its brown leather strap was completely worn out, and it didn't match my outfit, but I wore nothing else. Simple makeup. I thought Brandon would come up and we would go together, but he wrote we would meet there. It didn't deter me. I got in a taxi and had myself driven there. I suspected we were going to the art district. That's where writers usually lived. Not the washed-up ones, but those who were successful. Each house had a considerable size and a swimming pool. The houses varied in their eccentricity. The creatively quirky writers lived in the most unusual cottages. Based on what I read about this writer, it was hard to determine how eccentric he was.

But judging from his house, it didn't seem too alarming. It wasn't a hippie house, but a relatively modest, snow-white, large, towered house. It even had two parking spaces. If he had to come to his house for the meeting, I didn't think he would leave his home too often. And I deduced this from the cars as well. Not a speck of dust could be found on any of them. I didn't know if Brandon was already here, but I announced my arrival. Stepping into the house, I found what I expected. Handmade wall decorations. Paintings. Books. Deep, soft carpets. I was led into a room that looked like a dentist's waiting area. I guess I don't need to explain. There were still five minutes until two. Brandon was nowhere to be seen, but I didn't mind. At exactly two o'clock, the door of the "dentist's office" swung open, and the writer himself came out. He looked just like in the pictures, the same as in real life. An elderly guy with grey hair, a look that says, "I've seen it all." "Are you Jade Donovan? "He asked.

"Yes. Nice to meet you! 'I put on my most enchanting smile.

"Unfortunately, something came up for Brandon, but please come in. Have a seat. "He pointed to a couch; this room resembled more of a psychologist's office than a dentist. Sofas, soft pillows, bookshelves. There was a table at the other end of the room, but it didn't seem like anyone used it. He said nothing, just scrutinised me with his gaze. I handed him my portfolio, but he didn't flip through it. I stood there, meeting his gaze. It wasn't the first time, and probably not the last time, that I found myself in such a situation. It was uncomfortable, but I showed nothing on the outside. "What would you do for the role? "I tried not to interpret it in the way he intended. I kept smiling incessantly.

"What would I do to get the role? 'I asked back, but I also answered. "If my foot didn't hurt this much, for example, I could hop on one leg or go to the store to get some milk, "I continued to smile without a hint of expression. Maybe I'll mess up the role of a lifetime, but I wasn't willing to make the same mistake as before. Regardless of money or fame. And then I won't be able to look at myself in the mirror again. I didn't ask for that. "But if I get the role, which, by the way, perfectly describes my entire life, I will do everything to deliver the best performance. "He said nothing. I thought we were done with this. Maybe someone else will be more daring after me. I stood up. "You'll find all the information in the folder. Goodbye! "With that, I walked out the way I came. I called a taxi and went to Brandon's place because I left my bag with my laptop and clothes there. I found Brandon there too, drinking and using drugs, even though it was only half-past three in the afternoon. As soon as I entered, he attacked me.

"What happened? "His tone wasn't kind, and he didn't even greet me.
"I'm glad to see you, too. Why do you have to get high at half-past three in the afternoon?"
"What happened? Answer me! "He squeezed my neck and forced me to look at him. He didn't want to do this as much as he did.
"Nothing happened. "I realised the reason he didn't show up was for me to decide what to do with the old man. How I would react to his offer. But the way he was behaving right now, I wasn't sure if I wanted to reassure him.
"You're lying! Tell me what happened! "He was raging. Where was that kind man?
"I'm leaving "I said. I started gathering my things, but he caught hold of my hand. "Brandon, let go. Brandon, these hurts. "I told him and wasn't even that concerned about my stuff anymore; I just wanted to leave. There was a raging fire in his eyes. And although I knew it was because of the cocaine, it didn't reassure me. I was afraid of him.
"Tell me what happened! "He gritted his teeth, but I could still feel his anger.
"Nothing happened. Let go, Brandon! "But he didn't let go; instead, he slapped me. My mouth burst open, and I tasted the blood in my mouth. Suddenly, tears burst out of me, even though I'm not a cry-baby, or at least I didn't think I was, but everything became too much at once. Then, upon seeing the blood or my tears, he snapped out of it.
"Jade, I'm sorry, please! Forgive me! Please, don't be angry "but I was determined. I didn't say a word; I grabbed my bag and started walking. He called after me a thousand times, but I acted as if I didn't hear him. At the entrance, the same old man, his empathetic gaze, burned into my retina. So here we are again?! Don't you learn? That's what his gaze asked. Is there anything in my life that's okay? Nothing, right? I wanted to go home, but of course, I had no home. I didn't know where I was headed. Where should I go with a bleeding

mouth, sore feet, when my home, which is already three hours away, burned down? Well, this is morbidly funny. I called a taxi and had myself taken to the Castle.

I hope Antoinette was still there. She was an aging, never-made-it actress whom many hated, but I liked her, and now I needed her. The taxi driver, an Indian guy, probably had seen more striking things than a crying woman with a bleeding mouth in his taxi, so he didn't say a word. I arrived. The building hadn't changed at all, except maybe it had become even more run-down. In the hallway, there were giggling naked girls and boys, completely wasted. They said at the entrance that Antoinette was in the bar, as usual. When I walked in, she was the only guest. She sat at the bar, flirting with a young bartender. When she saw me, she withdrew. Antoinette watched my arrival from the mirror. Nothing had changed in the bar, either. Maybe they replaced the tables because they had been danced on too much, or perhaps other things happened on them, so they were all wobbly now.

But I think my name and the year I graduated are still engraved in the chair in the corner. "The stray girl has returned. "She said without turning around. I stopped behind her. I said nothing. Tears ran down my cheeks. Finally, she turned around, and I threw myself into her arms, sobbing. "Jade, if you're crying over a man, I'll kick you out immediately, "she said, making me smile. "If a man did this to your mouth, then I'll track him down. Come on, tell me, for heaven's sake! Stop crying. Give the lady a double whiskey, Roberto."
"What should I tell you? You know everything, don't you?"
"That's true, but I want to hear it from you. How did the meeting go?
"It didn't. There was no meeting. I handed in my portfolio and left."
"Then what's on your mouth? "I didn't feel like telling her. Brandon was like her son. I knew, just like everyone else, but we never asked about it.

"Let it go. It's not important. Let's drink. It's much better now. How do you know everything? "I played dumb.
"That's a secret, baby. "She had aged little since the last time I saw her. She must have been around sixty, but that's how she always looked since I knew her. Excessive makeup. Over-teased hair. Tight clothes. "By the way, will you have any problem downing this double whiskey with your skinny little ass?"
"I don't care. Can I sleep here?"
"Of course, my dear. "I downed the drink, and soon enough, it felt like I had been knocked out and asked which room I could go to. I got a VIP suite, which was only slightly better than the other rooms. Its only advantage was that I was alone in it and could lock the door.

Brandon kept texting and calling non-stop, but I didn't respond. I was so exhausted and frightened. Then I went to bed, but suddenly I woke up with the feeling of what if he hurts himself. I gasped for air and tried to dismiss the thought. I couldn't calm down. He didn't believe me. He couldn't believe that I didn't do it. Well, considering my past actions, it's not that surprising. He didn't know me before and didn't know the girl who had her own pride. He only knew the actress who would do anything for a role. Then the thought crossed my mind: I'll take out a loan. My thoughts raced. I don't need a role at any cost. At this age, it's time for me to commit, even if it's just to a mortgage. With this idea, I was satisfied and was about to go home, but the alcohol in my bloodstream was stronger, and it was still nighttime. However, my conscience wouldn't let me go back to sleep, so I called him.
"Brandon?"
"I'm sorry, Jade! Please. I didn't go because I wanted you to make your own decision, but I can't stand the thought now that you did it. I'm sorry. It's driving me crazy. Of course, this is not an excuse. "His voice was completely calm, which worried me even more. It felt like a farewell. How did we go

from him sharing me with his friends to him going crazy if someone touches me?

"Brandon, nothing happened. I left. I don't need the role if this is the price. Not anymore."

"Really? "Hope crept into his voice.

"Of course."

"Will you come to me? "He asked. I think he knew where I was.

"No. I drank quite a bit; I'm not feeling well. My feet hurt. I'll go home in the morning."

"Okay. And can I visit you," – hesitated.

"Yes, if you want to, "I finally blurted out. Has he already got over it? Or will he lose his mind again? It was as if he had been waiting in the hallway because there was a knock on the door almost immediately.

"Hi "I greeted him shyly; I was a little afraid of him. Although I had washed off the blood, my mouth was still swollen. His handprint was visible on my neck. I got a shirt to put on as a makeshift. He came in but didn't approach me. There was only a small lamp on. He changed his clothes and took a shower. He was wearing different clothes, and I could smell his shower gel.

"Hi, Jade! I brought this for you. "He opened a box, and there was a beautiful white gold necklace inside. Three intertwined strands, and even those were intertwined with three chains.

"Can I put it on? "He asked.

"Of course, "I said. The air got trapped in me as he approached closer. He stepped behind me.

I lifted my hair to give him better access to my neck. He clasped it and left his hand on my neck for a moment longer than necessary. Then he kissed my neck. "I can't control myself when you're near me, "he whispered in my ear, still from behind. He gently turned me around. I looked into his eyes, and all I saw was pure desire. "Is it allowed? "He asked. I nodded. He kissed me gently, as if I could break. He pulled me tightly into his arms. This was more than just a kiss.

Every feeling was contained in this shy yet passionate kiss. Reluctantly, he stopped. He went to the window and stared out. He couldn't see anything; the garden was pitch black, yet he stood there for minutes, looking at nothing. I watched from the bed, which resembled more of a couch than a bed. He turned around but didn't move away from the window.

"There are moments when I think I don't care about Lilly anymore, and I should get a divorce. But of course, I couldn't do it. When a person has a child, everything changes. I never believed in these clichés, but then Lilly came along, and I became one of those who only talk about their children and rush home to be with them or those who must adjust everything because of their children. When I look at her, everything else fades away, and such immense love fills me. I can't see anything else, and I would do anything for her. Anything. So, when I think about wanting to be happy myself, I consider myself selfish and a shitty person. Of course, most of the time, I was exactly that, and if this is my punishment, then I deserve it. But I still want it. Or I would make up for anything just to not have to suffer anymore. For a long time, I thought I was given this love to experience how miserable I made people and to become one of them. Do you understand?"

"Of course, "I said, and I did. There were many actresses who had children, and I knew what they went through. I had nothing to add to the rest. I didn't know what he was trying to achieve with all this.

"But this can't go on like this. What did I do to you this afternoon? Oh god. I hate myself for it. "He glanced out the window again. I felt sorry for what he was feeling, but I couldn't help him with that; he could only do it himself. "I know I must let you go, and that was the plan, but then you called me last week, and then we made love, and my god! I can't be without you; you're like a drug to me. But I know, and I don't know. Do you understand?"

"Yes, Brandon. What do you want me to say? "I asked. "You treated me the way you did back then, and then in the afternoon. Of course, I understand you can't get a divorce. It's completely understandable. Really. Wait, a minute "I got myself worked up "there was a guy who shared me with his friends, who turned me into a whore, then a man who, after sleeping with me, went and married another woman, oh, not just any woman, the one who is my biggest enemy at home. Then the first man declares his love but tells me he can't divorce. After that, he physically abuses me because he thinks I will fall back into the role of a whore for another role. Meanwhile, I forgot that while I was your bitch, I pushed everyone away, and by the time I came to my senses, I no longer had a family. Someone set my house on fire, and my manager was beaten up, and they post everywhere for me to go back where I came from, where I was once a nobody. "Shame was as present in his eyes as pain. "What do you want? Because last time I came back to tell you I don't want to come back, that I'm done. But then you declared your love, and after Steve, I thought, why not give myself to you when you know me and want me to? But what do I have? A married man who physically abuses me. So?"

"You're right, Jade. I know very well, and I said I'm sorry. I just can't stay away from you. "His expression completely changed. He looked helpless, and I felt so sorry for him, but I still knew I was right. Or rather, not that I was right, I simply didn't want to humiliate myself again and put myself into a situation when I wouldn't come out as a winner; it had to end. Even if I wasn't over it, even if I didn't enjoy suffering. I would forget.

"Oh, but you can, Brandon. Just give yourself some time. I'm not any more special than anyone else. In fact, less. Go, please."

"Jade..."

"Go, Brandon, we both know it's the right thing. We just proved it. Please. "He stepped closer, placed his hand on the back of my neck. He looked deep into my eyes. I remained resolute. I pressed my lips together, averted my gaze. He said nothing, just left.

My heart clenched at the sound of the door slamming. I held myself back from crying. He's probably going home, calling some other girl, getting high, and tomorrow I won't even cross his mind. I hoped it would be that way. I didn't want him to suffer. In fact, I never wished that upon anyone. Dawn came slowly, but as soon as it touched my window, I was already outside the building. I had myself driven to the airport. I was already waiting for take-off on the plane when my phone rang. It was the writer.

He said the role was mine, and he was sorry to hear that Brandon was no longer my agent, but he wished me good luck in finding another one. He said they were eagerly waiting for me on set next Monday. I should learn the role and everything necessary. I was happy, yet not entirely. Because it meant I had to come back, I would meet Brandon again, no matter how much we avoided each other, even if he's no longer my agent. I could deal with that later. When I landed and turned on my phone, I had a thousand and one messages from various agents. I thought Brandon had arranged for someone else to take his place. I had myself driven from the airport to the farm, even though I was in a shabby state, and I knew there was nothing there. The workers were busy at the stables, the poultry yard, and the lamb pen. Katie and Tom were thrilled to see me. With professional makeup, nothing showed on my face. They didn't even notice.

They were bustling around the workers until my taxi stopped, and then they practically ran towards me. I didn't know they felt so close to me.
"Hi, guys, "I greeted them with a smile. Suddenly, all the tiredness left me. Katie, with her petite and always helpful attitude, and the ever-shy Tom, made a pleasant couple.

Typical protagonists of a married comic strip. The loudmouthed wife and the submissive husband.

"Jade, what's new? Why were you in the big city? It's the second time already?"

"I got a role, "said, and both looked shocked, then pretended to be happy. "I'll be here and there and won't leave the farm.

"Phew. That's good then. I was worried. Congratulations. What movie is it?"

"You'll see when it comes out. What happened here?"

"Nothing. The work is ongoing. Steve said that when you get home, be kind and drop by."

"Why didn't he call me?"

"I don't know. "Katie shrugged her shoulders and grinned.

"If you're here, then I'll go over."

"Sure, go ahead. Take my car." Oh right, the car! Damn it, it was burnt to a crisp in the fire. Damn.

"Thank you. I won't be long." What does he want? I really need to buy a car. It's a lot of expenses. I calculated, divided, multiplied. Of course, Brandon also sneaked into my thoughts. He hasn't written or called since. When I pulled into the fancy house, the gate immediately opened. Well, isn't it great when you fuck the owner? I thought bitterly. I parked the car in front of the entrance, never thinking that I would stay here. The house still looked beautiful. I saw no sign of a woman living there. The door swung open before I could even knock. There was something unsettling about this place: the butler. I suppose it was the last night I spent here a month ago that pushed me over the edge. Of course, it was the butler who was at the door, and he ushered me into the study, promising that his lord would be here shortly. He offered me a drink if I wanted. I declined. I stared at the garden again. And I waited, just like last time. His lord finally arrived. He said nothing. My gaze sought his.

"Hi, Jade! "He finally blurted out. Nothing had changed since we last met. You couldn't tell he was married now. Because on the night of the fire, it was dark, and I couldn't see that well, but now I see clearly, and there's no "married" sign flashing on his head. Well, Brandon's head didn't have one either.

"Steve?! "I spoke, but I didn't continue. Let him say why he summoned me here.

"Come, have a seat! "He pointed to the chair across from his desk. From that, I assumed it was a business matter; otherwise, he would have sat on the couch for a friendly chat. I took a seat at the heavy oak table. There was an air of dignity about the table. No pictures or any mementos anywhere. "I wanted to apologise for the last time. "My eyes widened in surprise. Steve Stark was apologising to me.

"Please, tell me that's not why you called me here?! "I stood up and turned away. I felt ashamed. I had given myself away, had been used, deceived. Even if I wasn't the jerk, I still felt ashamed because I was the woman who was deceived. Those who can deceive someone are less ashamed of themselves. "Forget it, Steve. You weren't the first, and you won't be the last."

"Look at me, Jade. Please. "I looked at him. I didn't give him the satisfaction of seeing tears or anger.

"Tell me, Steve. "I waved my hand dismissively. "I'll be your emotional dumping ground, too. Do you regret sleeping with me twice and then choosing someone else? Of course, when you said on the plane that we'll see if it's worth it, or if it's worth everything, you already knew, didn't you? That I'm not worth everything. Not to you. Right? So now you want to ease your conscience? Nothing happened. Just a casting couch. Ring a bell? I'm already used to it, everywhere. May you have sleepless nights?"

"What happened to your neck? And with your mouth? "He saw it anyway. Professional make-up here or there. He knew every inch of me. That's right, just my body.

"I'm telling you now, I'm used to it. What do you want?" I completely freaked out, even though I didn't want to. Damn, I didn't want him to see me as weak.

"Jade, would you stop? Can I say what I want?"
"I'm too angry now. I've had enough of all of you. Is this why you called me here? Because I don't have a place to stay, my car is on loan. These are more burning issues than your little soul. Why didn't you think about this when you brought me to your bed? Was that all you wanted? I need to go."
"Go, Jade. I'm sorry. "I practically stormed out of the door and annoyed myself.

He wanted to apologise, too. But that doesn't make it all go away. Maybe he feels relieved, but it still happened. I still went through it. And I felt miserable. Well, I was. Whatever. I took the car home, called a taxi, and went to the hotel; I took the same room where Brandon and I stayed. At least I knew that one somewhat. All my stuff fit into a bag. Well, a big bag, but it fit. Laptop, phone, a few clothes I bought since then. I took them off, showered, washed them, and put on the hotel robe, called the sympathetic agents and scheduled a meeting with them for Friday, which meant I had to go back on Friday morning, and I need to buy a car. I can't keep flying around all the time. There was a knock on the door, but I ordered nothing. They must have given my room number to someone else. When I opened it, Steve was standing there. I'm going to complain about this. Last time they didn't give me Brandon's room number.
"I want to file a complaint. I thought they couldn't give out my room number without my consent."
"Unless it comes to me, because everyone loves me, "he said with a huge grin on his face. He entered as I moved out of the way. He sat down in the only armchair in the room. I sat on the bed. I requested coffee for both of us.
"Tell me, Steve. I won't interrupt you. You won't leave me alone, anyway."
"True. "He flashed his charming smile. "My father is in prison. Tax evasion. My brother is in rehab. My mother is in a mental institution. Well, I finance them all. My sister couldn't handle this stress, she ran away. I understand. And she never came

back. I wouldn't have taken her, but she didn't reach out to anyone in the family. I run the farm. That's why I had to come back to the city, to take over. "It rang a bell now. My parents seemed to have talked about something like this. Or similar things. Of course, I didn't understand how this was relevant. Or what he was getting at. "The farm is running, of course, but now you know you don't earn as much from it as you should. All the treatments cost a lot of money. And I wanted to marry Samantha..."

"Because of the money... "I groaned.

"It's pretty harsh, but yes."

"Great, and why do I need to know this? "There was a knock on the door, and suddenly I saw the occurrences in front of me. It's Brandon, and he's going to beat Steve to a pulp for how he acted yesterday. There was another knock on the door, but Steve noticed the change in my gaze. As I looked down at myself. I wasn't wearing anything, just the gown. Well, he was dressed, but that meant nothing. "I'm going, "said fearfully and wrapped the surrounding robe as much as I could. I gestured for Steve to stay there. It wasn't a moral decision; it wasn't a good move if it turns out like yesterday. Then it doesn't matter what I do. It's too late. I opened the door, and Brandon was really standing there. Fear was visible in my eyes, and he knew someone was in the room. He entered. Without a question, he headed towards Steve. "Brandon! "I called out. "Brandon! Baby, nothing happened. "I jumped in front of Steve through the bed. "Brandon, stop! Please. Baby, nothing happened. "He grabbed my neck again, shoved me aside as if I were a rag doll. I hit my head, so I passed out.

## Chapter thirteen

*Brandon saw nothing else but someone trying to take away the person he could finally love. He loved her so much that it hurt. When she smiled at him, it was as if he saw Christine. As if she was here, as if they could create a wonderful future together. And someone wants to take her away from him. Again. He couldn't allow that. With boiling anger, he lunged at the man. Without hesitation, he landed a punch on him in his three-piece suit. He wants to dizzy Jade with his actions. He can't let that happen. She will be his, no matter the cost. He couldn't even say a word, just wiped the blood from his nose. Then he pointed at Jade.*

*Jade hit her head on the nightstand, blood dripping from the back of her head. They both rushed to her. Brandon just stared at his hands, his face reflecting deep hatred. He caused this again. The immeasurable rage, the uncontrollable anger that he didn't know how to deal with.*

"What do you want from her? "The man asked.

"I just want her; I want nothing else."

"Fine. She can be yours. I want the Farm, but now you must leave. I must call the ambulance, and they will surely ask what happened. They know me here, there won't be any problems. I'll take care of everything. Just go."

"I'm leaving my car for Jade. She doesn't have one right now."

"Fine, just go! "With that, Brandon left. He hoped it wasn't too late. He flew back home and sought a psychologist. This couldn't go on like this...

## Chapter fourteen

I woke up with terrified, as usual when I oversleep. I slowly gathered my thoughts. But as I suddenly sat up, a sharp pain shot through my head, and I could feel the bandage on it. Slowly, it became clear what had happened. I was in a room. Steve's house. Wearing a robe. Suddenly, I did not know what day it was. I couldn't understand why I was there, remembered the hotel, Brandon, and Steve. I wanted to get out of bed, but my throbbing headache prevented me from doing so. There was no one in the room. I slowly struggled to get out of bed, but I didn't remember it being this high. I fell to the floor, intensifying the pain in my head. It felt like it was going to explode. And now, do Samantha, Steve, and I share this bed? What is happening? And where is Brandon? I need to leave. What day is it? I must go to L.A. on Friday. And why is there a bandage on my head? In response to the noise, a nurse or something similar entered. I understood nothing, but to be fair, my head was still fuzzy. Or is this a private hospital?

"Good morning! So, you're awake? How are you? "She asked while rushing over to help me up. She looked like a kind, blonde woman in her forties, at least that's what I could gather.

"Good morning? What day is it? "I slowly and groggily formed the words. "Who are you? Where am I? Where are my things? "I wanted to know everything all at once, but the words came out slowly, and my head was throbbing.

"Just take it easy. Lie back down nicely, "she said. "I'll let Steve know. Just lie back down. Don't get yourself worked up."

"I need to leave. I want to leave. My head hurts. "I gave in and slumped onto the nearest seating, which was the edge of the bed.

"You see, miss, lie back down."

"I won't lie down. I'm staying here. Just give me something for my head."

"I will, miss, but I need to call Steve."

"He can wait. Just give me something for my head. I'm going crazy. Please."

"Lie back down. If I administer it, you might get drowsy. "I complied with her words, but only because of my head. She brought a syringe and swiftly pricked me; by the time I regained consciousness, it was already over. The headache hadn't completely subsided, and I could hear her speaking in hushed tones on the phone, but I couldn't understand anything. As the pain gradually faded, I fell asleep. When I woke up again, it was dark. Once again, I woke up with the same sense of horror that I had overslept. But this time, my head didn't hurt as much, just a dull throbbing. A small lamp was lit in the room, next to which Steve was sleeping, or at least he was until he abruptly woke up. Then he rushed over to the bed. He seemed tired and had some injuries on his face.

"Hi, Jade! "He greeted and smiled. "Now I can finally tell you what I wanted to say."

"You're kidding, right? "I replied. "I must leave, Steve. Can't stay here! Must go to L.A. on Friday. What day is it?"

"Jade! Please calm down."

"What happened? "I couldn't stop asking questions and feeling scared.

"Jade, take it easy! I'll explain everything. I thought you and Brandon weren't together anymore."

"Brandon... "I became even more terrified. "Must go. "I covered myself and realised was naked under the robe, which now opened, but I only realised it from the change in his expression. I was so frantic, lost my mind. But I could tell from his eyes. I quickly covered myself again. My gaze darted around in fear. "Jade, please calm down. It's Thursday. Your knight left his car here. He said he's giving it to you."

"Is it Thursday night? Or Wednesday night?

"It's Thursday because it's past midnight. After he knocked you out and me took a bit. That guy is a real troublemaker. Anyway, during the show of strength, we realised something was wrong because you didn't wake up. That's when we called for an ambulance. While we were waiting for the ambulance, we had a little chat. To put it mildly."
"Where is he now? "I pulled the blanket up even higher.
"He went home after they took you to the hospital. But you'll discuss that with him later. He said he's giving you the car. Because you're always on his mind, he said. That guy is not ordinary, "he smiled. "I'll really finish what I started, because until then I won't leave you alone."
"Do you have something for my head? Like medicine or something? "The pain started creeping back, or maybe I was just getting myself worked up.
"Yes. I'll give it to you. "He went to the nightstand and handed me a glass of water and two pills. I took them and waited for him to continue. But he just looked at me.
"Go on, I am not disturbing you. We were at the point where you married Samantha because of the money."
"Yes, because there are too many expenses, and I got used to a certain lifestyle; you know how it is, "he apologised.
"Continue. "I lifted my gaze to the sky.
"I didn't marry Samantha, "he blurted out.
"Excuse me? But I saw the wedding photos."
"Because those were taken before the ceremony. After that, when Kyra ended up in the hospital, I thought. If Samantha could do that, I couldn't back down because she wouldn't stop. What could I do? She's completely infatuated with me. "He let out a charming smile. "But in the end, I couldn't go through with it."
"Please tell me you're not about to declare your love now. "I almost burst into tears. I felt like I couldn't handle this anymore. And then the beast inside him unleashed the love-stricken man lashes out in jealousy, and if the man isn't in love, he takes advantage.

"Declare my love? "He savoured the words. "I just want to sleep."

"Yes, I'm sorry, I'll leave. I'm fine. I'll go to a hotel or something..." "I would have got out of bed, but he didn't let me.

"Jade, you can stay here. I didn't say that to you to leave. I'm just tired."

"But this is your bed. And why did you bring me here, anyway?"

"Because it was my fault, Samantha."

"Did you admit it?"

"No. Stay here, really. I'll go to the guest room."

"No, that would look strange. This is your house, your room, your bed. I can leave."

"What if I just lie down next to you? "He asked. I may have looked frightened; he saw it on my face, but he didn't back down, waiting for my answer. "I won't do anything you don't want, Jade."

"Okay." Lie down peacefully. "He didn't waste any time, get undressed and was already in bed and didn't need to be put to sleep; he dropped into a deep sleep and really didn't bother me. And when I finally calmed down, I fell asleep too. I woke up in the morning feeling quite refreshed. He might have felt the same, but he wasn't there anymore. It was the nurse from yesterday. I could easily get up. I went to take a shower and put on my clothes. Of course, I took two pills like the ones I received yesterday. After I finished, I sent him a message thanking him for everything and suggesting we have dinner together somewhere if he's available. He replied with a yes.

Although I didn't want to accept Brandon's new car, which he wanted to give me out of guilt once again, I still took it into use. I went to the farm where work was progressing smoothly and talked to Tom and Katie and called back to everyone else from Monday, also told them I wouldn't be around for a few weeks, but I created an online group where we can chat; I want to know everything. After that, I headed to the bank. The bandage was removed from my head, and I had my human appearance back. So, I wasn't worried that they wouldn't talk to me. I explained what I wanted and was directed to a sympathetic young man who turned out to be my former classmate. I told him about my request, and he assured me that there was no obstacle, but needed a guarantor, but he overlooked that, considering my situation. He promised that the desired amount would be transferred to my account later that day. They could start building the apartment. Quickly called the construction supervisor to discuss my plan and told him about my wishes, and he said that by the time I returned from the filming in the city, most of it would already be done. I hoped it would turn out that way because I didn't want to spend all my money on a hotel.

In the evening, I waited for Steve at the restaurant where we were supposed to have dinner on our last night. I couldn't come in my hoodie this time, so I wore the same dress I wore for the meeting with the writer. Steve also dressed up nicely in a three-piece suit. He looked incredible. I hoped he didn't want to seduce me. We ordered a bottle of wine. Just what I wanted.

"Why did you want to tell me? "Asked while scrutinising his face.

"Wanted you to know that I'm not such a jerk."

"I understand and don't know why it's so important for you guys to care about what we think when we're done, anyway."

"We're done? "He asked with a curious look.

"I don't know what you mean. About sex?"

"Not necessarily. But do we have to hate each other?"

"Oh, no, of course not. It wouldn't be good because next time it would be you who sets the Farm on fire."

"Do you know who it was? "He asked. "Would never do such a thing.

"I know. Steve was just a joke. I have an idea will rebuild it according to my taste."

"Aren't you going after them? You would get the insurance if you found the culprit."

"I haven't decided yet."

"You're beautiful, "he said, and even though it was obvious what he wanted, he said nothing, and I didn't react to it.

"Thank you, you can't complain either."

"Why are you going to L. A? To Brandon?"

"No. I got a role."

"Are you leaving us again? "He asked. No malice, no jealousy, just curiosity.

"I'm just going for a few weeks. And I'll come back to the farm, I think on weekends when there's no filming. When I went back, I realised I missed it. It pays well, and I could really use the money now. Besides, I can't be in just one place. It drives me crazy."

"And Brandon?"

"He's not my agent anymore. Maybe we can avoid each other."

"But then what was it, after all?"

"Well, he was my casting couch, so to speak, and then I left, and he fell madly in love with me, or so he says. I mean, I really felt that, but, you know, he's married and has a daughter, and he can't get a divorce. Of course, I know that now, but I'm an idiot, as the examples show. I slept with him again. "He swallowed hard, but there was no other reaction. "Only this time it wasn't under the influence of drugs, and it was my will, not for a role, and I thought he knows me, knows everything about me, and he really wants me, me specifically. Not the extras. Me. It's just expressed poorly."

"Why do you think this is happening? "We had finished our meal and were still sipping our drinks.

"Why is he losing his mind? Because he's never had to follow any rules in a relationship. It's like he grew up in some cave, which is almost true, but not because of that, but because he became successful as an agent quickly, and he never had to ask a girl twice. They were all his. And then I left. I walked away, and it excited him. I think that's all there is to it. "He pondered what I said. "What did you talk about after the knockout?"

"That he can't control himself and doesn't know what to do. Should you report him?"

"Are you going to report him? "I asked back, a little worried that he might consider it.

"Me? Not because of me, but I considered it."

"Please don't do it because of me. I feel like this feeling is enough punishment for him."

"You're too kind. Will you come over to my place? "We were already by my car. I wanted to pay, but he didn't allow it. It was a beautiful evening. The sky was full of stars. A pleasant breeze was blowing. Some people were still waiting in line outside the restaurant. The street was otherwise quiet. "Why go to the hotel? We don't have to sleep together. You can leave from there in the morning.

"I don't know if it's a good idea. People will talk."

"You're already on their favourites list anyway, and I don't care. Besides, the TV interview was good."

"Oh, don't even mention it. Alright, let's go. "I thought he would go to his chauffeured car, but he sat next to me. He was strange being in the passenger seat and didn't criticise my driving style, although it left something to be desired. He said nothing else. I thought he would need to be watered afterward, but he didn't. He just said:

"You didn't tell me you're a part-time race car driver, "he said with a sigh as we got out of the car."

"I don't like to drive at grandma's pace."

"I heard once that everyone has an acquaintance who crosses the street as if they want to die. Well, you drive just like that."

We laugh as we walked towards the entrance. The butler was standing at the door and informed us that Samantha was waiting for us in the living room. Panic flashed across my face. But Steve remained completely calm. He grabbed my arm,

not forcefully, kindly, as if I would attempt to escape. I would say he's figuring me out. "Relax, Jade. Come on."
"In the meantime, I'll hide in the kitchen or the bathroom."
"No need to hide. Come on. "Smiling nicely, we entered the living room. I examined Samantha's face for a reaction towards me, but she didn't react at all. She was also smiling. She looked good, as always, had wrapped her feminine figure in black leather pants and a pink blouse, had light makeup on.
"Hi "she said. "I didn't know you two were together. How's your head, Jade?
"Thank you, I'm fine. How about you? "If she's being nice, then I'll be nice too, even if it's fake.
"I'm okay. Sorry, Steve, for summoning you like this. I thought you'd want to get the paperwork done as soon as possible. "She waited for a response, but Steve didn't answer. I also looked at him now. He was looking at me. I raised my eyebrows in questioning. I didn't even know what they were talking about.
"Jade is leaving tomorrow for a while. Could we handle this tomorrow?
"Of course. I'm sorry, then tomorrow. Goodnight. "With that, she fled.
"Give me a whiskey "I said. "I'm not joking. What was that?"
"What are you talking about? "His behaviour changed. It was as if he got caught with something. I understood nothing.
"How did that woman who used to hate me become the one who is acting towards me the way this woman did now? And what papers were they talking about? And how did she take it so easily that there was no reconciliation?"
"You always want to know everything, don't you?"
"No. If I weren't here right now, I wouldn't want to know. And you hadn't had me taken care of here for two days. I wouldn't be here. If you hadn't called me, I wouldn't be here, and then I wouldn't want to know."
"Yes. So "it was difficult for him to tell the truth. Or come up with something I would believe. I don't know. "I wasn't

completely honest. She did all those things with your fence, and she had Kyra beaten up, and she vandalised her car. I exposed her. But I didn't go to the police. I blackmailed her."

"With what? Have you completely lost your mind? Steve, this is being an accomplice to a crime. And didn't you feel sorry for Kyra?"

"Jade, you just said that you wouldn't report Brandon."

"But that's only about me! And I decided I didn't want to, but he didn't endanger anyone else."

"Not now. Who knows what will happen next time?"

"Don't change the subject, Steve. And did you even write a contract about it?"

"Jade, please understand. I didn't marry her because I didn't. But I don't want to lose everything either."

"It's as if you said earlier that you're not that much of a jerk."

"She won't come near you again; she won't be rude to you ever again. And you wouldn't report her, right? "He stared out the window. He was right. I wouldn't report her. "Why would it be better if I took her down out of self-interest, rather than using her exposure to my advantage and considering my own interests?"

"You do what you want, but I don't agree with it."

"I don't agree with a lot of things you do, Jade, but I try to accept them.

"But what do you want to achieve with all of this? "I asked.

"Are you in love with Brandon? "He asked abruptly, with no transition. He turned towards me from the window. I was sitting on the couch inspecting my drink. I didn't want to look at him and knew what I would see. And I didn't want to see it.

"Would you look at me if I talked to you? "I looked up.

"I'm not over it. And you?"

"I'm not in love with him. He's not my type with his blond, cheesy style."

"You're hilarious."

"Since you said that I won't declare my love now, it has been on my mind. I pondered and tasted the word, and I had to realise that I haven't been in love yet, and I don't really know what it's like. Or rather, I often thought I felt it, but if I compare it to what I feel now, I don't know what this is. It could be love."

"What do you feel? Or what do you think you feel? "I slowly thought that I could afford a scream. Justifiably. No one would believe this.

"I crave you like crazy. I like your fiery nature, or the way you want to handle everything on your own, or your acting side that drives me a little crazy. "He smiled.

"I don't... Steve, I... you can't do this to me. What do you expect from me? "I got a little upset. If I tell this in the club... It's already a comedy, and I'm the protagonist...

"I expect nothing, Jade. I went to help. You didn't ask for it. I didn't stage a scene. I came back home and left you alone and won't come after you because you're going back tomorrow. Or should I not mention the rest? You give what you want to give, and what you don't, you don't. It's that simple. My life has been going on like this so far, and it will continue like this. I just told you what I feel."

"I can't do it. Not now, not today. Or tomorrow. I keep making mistakes or rather, making one poor decision after another. I need to put an end to this, Steve. Do you understand?"

"Of course. "He sighed and spread his arms and accepts it. He's not happy, but he accepts it.

"Would you like me to leave?"

"No, Jade, of course not. I behaved very well yesterday."

"Maybe by the time I come back, you won't even know who I am anymore."

"Maybe, "but he didn't seem convinced. "Let's go to bed."

I went to take a shower. The bathroom had black tiles with a white border. It looked incredible. Although I would never have such a bathroom myself because I would be afraid of having to clean it every day, as water drops would show on it. But I guess he had someone to clean it, so it wasn't a problem. A huge massaging bathtub. But I just took a shower. Mirror, green flowers. Well, that was throughout the house. It looked like a jungle. The entire house was tastefully decorated and filled with flowers. I didn't think this was his handiwork.

Each room had its own style, the living room had an old-fashioned style with antique furniture, thick Persian rugs, and a fireplace. The kitchen wasn't antique, but it was made entirely of wood, giving it a loving atmosphere, which it truly was. The bathroom and his room had a modern style, with marble, glass, and metal. It was also tastefully furnished. What was common everywhere was flowers. The exterior of the house had a modern style. I didn't remember seeing this house before. I didn't know when they moved here or if this was their family home, but it seemed to reflect Steve's taste. The garden was also impressive and filled with flowers. I liked both the house and the garden. As a makeshift solution, I put on a T-shirt after I was done. He also took a shower. I didn't know what he wanted, where I should sleep. Well, I had an idea. I stood in the middle of the room, feeling idle until he came back from the shower and felt naked in that T-shirt. I tugged it down as much as I could.

"What are you standing there for? Can you sleep standing? "He asked and had a towel around his waist. He still had a good body, as I remembered. Not the body you get from a gym like Brandon's or from bar fights. He achieved it through hard work. His forearms were covered in scars from the doors of the pens, just like mine, from when I also took on more of the outdoor work.

"I didn't know what you wanted, where I should sleep."

"Well, here, if you don't mind. You already know this bed, and at least we won't give Cassey any extra work."

"I know quite a few beds already, "I joked with him.

"You're hilarious. "He went into the hidden, built-in wardrobe, which had a mirrored side that almost blended into the wall and came out wearing a pair of pants. "Come on, "he gestured towards the bed. While we weren't here, someone had changed the bedsheets. They were black too, like almost everything in the room, but they were crisp, and I could smell the fabric softener on them. I settled in, pulling the covers up to my chin, and tried to fall asleep quickly. He really didn't touch me. I slept peacefully all night. My thoughts didn't race, maybe because the collision between my head and the wardrobe was still fresh in my mind. When my alarm went off, he wasn't in bed anymore, but there was a message waiting for me to say he was with the animals and if I was leaving, should say goodbye. I got ready, gathered all my belongings, went downstairs and asked Cassey for a coffee. She was bustling in the kitchen and gladly poured me a cup and asked if she could get her daughter's autograph. I smiled and gladly fulfilled the request. I also wrote one for Christine, since I had a pen and paper in my hand, anyway. By the time I was done, I had just enough time to say goodbye. I found Steve in the corral behind the house; I hadn't even noticed that building before. Perhaps because of the massive line of trees that separated the rear property from the house, and their foliage was so dense that they were barely visible. He was cleaning a horse. Many people were working all around, and there were many vehicles and even more animals. All kinds of them. Mostly small ones, and of course, the horses. I didn't know how large his farm was or how many animals there were. Amidst the loud noise, he didn't hear me approaching, but a man stood opposite him, opened his mouth when he saw me, and started nudging Steve, who guessed that someone was looking for him.

"Good morning, "I greeted. A sad smile played on his face. We walked out of the pen.

"Thank you for everything, Steve, "I said. I was a bit choked up, too. I don't like goodbyes.

"It's alright, Jade. When are you coming home?"

"I don't know. Maybe in a week."

"We'll talk, right? "He asked.

"Of course, "I said, but that's not what I meant.
"Drive safely! "He said.
"Always, Steve, "and with that, I zoomed away in my rental car.

I would have liked to keep Brandon's car; I liked its massive size and shiny black colour. Its masculinity appealed to me. It effortlessly cut through the miles. I hadn't planned to stop anywhere, just one stop. I was making good progress; if I continued at this pace, I would have set a record for this distance by the end of the month.

Upon reaching the city, I looked for a hotel that was close enough to the filming location but not too expensive. There were many people walking on the streets, which could be attributed to the pleasant weather and the nature of the city. Palm trees, girls in summer dresses, and very fit boys— this was what the city was all about. They said that my male co-star was also staying in this hotel, although I didn't understand why he was trying to save money. It belonged to the same hotel chain as the one we have back home. I requested the same room number we had with Brandon, hoping that it would ease my aversion to sleeping in unfamiliar beds. My afternoon was filled with appointments with agents. Before that, I wanted to go out and buy some clothes. I quickly unpacked and headed out. I visited my favourite places and successfully bought everything I wanted. It was strange that I didn't run into anyone I knew, which I found somewhat surprising. When I returned, there was one more call I had to make. I wasn't really in the mood, but I owed that much to her. I took a deep breath.
"Hi, Jess! "I said after she answered my call.
"Hi, Jade! So, it's true? You're back?"
"I just got a role. That's why I came back."
"Did you really get the lead role in that movie?"
"How do you know?"
"I bumped into Brandon earlier. He told me. I'm happy for you, sweetheart. It's better for you than those new bimbos."

"How's everything going for you?"

"No complaints. I got a couple of commercials this month. And I have a photoshoot. I'll manage. We should catch up soon."

"Of course, Jess! Bye."

"Bye."

I had a guilty conscience about getting this role. Of course, I was happy about it, and felt like I deserved it, but I knew that there might be someone who needed it much more than I did—like Jess. She didn't have a farm to hold on to. Well, mine burned down, but there was still hope for rebuilding it. I had to restore it or make it even better than before. Make it successful, just like it used to be. Beyond just enjoying acting, my life once depended on it, but now it was mostly motivated by money for the sake of the Farm.

I had three agents on my list. I encouraged myself to get started and keep the Farm floating as a goal in my mind. Unfortunately, there were more aspiring actors trying to climb up than established agents. I had heard about two of them, and they weren't bad, at least from rumour. I chose the third one just like that. Brandon recommended me to them, and I hoped the woman would be the winner.

First, I had to meet with Joseph at a downtown cafe. I was already on edge, waiting for him while he was nowhere to be seen. He didn't even send a message or call. He seemed like a big asshole already. Then he showed up twenty minutes late but didn't apologise. He looked like a dream come true for teenage girls. Blonde hair, grown longer in a Nick Carter-like style, with a baby face to match. A well-toned body from the gym. Gucci sunglasses, Armani watch. A Louis Vuitton clutch. He asked for a soy latte, which didn't make him any more likable. After scanning the room, he only glanced at me. "I'm busy, but I came here because Brandon asked me to. I have little room for a new actress, especially one with such a reputation."

"Then we don't really have much to talk about, do we? Let's not waste each other's time unnecessarily, "I said, and I was already fed up with him. Did I even need an agent if I wanted to leave all of this behind? I don't think so.
"When was the last time you had any role at all?"
"I have one now."
"Oh, and what is it? A detergent commercial? "He asked with so much contempt as possible. Brandon was never like that. He treated all his actors with equal attention, or rather, with equal lack of attention. I never thought I'd say this, but Brandon was an excellent agent.
"Have you heard about the new film with Richard O'Riley?"
"Of course, I have. Everyone's talking about it. They're going to shoot it here."
"Well, I play the lead role in that film. "His jaw dropped, but by then, he had already lost me.
"You don't say. Why didn't you start with that? "He perked up immediately, and the condescending look vanished.
"But you're very busy, and so am I. I still have two meetings with other agents. You can watch the film later. "With that, I threw some money on the table and rushed off to my next appointment. An inflated ego.

This guy wanted to meet me in the bar of a hotel. He was already sitting in a booth when I approached and wasn't an attractive guy. He was big, with a pimply face and a short, greasy haircut. The place, of course, was a five-star hotel, and the bar looked the part. Shimmering disco balls scattered their light. The walls were covered in accordion mirrors. The floor was marble, and my shoes echoed on it. Glasses were being diligently polished by a boy in the corner. The bartender wore a perfectly white starched shirt, and I would bet that his manners were impeccable as well.
"Hey! Jade Donovan. "I extended my hand with a smile. The man accepted it and gave it a firm squeeze with his sausage-like fingers.

"Pleasure to meet you, miss. Please take a seat. "He devoted all his attention to me.

"On my way here, I realised I might not need an agent. This will be my last role, and then I'm done. I apologise for wasting your time, "I apologised.

"Brandon said you would need an agent. I've only just started, so I have plenty of time. But if you feel that way, alright."

"So, you don't have any clients yet? "I asked, astonished.

"I have two. They appear in commercials. I'm trying to get them something better."

"That's very kind of you. Are you close with Brandon?"

"Yes, you could say that. Or rather, I would say that I know him better than anyone here."

"Then talk to him and ask him how to get started. He is kind in his own way, and I really apologise for wasting your time."

"It's not worth mentioning. Good luck, miss!"

"Thank you. Same to you. "I went to my last meeting, which was with a woman in her forties who invited me to her apartment. But since it was a woman, it shouldn't be a big problem, I thought...

When I arrived at her house, I rang the doorbell. An exhausted-looking woman opened the door, holding a newborn baby in her arms, which she immediately handed over to me. Oh, my goodness, I had never held a newborn before, not even a child. The house was in complete chaos. Toys scattered everywhere, coffee mugs here and there in the house, some of them still half-full and the woman started walking away again, and I followed her into the kitchen, trying my best to hold the baby without dropping or making a cry. The woman looked a bit dishevelled, but beneath the surface, she was beautiful and would be again once she got to sleep for twelve consecutive hours, have a glass of wine, and take a soothing hot bath. The same applied to the house, which could turn into a modern, beautiful family home after a thorough cleaning.

"Oh, thank goodness you came. I need a coffee, "she groaned, "because otherwise, I'll die. The nanny didn't show up again."

"Uh" huh, "I say, feeling overwhelmed. What should I have said? I could barely take a breath, afraid of startling the baby. It was actually silent, barely making a sound.

"Would you like some coffee?"

"Yes, I'll have some. "She brewed a cup while starting twenty other things, thinking that since she had her hands free, she could do some tidying up. But she just started everything finishing nothing because she spotted something else and began working on that. Then the coffee machine beeped to show that the coffee was ready, so she put down the newspapers she was about to tidy up. I couldn't help but envy the dark circles under her eyes.

"It's interesting how the baby doesn't cry around you. You could stay here. "I think she was only half-joking. She swept a pile of things off the coffee table and placed the coffee in front of me. And didn't really pay attention to what was falling. She took the baby from my hands and gently placed it in a carrier. She made the sign of the cross, probably to seal this lying down state and the silence to be lasting for the baby.

"Alright, let's get started. Thank you for your patience. I'm Holly Johnson. Nice to meet you."

"Jade Donovan, "I tried to whisper.

"Brandon called and said I should take his place. What happened? He didn't elaborate."

"Well, I guess you were obviously giving birth... Let's just say his wife wasn't too thrilled about me satisfying her husband orally in the newspaper."

"Holy shit! "She was completely shocked. "I wouldn't be too happy either."

"I didn't know he had a wife and a child, and I guess I didn't want to know. Anyway, it doesn't matter. It seems like you have enough on your plate, and I don't need an agent because I want to quit after this show."

"Well, tell me something. Since I got out of the hospital, I have met no one who didn't want to talk about breastfeeding or metabolism. Please entertain me. Tell me something about the outside world. I disappeared a year ago, and even before that, I wasn't exactly a remarkable presence."

"What are you curious about? I know little more than you do. I left here a few months ago too and just got a role, so I came back, but don't plan on staying afterwards."

"I saw your portfolio and watched the film Kyra Reynolds made at the Farm. It turned out good. It convinced me."

"I haven't seen it, but I'm glad. How do you know Brandon?"

"We went to school together back in the day, "she drifted off into the past. "Many people said he had a lot of girls, but I didn't believe it. Somehow, I couldn't picture it. That's not how I knew him back then."

"He has a lot of whores, not a lot of girls. You must care about a girl, but he just fucks them. If possible, always someone different. That's how it was until now. I don't know what he was like before or what he's doing now, but that was my experience."

"And why did you leave?"

"Isn't it obvious? Well, maybe not. I didn't come here to be a whore a long time ago. I wanted to be an actress. It didn't work out."

"So, how did you get this role now?"

"Brandon reached out to me and offered me a role. I accepted because someone set the Farm on fire, and I need to restore it."

"You got such a good role?"

"Yes, I think so. "I didn't want to brag about it. She had already finished her coffee, but she seemed no more alert.

"I'm sorry to take up your time, but I must go now. I need to learn my lines."

"If you change your mind or just want to talk, call me."

"Sure. Thank you. Good luck with the baby. "I couldn't wait to lock myself in my hotel room. And that's what I did. I ordered some food, ate, and went to sleep. I didn't leave the room all weekend, just learned the script. Although I suspected Monday would only involve a photoshoot and no actual filming, it was still a relief to get through it. Everyone gets to know everyone. We take a million pictures: everyone with everyone. The official opening will be online in the evening. And if everyone is in good spirits, we can start filming on Tuesday.

The lines weren't difficult, although some parts were boring, but that was to be expected. I liked the main character's sharp tongue. She never played the meek one, always outsmarting some bad guy until this handsome guy showed up, and from then on, everything would be happy. But many people want to see them apart, so there's a lot of scheming going on. But in the end, there will be a grand reunion of the great lovers. A happy ending, of course. Not a bad dream. Steve had been messaging me since Friday, but I didn't want to reply. Somehow, I didn't want to establish a connection with him. Not with that scum that was my life. Or with the way he behaved last time. I hadn't forgotten the pictures either, or many things seemed uncertain about him. Sometimes he seemed like an angel, other times like a devil in disguise. Did I need that? It was hard to put it into words, even for myself. But on Sunday, I ended up sending him a message, and he called me right away.
"Hi, Jade! How are you? "He asked. His voice sounded casual and curious.
"I'm fine. I spent the entire weekend studying my lines."
"Who's your agent?"
"No one. I don't need one. I'll manage this film on my own. And at least I won't have to pay for someone who won't do the job properly. Let's leave it at that."
"Are you upset?"

"No. Okay, maybe a little. How about you? Have you heard anything about the Farm?"
"When I was there, they were just bringing in a hundred crates of beer for the evening party. I'm doing well, especially since I was also invited. And a hundred dancers too."
"You're a funny guy."
"You think I'm joking... No. I told them that the unicorn is a bit too much."
"Alright, Steve. Sleep well. I'm going to bed too. It's going to be a tough day tomorrow."
"You're awesome. No need to worry."
"Thank you. Goodnight."

# Chapter fifteen

I woke up feeling refreshed the next morning. I didn't bother with makeup; they'll probably use their own makeup artist and put on one of the light summer dresses I bought, grabbed my lines, my phone, not much else and took Brandon's car; I did not know how long it would last and didn't want to keep spending money on taxis when I had this car available and return it to him once filming was over. And by then, his conscience should be at ease. I hoped the male lead wouldn't be unbearable either. I can play along, but it would be easier if he wasn't. When I arrived, parked in the staff parking lot. There were already plenty of cars there. My stomach tightened into its usual knot. Well, the good kind. The excitement.

The filming location looked like any other. Half-built houses, half-furnished rooms, half-furnished cafes. Cameras. Golf carts. Lots of people. I was immediately ushered to the makeup artists, what felt like an eternity to finish. It was only an hour, of course, but it felt long to me. Although I never used to talk to anyone before, I confidently chatted with the makeup girls. Maybe it was because I was prepared for this to be the last one. The hairstylist was a man, and he was very kind. He immediately knew what would work well for the role and for me, and I agreed with him. The amount of hairspray weighed my hair down, and the makeup was uncomfortably heavy, but I smiled continuously, as a talented actor should. Not to mention my outfit. It barely covered my nipples on top, and the skirt offended all senses of decency.

Then they sent me to the cafe. The cameraman was rushing around like a poisoned mouse. Richard was already there, looking magnificent. He really looked fantastic. I think he must have had some Native American blood flowing in his veins, with his slightly Creole skin, broad cheekbones, brown hair, and remarkably muscular body. A flirtatious and friendly gaze. If this wasn't a facade, then filming was going to be great. He had such a kind smile. I had heard about him, but only that every woman melted for him, and what a great actor he was, but nothing specific, and being a great actor is a matter of perspective. I cautiously sneaked closer, as they were taking pictures of him. The cameraman was bustling around him, which was quite annoying even to watch, but Richard just kept smiling and paid no attention to it.

"Ahh, who do we have here? "He shouted, and I looked back in alarm to see who he was talking to. The writer was also there, but he said nothing, just sat in a chair and watched the photoshoot. Richard was sitting on a chair in the cafe, with a coffee in front of him, and arranged props to make the photo more marketable in magazines. "Jade! "He exclaimed. "Well, here you are."

"Hello "I said as I slowly approached him.

"Come on over, you're needed for these one million and two more photos. "I'm coming "I said. I was dragged to a table as well, posed in various ways, and they took a million pictures of me. My table required pink props. Now the cameraman was hopping around me. It was extremely annoying, but I kept smiling or did whatever they told me to do and sat and stood like this for hours. We changed clothes and poses. We changed makeup. For hours on end. There were a few hundred group shots as well. In different outfits and different poses again. Romantic, cuddly, quarrelsome, passionate. We acted out every kind of emotion projected onto a photo today. Each moment was a scene from the film. For commercials, teasers.

    I hope to please everyone and tried very hard and didn't complain when had to change makeup and clothes for the hundredth time. I thought it would at least save the crew some trouble because it couldn't have been much easier for them than it was for me, was tired. It was already dark, but there was still a need for night-time shots. Richard didn't complain either. His effortless, relaxed style charmed everyone and especially helped endure the whole hustle and bustle more easily. Then, around ten o'clock, we were finally done. Even the cleaners were already there, urging us to leave so they could prepare the location for the morning. Slowly, everyone dispersed. The writer had left a long time ago. Richard's agent had been on his phone all day and had left much earlier, but he didn't mind at all. Their relationship seemed very good. The dressing rooms were empty. I quickly discarded my clothes and put on my own. I didn't bother washing off the makeup; thought I would do it at the hotel. Didn't want to make them wait for me. An older cleaning lady was already standing at the door. I apologised and left immediately.

    It was already ten o'clock. I was tired, and I was sure they were too. Even though the whole delay wasn't my fault, I still felt bad for them. Richard was leaning against my car outside, which surprised me quite a bit.

"Would you like to have a drink? "He asked. It couldn't have been too difficult for him to change. He was wearing jeans and a T-shirt that hugged his muscular upper body. I didn't want to refuse, but I was dead tired.

"Maybe one, I'm tired, "I said, telling the truth; I just hoped it wouldn't offend him. "Let's go to the hotel bar. I heard you're staying in the same place as me.

"Chee Rokee?

"Yes. "He sat down next to me. No driver or any car came for him.

"Where's your car?"

"I don't have a car, don't even have a license. "I looked at him in surprise.

"Well then, hold on and buckle up! "I smiled. He's in for a ride with my driving style. But he didn't show any signs of being scared; he didn't make any comments about the driving at all. In the meantime, we chatted casually, mostly about L.A. Then we continued over a drink.

"And when did you decide to pursue acting? "He asked, giving me his full attention. He didn't look around the bar to assess the crowd. But everyone was staring at him. It didn't bother him; he devoted his full attention to what I had to say.

"I think it was when I was in seventh grade. I probably saw a dumb movie and thought it would be great."

"And it didn't turn out great?"

"I guess you heard about the nothing I've accomplished, "I smiled self-ironically. "But at least I got on a casting couch. Anyway, it doesn't matter now. "I shrugged.

"From what I saw today, you really know what you're doing, and it seemed like you enjoy it too."

"The price was too high, but yes, I loved it. This is my last movie."

"I'm sorry to hear that. I know little about actors, which may sound conceited, but not because I'm not interested, but

because I don't have time for it. Either I'm shooting, or I'm with my family. My daughter was born recently."
"Congratulations. What's it like being a father? And how do you juggle it with work? Especially with this kind of work?"
"It's difficult. My wife is an agent, that's how we met. She was my agent."
"Holly Johnson? "I asked, astonished.
"Yes. I heard you were with her yesterday. What a small world!"
"She's a very adorable baby. Honestly, I know little about babies, but she was cute."
"I heard you managed well; she didn't cry with you. Holly said so. Poor thing, she was really exhausted. "I didn't understand why he stayed at the hotel and didn't go home to his family. Maybe he read it in my expression.
"I'm not going home, just for the weekend and not bringing work home with me. I am more tense during these times; can't focus on them the way I want to. We often argue during these periods. So, we decided that when I'm shooting, I'll take a brief break."
"Is not she jealous?"
"Not anymore. And I'm not either. We trust each other, and we know that we're the most important to each other."
"It's admirable. "I had a whiskey, but the world was already spinning with me and wanted to go upstairs and sleep, knowing that tomorrow wouldn't be much easier. "I'm going, Richard. Thank you for the pleasant company, but I'm tired now."
"I'm leaving too. "He dropped some money on the table, and we went up together. He went higher than me, I thought, to the VIP section. I wished him goodnight and went to my room.

Once in there, I quickly took a shower and got into bed. It just occurred to me I had eaten nothing all day. I quickly checked my phone but couldn't reply to anyone anymore. Fell into a deep, dreamless sleep and woke up to my alarm in the morning and got ready for the first day of shooting. I was nervous. It had been a while since my last day of shooting. It was for a commercial. Today, I wore sweatpants and sneakers and responded to everyone's messages at red lights. The distance wasn't too long, but there were many traffic lights. I hoped I wouldn't get any tickets in Brandon's car. I texted Steve and the Farm group as well. The advancement of technology. It made people busier but also lonelier. I had to call the builder because he wanted to ask something, but maybe I'll have time during lunch break.

It started, and I enjoyed every moment. We quickly got a feel for each other's style, and we didn't have to redo many scenes with Richard. He was very experienced, and I compensated for my lack of experience with determination. I got along well with the other actors too. We had a good team. They were skilled. There was no weak link. It seemed like everyone understood their role and everyone was focused. Today, I didn't have to change costumes as often as for the photoshoot, but this film promising to be a box office hit was still somewhat new to me. They tried to shoot similar scenes simultaneously, but everyone knew their part, so there were no hiccups with that either. During lunch break, I stepped aside to make some phone calls and recharge while the others huddled together and laughed. They had already planned to go out partying in the evening, but they whispered it because the producer would have freaked out. In the afternoon session of shooting, Brandon showed up. I tried to ignore him, but it wasn't going so well, and Richard noticed it, as did the producer. We had to redo a scene because of me, and I felt sorry about it. But then Richard saved the day.

"Nick, we can record this later. Now let's record mine. Jade could use some rest."

"Fine," says Nick, who was an annoying little pelican anyway, but he was eating out of Richard's hand like a bird, so it was a win if I had Richard by my side. I went to the locker room, didn't want to be near Brandon, but somehow, he sneaked in. I stood there in my little dress, my face smeared and the door open, dreading the Brandon I was facing now. There was a security guard outside my door, but in this case, I wasn't sure he would come to my aid. Still, Brandon is just an agent, while I'm an actress.

"What do you want, Brandon? "I asked as he closed the door behind him.

"Hi, Jade! How are you? "He asked. His mere presence still unsettled me, and it wasn't good.

"Fine."

"Sorry about last time. I didn't mean to hurt you."

"I will not report you, if that's what you're worried about."

"I just wanted to know how you're doing and saw the pictures in the magazine. You're beautiful, and I wanted to see you."

"Go away, Brandon. Please. "He stepped closer. I backed away. "Please, Brandon. Go away. "He continued to inch closer to me. I kept backing away, looked for escape routes, but there were none, only the door, which was blocked from me.

"Baby, Jade, it doesn't go away. No matter what I do, it doesn't go away. I want you. Jade, please."

"No, Brandon, go away, please. "But he didn't leave. I was already against the wall, and he was standing close in front of me, didn't know if I should call for help or what to do. I didn't want a scene on set, especially not caused by me, already felt like my role was on shaky ground. They could have easily given it to someone else. I didn't want to lose it. Neither the money nor the role. He pressed himself against me and tried to find my mouth with his.

"Please, Jade. Kiss me! "I tried to free myself from his grip, but he was much stronger than me. His hands roamed up and down my body, touching me wherever he could. Richard suddenly burst in.

"Now it's your turn... "he was about to say that it's my turn now, but he seized the situation, not wanting to cause a scene either. He closed the door behind him.

"Let go, Brandon. She doesn't want it. I don't want a scene, and neither do you. Go away, Brandon. "He listened to him and left. Instead of bursting into tears, I adjusted my clothes and tried to act as if nothing had happened.

"Are you okay? "He asked. I felt ashamed, but I showed nothing.

"Of course. We can go, "I said and went out. The rest of the afternoon went smoothly. I didn't dare to look at Richard; I didn't want to see his pity. Time passed quickly. In the evening, they asked if I wanted to go partying with them, but I shook my head and headed back to the hotel. I thought Richard would bring it up, but he didn't. He didn't say a word about it. The next day, however, I got a bodyguard. One guy said they think the movie will be even more successful than they thought, and caution wouldn't hurt. Of course, I knew Richard had something to do with it. But I had no objections. There were only two days left for filming this week, and I didn't know how I would get home after shooting on Friday, but I was already homesick. I missed a lot of time, and even for me, this whole commotion was new. I was getting tired. So far, every day had been incredibly draining. Everything was going well at the Farm, but it would still take at least another month for the house to be completed. Today, I had to call Steve. We exchanged messages every day, and he always asked when we could talk. Today went smoothly as well. Everything was going well, we didn't have to redo any scenes, and the producer was very pleased. He said we were progressing much better than expected, so we might finish filming on Thursday this week. I was thrilled about that, but I wasn't happy about not having a home to go to.

"Hi, Steve, "he answered the call on the first ring. True, it was only ten. "Am I calling too late? Am I disturbing you?"

"Not at all! Hi Jade! How are you? I saw the pictures."

"Everything's fine. I'm tired."
"When are you coming home?"
"We'll finish filming on Thursday. Oh, that's tomorrow because we're progressing well, but we usually finish around this time. I don't know if I'll be able to drive home afterwards. Besides, I don't have a home right now."
"Didn't I tell you? I love sheltering beautiful homeless actresses. It's my hobby."
"Really? You've never told me about that. Brandon showed up on the set. "He paused, waiting for me to continue. "So, I got a bodyguard. He's standing outside my room right now. I feel sorry for him. He must be tired."
"But everything's fine?"
"Of course.
"Okay then.
"I'm going to bed. "I left the question hanging about whether I'm coming to see him or what should happen next, whether I'll even leave tomorrow.

*Thirty years old. He became an agent thanks to his connections in the acting industry and his schooling. Most of the time, he could suppress his uncontrollable anger. Here, he could exploit more girls than when he was a bodyguard.*

*Power was in his hands. Meanwhile, he had a wife whom he treated kindly, but he cared little about her. There were always new girls coming in, whom he could get hooked on drugs, and then they would do anything for him in exchange for the drugs or a role. They were no longer beautiful and happy. And they weren't rich either. He determined who got what role. And how much money. He particularly enjoyed this and didn't consider himself evil, just taking back what was once taken from him. Then Lilly came along, and everything changed. He didn't want the child. But when he held her in his hands, everything became different. He became a father and took it seriously. His anger transformed into immeasurable love for his daughter, and he will do anything to ensure that she had everything and didn't have to grow up like him. In the girls he had exploited before, he saw his own daughter, and he felt ashamed. But he couldn't stop these activities in front of his friends; word would spread among the agents immediately. So, he always kept one girl among the aspiring actors and treated her with respect. Then little Jade came along, and everything turned upside down.*

## Chapter sixteen

The next day arrived quickly. I checked out of the hotel and prepared to leave in the evening and didn't want to stay here anymore. I needed a change of scenery; and had been here for almost a week. I was tiring of the big city. The morning went smoothly. On set, I had to argue with my former on-screen lover to break up; these words could have been spoken not too long ago between Brandon and me. The guy didn't want to break up, and he used every low tactic to win me back. There was no violence involved; not that kind of movie, but I felt a strong connection to the role. In the afternoon, I had to dismiss some jealous girls to make sure my on-screen sweetheart would finally be mine alone. It wasn't mudding wrestling, but the crew would have probably enjoyed it. The girls, one by one, were beautiful, blonde, and stunning, unlike me, with my black hair and slender figure. The male lead must have fallen out of love with the previous blonde bombshells of his genre and switched to the dark-haired actresses. It worked well for me.

Richard was preoccupied with something today, so there were scenes that had to be reshot, but no one was upset about it. In the afternoon, someone came looking for me at the gate. I thought it was Jess, but I was taken back—it was Steve standing there. I invited him in and quickly showed him around; then I had to go back to shooting. He found his place and soon sat behind the cameraman, watching us. I guess he sweet-talked to someone and got in. Everyone was very kind to him. There were a few more scenes left. It had been dark for a while. Everyone was tired. Richard and I were filming our joint scenes. I didn't know how he would react after what Steve said. Even the cameraman was getting tired because he considered it a wrap for the week. Everyone hurried to their dressing rooms. Steve was waiting for me by the car. Richard was near the dressing rooms. So, I went with him to the car.

"Will you be okay without a bodyguard? "He asked, concern flickering in his eyes.

"Of course, "I said. I didn't think Brandon would come to the Farm again. Or go to Steve.

"Then we'll meet on Monday."

"Yes, on Monday. Have a great weekend! "With that, he started walking with the others. And I joined Steve in the car.

"Hi, Jade! "He smiled. It was clear he was happy to see me.

"Hi, Steve! How did you like it?"

"It's not something I would do, but I really enjoyed it. And you were great."

"Sure. I think Richard played a trick on you. "
"Must admit, I'm quite into him, but don't be jealous." I laugh as got into the car.
"How are you? "I asked as fastened my seatbelt and got ready to drive.
"Fine. I missed you," he replies.
"And the Farm?"
"Well, after the party, there was nothing left standing. The next day, even the horses were drunk."
"Enough talking, let's go!" I tell him. I liked easy-going and funny Steve; he relieved the stress in me in a way I hadn't experienced before. He cracked jokes, talked nonsense, and before you knew it, you couldn't stop laughing. I don't remember ever laughing as much as I did with him. There was always some joke he had to tell or some way he could turn something into a joke.

I was driving slightly above the speed limit, but not by much, when we were pulled over by the police on the outskirts of the city; already had a bad feeling. I had never been stopped by the police before. Never in my life. I was in full costume, full makeup, and the outfit, wore for the ending scene, and I cursed myself for rushing so much; I should have changed clothes. We pulled over. I rolled down the window and already had the papers ready to show the officer.
"This car is wanted, "said the police officer. "Please step out of the vehicle." I put my hand on Steve's hand, signalling him to stay seated. I should have suspected something like this after what happened yesterday.
"Brandon White borrowed it for me to use."
"He himself filed a report stating that his car was stolen and identified you as the thief." I would say I was speechless, but that wasn't true. After this, I easily believed it. Since I wasn't going anywhere, he took revenge.
"There seems to be a misunderstanding here. Do you want to press charges?"

"He said that if you return the car, he doesn't wish to pursue any further action."
"Of course. Can I retrieve my belongings?"
"Certainly, miss." Now Steve was outside as well. I took my things out of the trunk and handed the key back to the officer. One got into the car and sped away with it while the other got into their patrol car and drove off.
"I'm sorry," I say to Steve. "It was to be expected." I was angry enough to do something stupid, to act like him.
"I suggest we go back to the hotel and head home tomorrow.
"Fine. But will you do something for me before that?"
"Do I want to? Jade, don't you want to do something stupid that you'll regret afterward?"
"But I do. You know I have this tendency to do things like that. But it won't hurt you. I promise." I caressed his chest, then his neck, and started kissing him slowly, growing more passionate. He didn't resist, not even when I took a picture of us. But I couldn't stop the kiss. I was breathless from his response. It excited me to see how I excited him. We were standing by the side of the road. Cars passed by, but we didn't care. We kissed passionately. Then he suddenly pulled away.
"Jade, if..."
"Let's call a taxi," I say. Then we didn't say a word in the taxi, nor at the reception. In the room, with the door closed, he watched me. He watched my gaze. With a casual move, I untied the piece of cloth called a top that I had on. He didn't need more. First, he devoured the sight, then he pounced on me as if I were a wild animal he wanted to capture. Urgently, he undressed me, and I did the same. We passionately and quickly made love. It was intense, but I think we were both in that mood, although I didn't know why he was. Then we caressed each other in bed, but we didn't say a word. Our clothes and belongings were in a pile on the floor. We didn't turn on the lights, but enough light came in through the window. There was a streetlamp just below our window. I felt ashamed that I wanted to use revenge. To take advantage of

the fact that he desires and loves me, or so he says. Maybe that's why he said nothing.

"Are you angry?" I broke the silence.

"Yes." But he says nothing else. "I deserved it, didn't I?"

"No. You can be angry. "He got out of bed and went to the window. He looked stunning, naked.

"I'm furious, but I don't want to argue with you. You're tired, and you've been through enough bad things. "He stared out the window. I stepped behind him and hugged him. He turned around, and I saw the anger in his eyes. I was scared for a moment, just a moment, enough for me to step back.

"Perhaps with me. I understand, and I'm sorry."

"I told you, don't want to argue with you. Just didn't like that you slept with me because of your revenge."

"That's not true, and you know it well. I kissed you with that intention, that's true, but it turned into something much more."

"And don't pull away. You know I would never hurt you. Right?" he asks irritably.

"Yes, I know. It's just a habit. I'm sorry."

"Doesn't matter, Jade. Lie down. You can barely stand on your feet," he says. This was true. When I lay down, he was still staring out the window. When I woke up in the morning, the bed next to me was empty. It was seven o'clock. Did he leave? Where is he? I went to shower and dressed properly and washed off the remaining makeup, asked for a coffee and was done in an hour, was sipping my coffee when the key turned in the lock.

"Good morning, Jade!" His smile again, which felt good.

"Good morning, Steve. Where were you?" He was wearing new clothes. He probably showered.

"Took a walk."

"And how do you like it? The city?"

"It's a beautiful place. Full of actors. Everywhere."

"Yes. And they're terrible, aren't they? Their manners, they make you lose your mind," I tease.

"you're telling me? I had an encounter with an actress, and boy, was she an unbearable bitch," he smiles. "Although she was superb in bed." He came over to the table, grabbed me by the hair, not painful, but with enough force for me to feel the intensity of his desire. He eagerly kissed me. Although he wanted to slow down, his masculinity didn't allow him to savour a slow, passionate kiss. He pressed his mouth firmly against mine. It was like a drug, the way I affected him. He practically tore my clothes off, and wherever a part of my body was exposed, he either grabbed or kissed it. With practiced moves, he undressed me, and I did the same to him. He didn't allow me to touch him and nuzzled me onto the bed. He penetrated me immediately and urgently. While thrusting forcefully, he interlocked our hands. We reached a point of pleasure quickly, and we didn't want to come back from there. We were sweaty, lying on top of each other. "If we keep this up, my average performance will be ruined."

"I give you an A+," I chuckle, "and let's not worry about the others. Short-term is a term too."

"I feel like we need a lot of practice to get back to our old performance."

"I'm in. Let's go shower," I say. "Let's save water." In the end, we let the water run for a good hour, not being mindful of our impact on nature. We washed each other, mostly with our tongues. It was quite time-consuming. Finally, we checked out of the hotel to head to the airport. But he mentioned he wanted to show me something he saw in the morning. Curiously, I went with him, and we walked up the hotel street towards the shopping centre. There were only a few people lingering around. I couldn't imagine what a man could have seen on the shopping street. Then, about thirty meters away, he stopped next to a pink SUV. It wasn't just pink; was sparkling. It was a beautiful Toyota CHR. The dashboard was half pink, half black, creating a sharp contrast. Black leather seats. It looked stunning, something I had never seen before.

"I don't know whose it is if you're curious," I say.

"I know," he says, and I raised an eyebrow. He just arrived in the city; how could he know whose car this was?
"How do you know?" I ask, amazed. I must be doing something very wrong.
"It's yours, Jade!" Now I couldn't believe my ears.
"Excuse me?"
"I bought it for you."
"Are you joking with me?" There I stood with my bag on my shoulder, in the middle of the shopping street, in a parking lot, and anger welled up inside me.
"No, Jade, I'm not joking."
"You think that because some asshole took his car back from me when I didn't sleep with him anymore, I would accept a car from you?"
"I would have been much happier with a thank you," he says solemnly.
"Do you think so?"
"Do you think I'm just as much of an asshole as the one who took your car away?"
"You threatened Samantha, not me. It was you who slept with me twice and told me you would leave me for her money. When are you going to take it back because money is more important to you?"
"I understand. You're right. I am just like Brandon. Because I want to keep my family, I am truly capable of anything. Almost anything because I didn't want to give up on love. I didn't want to give up on my happiness. I'm flawed, a parasite, "he retorted. And of course, I deeply hurt him. But I was angry too; of course, when he explained why he did things, it sounded different from when I explained them. "I'm leaving. I'm going home. All the car documents are in your bag. Do whatever you want with it. This makes no sense, Jade. "
"Steve, wait. Please. "He turned around, looked at me. His gaze was filled with sadness. I couldn't bring myself to say

anything. "I'm sorry. "He turned and walked away. He didn't look back. I watched until he disappeared.

I messed up again. Then, driven by a sudden idea, I retrieved the key from my bag. It was there, a shiny pink butterfly charm hanging from it. I hadn't paid attention to the license plate before. It read JADE001. I took a picture of it and sent it to Brandon. Let him have his car back. I got in, quickly familiarised myself with the controls, and started driving. I hoped to get home before he arrived by plane; he still had to wait for boarding, if there are any flights available these days. I sped through the kilometres.

Meanwhile, I paired my phone with the car radio and enjoyed listening to my own playlist. Everywhere inside the car, my name was displayed. Meanwhile, I wrote him an apologetic message. I've never been someone who takes advantage of people. And I didn't want to, not last night, not with this car either. I didn't want him to spend money because of me, and I didn't want to use it as revenge. I didn't want to become one of those people who, because of the negative experiences they've had, become absorbed by the same negativity. Those who become sceptical and disbelieving because they have encountered a few poor individuals in their lives. Anyway, I drove without stopping, so I arrived at my pace in two and a half hours.

Although I do not know how many pictures were taken of me along the way. After the usual hustle and bustle, the grand gate opened. Inside was the strange little man who finally introduced himself (his name was Simon). He remarked the master is not home yet, but if I want to go in, I should go ahead. I didn't want to. Instead, I waited in the car for the master. Then the cook came out and asked if I wanted a coffee; gratefully, I said yes. Minutes turned into hours, and I couldn't imagine where Steve could be. I knocked and asked Simon if the master had left any messages about when he would be back. He said there were no messages, but the master was probably visiting his family. And it might not be a good idea for me to stay here on a day like this because the master gets furious. He rarely goes to see them, that's why. Suddenly, guilt took hold of me.

Would he have taken me with him? Or if I were with him, would he not have gone and spared me from such an occasion? I didn't know, but the realisation didn't sit well with me. Then I didn't go anywhere; I got back in the car and waited. I fell asleep in the meantime, only to be awakened by shouting and darkness. Steve got out of his car and was arguing with his driver; no one else was around. I felt sorry for the poor guy. He was blaming him for nonsense, driving too slowly, too fast, and where does the fuel disappear too, anyway? I quickly got out to spare the guy. Steve didn't even glance at me; he just walked into the house while still arguing. The man stood there, broken, holding his hat, but didn't say a word. Steve slammed the door in front of my face, but I didn't let myself be shaken off that easily. Without knocking, I opened the door. The living room door was open, so I thought he would go there. I followed and found Steve arguing with Simon about why he let me in without questioning. That was too much.

"Simon, please, just leave. I'll talk to the master myself, " I said.

"You are nobody here, and Simon is not going anywhere! "Steve raged with anger. The poor butler didn't know what to do or not to do.

"That's true, and I'm nobody anywhere else. "I stood between the two of them. We locked eyes. His gaze didn't soften one bit. There was a drink in front of him. "Tell me, Steve, I'm listening. Tell me. Talk."

"I have nothing to say to you."

"Really? And how is your brother? Your mother? Your father? Are they all doing well?"

"It's none of your business, Jade. What do you know about responsibility? If you don't like something, you just grab yourself and run away. You didn't even come to your parents' funeral and left acting, left the Farm, and left Brandon and you drove me away."

"That's all true. "Meanwhile, Simon had left. And I turned away and went to the window. "It doesn't matter. I'm not enough for any of this. I'm sorry."

"See? Here you go again. Just running away."

"You've said it. You're right, can't change them. I want to, but it's no longer possible. I left and came after you, but I'm not enough for any of this. Sorry, Steve."

"Indeed, you're not enough. You're weak."

"Maybe. Good luck, Steve! "With that, I turned and left the living room. I tried not to stomp my feet until I reached the gate. Painful things were thrown at me; it doesn't mean they're not true. I knew they were, but it didn't sit well coming from the person I thought loved and wanted to protect me. It was already nine in the evening. I took my things out of the car and the papers tossed on the seat with the key. I was just about to slam the car door shut when he hurried down the few steps leading to the house. The top two buttons of his shirt were already unbuttoned.

"Is this what we're going to do? "He asked. "Fight constantly?

"No. I'm done, as you can see. And it's not about the arguments, it's about your inability to accept. You are closer to it than anyone before, but still not close enough. It was expected that you would lose your temper. You lasted quite a while, I must say. Nobody will put up with me. And this is not a self-pitying speech. It's just that everyone eventually reaches their breaking point with me. That's how it is."

"Jade. Baby. Come here. "He leaned on the car, stood with his legs apart, and beckoned me into his arms.

"No, Steve. I came because I knew that in my whole life, you were the only person who saw me, treated me like a human being, and not to mention how you behaved towards me. But you still threw those things at me. I already beat myself up enough for those things, and I don't need a man to throw them at me, either. So, you're no better than anyone else."

"I was just angry. And not really at you. Well, at you too, but it was just a release of tension."
"So, what are you going to throw at me when you get angry at me? I can't even imagine. What do you want to build on this? In this anger? In these words? Or am I not entitled to a clean relationship?"
"Shall we try? We haven't really tried yet."
"I feel like we've tried twice already."
"Please. Let's go have dinner and stay here. Jade. Come. "He finally pulled me into his arms. He buried his face in my hair, took a deep breath, and held me tight. Almost crushing me. I said nothing. I let this feeling wash over me. It reassured me.
"When will you get upset again when... "He silenced me with a long and passionate kiss.
"Let's go inside, "he said when the kiss ended. He didn't apologise to anyone inside and didn't even speak to anyone. He only talked to me, and he was still grumpy. We ate in silence in the kitchen. He seemed quite lost in thought. He said nothing in the bedroom either. I took a shower, and then he did too. We lay in bed: I rested my head on his chest, unsure whether to mention the recent scene and the family visit or not.
"What happens in moments like this that you become so grumpy? You, Steve, who always jokes around and is always cheerful?"
"Well, that's hard to explain. After my father's case, my brother became an addict almost immediately. At first, we still deluded ourselves that it would pass, he would grow out of it, or just leave it behind, or anything, but then he got so involved he started stealing from our mother, selling things. In the end, we took him to a rehab centre, and he's been there ever since. It's been several years now. He comes out from time to time, but he always relapses. He'll never fit back into society. I left earlier, only going home on weekends. My mother went crazy. Linda ran away. The lawyer called and said I was taking over the Farm. That was around seven years

ago. My father will be released in five years, but I don't think he'll ever come back. "The words and disappointment poured out of him. I felt sorry for him. My life story seemed insignificant next to his, or my problems diminished to trivialities. "And my mother can't move on from the past. When I visit her, she still acts as if I'm fifteen and she talks to everyone like that. They say she's defending herself against the bad things that happened to her, that she's stuck in a state when she was happy. If I hadn't left, maybe things would have turned out differently."

"It wasn't your fault at all, Steve."

"You say that, always blaming yourself for something."

"I have reasons for it. It's irrelevant now. And what do you want? "I asked him in the dark room.

"If everything could be good again. I don't want the Farm, I never did. I wanted to be an engineer. A designer, an architect. No deal with the Farm. Not because I'm a spoiled rich kid or don't love it, but because I love that more. Do you understand?"

"Of course. I love it very much. I've realised that. True, I have little time for actual work anymore, but I love being out there. When I came back home, and there was a storm on the first day, and there was no one around, even though ten years had passed, everything came back as if I had only missed a day. And it felt so good! I love both, and both are mine now, in a way. There's a great guy underneath me, and I can't say a word. "He laughed wholeheartedly, and it was worth it just for that. I leaned over, and he didn't resist. Today, I wanted to pamper him. He let it happen for a while, but then he couldn't resist anymore. The anger that was inside him was long gone. He made love to me gently. Deep sighs escaped his lips. Now it was me who was greedy and could barely get enough of him. Then we fell asleep in each other's arms, naked. It was a deep, dreamless, restful sleep. And when I woke up, he was still sleeping next to me. But it wasn't early, and I found it strange. I carefully slipped out of bed. I didn't want to make any noise, so I just put on a robe and went to the kitchen. Cassie had already been there and immediately served me coffee and pastries. I mumbled something, but at this time, I'm not capable of conversation. I asked her if anyone smokes in the house, and she said George, the driver, does.

So, I found George, who was washing the car, and begged him for a cigarette. Of course, I first apologised to him for last night. He was a sweet little old man, not like Bobby, who came for me last time. George was a grey-haired, thin, broken-faced man. He said he had been the driver for thirty-five years. And Master Steve is a very kind gentleman. The mentioned gentleman appeared behind me and embraced me. He caressed me through the robe.

"Good morning, Jade! "He said with a smile. He was already dressed in work clothes, so I assumed he would work on the Farm this time. Green cargo pants, a denim shirt, boots. Of course, he looked perfect, even like that. "I didn't know you smoke, "he frowned.

"Only occasionally. I didn't want to wake you up, so I asked George for one."

"Great, but you shouldn't smoke."

"The things on my 'shouldn't do' list are quite long, so I didn't have time to read it through this morning."

"There's room in my closet for your stuff if you want to unpack."

"Today, I'm also going to the Farm to have a look around. "I left his statement hanging, needed a few more hours of sleep for that. "I sent him a picture of the car, huh?"

"Ah, still him."

"Excuse me? I just wanted you to know about it."

"I don't mind. Do you like it?"

"I love it. It's beautiful."

"Then please, use it. It's yours. Regardless of whether we fight."

"I understand."

"Really? Because yesterday you wanted to leave it here."

"That's true."

"Jade, I bought it for you. If you leave it here, I can't do anything with it because it's registered in your name."

"Okay. Thank you."

Jade caught him right away, with her always defiant nature and naivety. She did everything for him as if she was having a tooth pulled, but never uttered a complaint. If he brought up his rudest friend to have sex, she did it. She never said no to anything. When she acted, because she had to get a role after such an occasion, she acted as if her life depended on it. He found her attitude, her personality, very likable. She was strong of anything to achieve her dreams. She never became dependent on drugs. If they didn't meet for two weeks, she didn't use for two weeks. The other girls demanded a second dose after the first one.

She was completely different. After a while, he no longer wanted anyone else to touch her, and the anger crept back into his heart. Immeasurable hatred and anger reigned within him again. It was a bittersweet feeling. As much as he wanted that kind of love, he didn't want hatred to take over again. As soon as someone else touched her, he could have screamed. Then that article appeared in the newspaper, and he was afraid of losing Lilly. But he lost Jade. She left. He drove her away. He could barely cope with her absence and finally felt the same love he once felt for his first love, and now she was gone. How much he missed that feeling. And now he had it, and he wasted it. Hatred coursed through him once again. Even Lilly no longer offered his consolation. Usually, if he got angry, all he had to do was look at her little girl, and all his anger evaporated. But that didn't work anymore. And now he lost her. Again, but he didn't want to leave it at that. Not this time. He would do anything to get her love back.

## Chapter seventeen

I went to the Farm. Everyone was plying. The stable was ready, the poultry yard was done, and the cows' dwelling was almost finished. They had also started building the house. The foundation remained the same, but I wanted it to reflect my taste. A small house that would be just enough for me. The workers immediately gathered around me, asking about the filming and my car. I told them everything. Thomas and Katie looked lovingly at each other and always stood close to each other. Now they had bonded well with Linda, too. Meanwhile, I had to talk to people about what and how things should be. They had a few questions about colour, pattern, material, but overall, I was satisfied with the progress. It would still take some time before the house becomes move-in ready. It was already Saturday, and I had to leave tomorrow evening. I went through the letters; when Katie and Thomas went back to help, Linda came over for a managerial meeting.

"How are things?" I ask.

"Everything is going fine. We didn't miss that many animals. We sold a few this week. They are doing well, eating, and they like the new place."

"How are we doing financially?"

"We're in a bit of a deficit right now, but once they finish and we work at full speed again, it will be good. Have you thought about opening a riding school?"

"No, but I like the idea."

"You could teach in it. It would be an additional income, and you're the real advertisement."

"I like it. Do you think I would go wrong with milk? Or apples? Or eggs?" I ask, genuinely interested in her opinion because she was an expert, and I was just brainstorming. Now that I look at her more closely, she really resembled her brother, but not enough for anyone to tell. Although I was never good at determining who looks like whom. They always told me I looked just like my father in terms of nature, but like my mother in terms of appearance. I didn't see it, and I didn't care. Not until now. Back then, I took offense at everything in my stupid age... well, at everything, anyway.

"No daring ideas, and I support you. Everything depends on advertising. But there is no profit without risks."

"True, I just don't know how to advertise."

"Jade, you're an actress. I think you'll figure it out. I don't know how my brother will take it, but this is business, right?"

"Yes." I didn't mention that I would share a bed with her brother. "I would like to be here more, but that will not happen. The filming will last at least a couple more weeks."

"No problem at all."

"But if anything happens, please write to me. I would like to know everything."

"Of course."

"By the way, Steve was here the other day," I brought it up to her. "Nobody mentioned it."

"Yes, I didn't mention it because you're not on good terms. He just came to check if everything was going well, not because of me. "I didn't even realise it. I was so busy with the filming and everything else, having his sister here.

"But Linda, everything, that's everything. If something urgent comes up, call me. There's a better chance I'll respond faster, but if it's not that important, please write it down. I know it's not in the job description, but... "My statement was interrupted by the police. Linda went back to work, so I could speak with them privately. They didn't come inside the gate; they just drove up to the driveway and stopped there. I went out to meet them, thinking they didn't want anyone else to hear what they were saying. There was no one nearby. The employees were already with the animals, and the workers were at the cattle shed, hammering, drilling, and carving so intensely that I didn't think they could hear anything.

"Jade Donovan? "Asked the younger police officer.

"Yes. "The other guy was sorting through papers on the car roof. He was older, in his forties, and he wasn't wearing a uniform, so I assumed he was the boss. The younger officer seemed like he had just come out of the police academy with some stubble on his chin. He was very young. His uniform was almost new and perfectly ironed.
"Can you identify yourself? "The younger one asked.
"Of course. "I reached into my bag, which I always carry with me, or if I don't have it, I feel naked, and I handed him my driver's license.
"Thank you. Well, the investigation concluded that it was an intentional arson. In the second round, we determined who did it. You'll find everything in the papers. Regarding the person involved, we can't start legal proceedings. Only you can file a complaint."
"Who is it? "I asked, shocked.
"Everything is in the documents, and you can decide whether to file a complaint. If you do, you'll receive the insurance money, but if you don't, you won't."
"Alright. Thank you. "With that, the older man handed me the papers. They thanked me for my attention and left. I was devastated and curious at the same time to find out who it was. Until I knew this, it didn't feel real that someone wanted to set fire to and destroy a lifetime of work just out of revenge or some other fabricated reason. If they had a problem with me, why didn't they confront me? Why did they have to target the Farm? I didn't want to read it there, got in the car and went to the nearest cafe and sat in the corner with the wall behind me, so I could see everyone, but no one could accidentally read what I was reading. I ordered a coffee and took a deep breath. My eyes devoured the words. In the end, I didn't get the result I expected. I sat there for a few more long minutes, contemplating everything. I called someone and found confirmation of something that had been on my mind for a long time. Well, Jade Donovan, here you go again. In my imagination, I rolled up my sleeves and said,

"Let's begin." Maybe they didn't know what kind of material the Donovan's were made of.

I went back to the Farm and inspected everything more closely and hopped on one horse and galloped around in a circle. I rode around the entire farm twice. It was magnificent.

The shrubs had already been planted, and the sheep were grazing in their own paddock, as were the cows. The Farm was designed in a way could enter everywhere on horseback, touching no enclosure, but being able also go around the entire Farm without touching a single pen. I liked it. I really liked it. And there was enough space for riding lessons and for someone experienced to go out. Katie and Tom were wandering around with the horses. Tony was with the cows. Linda was grooming the horses. The workers were here and there. Since I hadn't been here much, I felt like a guest for a little while. I noticed shouting from the neighbouring farm.

Steve rode towards me. He was wearing the same riding outfit as when I first saw him, and he looked just as handsome. He smiled, seemed happy to see me. I went to the nearest point between us. He rode up to the fence with his horse, and we could easily exchange a kiss over the fence. If he's not hiding anything, then I don't need to either.

"What's the situation, Jade? "He pronounced my name in such a sexy way, as he always did.

"Everything is fine. I like how things are progressing here. And it's good to be here."

"But you'll come back home, right?"

"Of course. What's for dinner? I'm starving."

"Haven't you eaten yet?"

"No. I need to go on a diet."

"Excuse me?"

"Just kidding. I didn't have time."

"Well, good. I was almost getting a heart attack. When are you coming? I'm heading home from here. It'll be dark soon, and you must go back tomorrow. "There was a sad expression in his eyes.

"I'll be leaving soon. I'll say goodbye to everyone and then go."

"Okay, Jade. Then come to my place. "One more kiss, but this one already included the promise of the night.

And so it was. I went back. I said goodbye to everyone and left. The gate was already open. Steve had already showered and was wearing a tracksuit. I quickly went to shower as well. We met in the dining room. He was sitting at the head of the six-person table, and I was on his right. They had prepared a huge dinner. We talked about my farm and his. He no longer needed to go out there unless he felt like it. Otherwise, he only deals with business and procurement. Mail as well. He also tries to work on architecture, but so far, he hasn't had enough time to delve into it and generate income. But the plan is that once the Farm can operate completely independently, without him, he wants to design structures. He just thinks that this town is too small, and there's not much he can do here on his own. The idea of starting over is still fresh in his mind.

"Steve, "I said, "you mentioned you came over to my place while I was away, but it only occurred to me today that Linda was there."

"Yes, and? "He asked with a curious look. We were sipping our wine on the couch in the living room, the fire crackling in front of us in the fireplace. It cast a warm glow. I looked at him in amazement.

"I don't talk to her about family matters, or just I talk to her like anyone else."

"Why? Is it necessary for you two to be on bad terms?"

"No, but it just turned out that way."

"And why don't you hire a woman? "I asked.

"Because this is not a job for a woman, "he said simply.

"Well, I'm doing the same thing."

"But you're the boss. This is physically demanding work, and I don't think it's suitable for women. And I'm not an antifeminist. Before you beat me to death with a wine bottle, I simply feel sorry for how many women can't have children because they lifted themselves up."
"I understand. But a woman can decide for herself whether they want to take the risk. Some of them have brains, not just vaginas."
"I'll keep that in mind."

We drank wine and talked. About my plans for next week, about his plans.

Then another week of filming passed, which was also great. A better relationship was developing with the actors and everyone else who worked around us. The team was good, and it filled me with awe that being an actress could be like this. I wasn't worried about whether I would have enough roles this month, or if I could pay for everything, or if I was good enough for Brandon. We simply filmed a box office hit with professional actors and crew. Everyone hoped it would turn out that way. We didn't finish on Thursday this week, but it was fine. I was still quite exhausted, but I still enjoyed it. After the filming days, I collapsed into bed as if I had worked a whole day on the farm. Tired, but satisfied. No negative reviews reached my ears. Everyone seemed satisfied with the shots and everything. I thought a lot about Steve and the whole situation. When we were together, we had friendly conversations about everything, and sex was not neglected either. On Friday, we finished at four o'clock. I drove home, but at Steve, I could only fall into bed. The next day, I was at the Farm; the animals' spaces were already fully prepared, we just had to wait for the house, but progress was slow. But on Friday, the test results arrived, and from then on, everything changed completely...

It's fortunate that I studied acting. My mind was constantly racing with what the police said, or rather, what I read in the file and what I discovered afterwards, but none of it was noticeable on the outside. I weaved and discarded plans. I observed the signs and the evidence. Meanwhile, I just smiled and conversed, but my mind was feverishly working. I needed a lawyer, some help. I tried to push the thoughts away, but it didn't really succeed. Steve, after one of our evening drinks, invited me to the bedroom. It was a lazy encounter. Leisurely, savouring each moment, but it wasn't worse than the previous ones. We were getting to know each other's bodies and habits, and we knew how to entertain one another. We fell asleep, tightly intertwined. Morning came quickly, and Steve was still asleep when I got out of bed. I sneaked out for coffee and smoked a cigarette, quickly sent a few emails; I pocketed my phone just in time as Steve, groggy and wrapped in a robe, stumbled down to the terrace. He just sat next to me at the table, and his coffee, newspaper, and pastries were already brought to him. He didn't speak. I don't think it was out of rudeness; he was simply pondering.

"How are you, Jade? "He asked. He was still blinking away remnants of the night from his eyes. The whole situation saddened me.

"Thank you. Everything's fine. How about you, Steve? "I asked.

"Just hearing my name makes him rise." He pulled me into his lap, and I could be sure of it. "I desire you, can't get enough of you. I want you. Now." Suddenly, he stood up with me still in his arms, urgently pulling me through the back door that led to the kitchen. He didn't care who was there. Cassey fled in a panic. He placed me on the counter as if I were a baby. He pulled apart my robe, and he was inside me already. His eyes darkened, as if there was no soul present. Mad fire danced in his eyes. It made me quite uncomfortable to be there at that moment. I wasn't the same young, shameless girl anymore. Of course, it excited me, the way I excited him, but I couldn't completely detach myself from our surroundings. But they say the end justifies the means. Urgent thrusts pushed into me. He dictated an increasingly faster pace, deep sighs escaping his mouth. His hands moved up and down my body. I no longer had my nightgown on, neither down nor up. My exposed nipples he suckled whenever he had access to it. He reached the end quickly, perhaps because of the location, which made it feel longer to me. I tried not to escape like a shy little girl. Acting. I proudly straightened myself and adjusted my clothes, was about to return to the terrace when he grabbed my hand and pulled me towards him. "I'm sorry, baby, but you bring out the animal in me."

"It's okay, Steve," I say and stayed in his arms. I looked deep into his eyes, kissed him, and knew the effect it had on him. And I wasn't disappointed. He struggled with my kiss, convulsing throughout his body as one part tried to regain control while the other revealed in pleasure. I felt my power over him. I usually wasn't the one to take advantage of it... usually...

After the kiss, I withdrew to the terrace to finish my coffee and cigarette. He didn't join me. When I finished, I went upstairs to take a shower. But he wasn't in the room, and I suspected he wasn't in the house either. When I was done, I looked at him. Or rather, I would have looked for him, but he had already ridden off. I didn't want to disturb him with his self-flagellation. I wrote him a message and left. Before that, I wanted to say goodbye to the workers at the Farm.

Lost in my thoughts, I drove. My Farm was near to his by car. Back in the day, they used to live next to us as well. We even attended the same school. And then the same high school. Our town only had an elementary school, so we commuted to the bigger city for high school, where they already lived. We went to the same middle school, but not in the same class. We had some classes together, but he was more into the sciences while I preferred humanities subjects. It's hard for me to remember who his friends were back then. Or his girlfriend. Well, I'm not on good terms with any of them now, and honestly, I wasn't back then either. It wasn't a viable path. When I turned onto the access road to my farm, I received the response to my email I was expecting. Thanks to my father. Again.

I blurted goodbye to the guys and reminded them to reach out if there was anything. Despite it being Sunday, everyone was working and seemed to enjoy it. I was genuinely happy about that, would have preferred to stay here, not go into the city. I didn't want to go back now, knew that in the first few weeks, everyone gives their all, but then comes the decline, multiple retakes of scenes. Overtime stressed producer. It's always been like that. It loses some of its excitement. Then, in the following week, depending on the extent of the scolding and how each person takes it, either the enthusiasm remains until the end, or it doesn't. I wasn't in the mood for this game again. Even if I bring out my best, it won't matter if they don't.

The workers were there too, which surprised me because it was Sunday. They said they understood how urgent this was for me. I was grateful for that. The house won't be ready to move in for weeks. When I got into my car, Steve got in beside me.

"You couldn't leave without my kiss. Without it, I think they would have easily turned you back," he says, as we both got out of the car. His eyes were smiling, too.

"I was daring enough to take the risk," I reply, leaning against my car in a relaxed stance, and he pulled me into his arms. We looked at each other. I tried to read his face, to understand what his eyes were telling me.

But he just smiled, and all I saw was pure love. At that moment, I felt ashamed of myself. It was already two in the afternoon. The sun was scorching, but it didn't bother us. We looked at each other. I slowly approached his lips. He was slightly taken aback. It was a fraction of a moment, but I noticed, and I didn't retreat. I gently tasted his lower lip. Then the upper one before immersing myself in the taste of his kiss.

"It would have been foolish to leave without this," I smile at him after the kiss ended.

"I knew it. That's why I came. You'll get there quickly enough today."

"At least I don't have to drive like a race car driver."

"Do you know any other way?" he asks, laughing.

"No, not really. I'm off now."

"When will you come back?" his gaze turned serious.

"On Friday, this week I'm certain we won't finish on Thursday. But if you can, you can come up on Thursday, and we'll go home together on Friday."

"Alright. But we'll still talk until then, right?"

"Of course, Steve. Bye." I lightly kissed his lips and pulled away. I started towards the highway, but took the exit earlier than I should have. I had some business to attend to in another city, where my county interview was scheduled. I glanced in the mirror frequently, but I saw nothing suspicious behind me. Unfortunately, I couldn't remember the route by heart, but why else would I have a smartphone if not to help with that? Although I saw the love in Steve's face, and I knew he desired me, it didn't deter me from my goal. I arrived quickly, considering the heavier traffic here. Being Sunday, panic had gripped everyone, fearing the stores would close at five pm and maybe they wouldn't last until Monday morning without those two tons of flour. I never understood it. Anyway, the building where I had to stop was faintly illuminated. The county courthouse towered above me with all its beauty and grandeur. It was a red brick and massive, towered building. In the central tower's window stood a magnificent bronze statue of Lady Justice, holding scales in her hand.

The atmosphere exuded a lofty feeling, and a sense of foolish calm washed over me. I felt I was in the right place and entrusted my case to capable hands. After the obligatory frisking at the entrance, I was escorted to Judge's office. My shoes echoed loudly on the ancient tiles. Black-and-white tiles from the seventies. They had been patched up here and there; they tried their best not to stand out from the originals, but if someone observed closely, they would notice. The walls were adorned with enormous pictures, quotes, and the principles of justice. Several busts and evergreen plants. I already loved this building, only vaguely remembered that my father used to come here sometimes and have long conversations, while we had to wait, but afterwards, he always took us out for ice cream. I tried to push that memory aside. The court clerk was a thin man who wasn't thrilled about having to climb up to the top floor on a Sunday when he was deeply engrossed in analysing an interesting law. He was only here to fulfil his monthly Sunday duty, and he had already exceeded his daily tasks. When we arrived, he practically shoved me through the door and rushed away. Behind the heavy door sat an old man behind his desk, staring out of the window. Lost in thought. He was just a lawyer back when we used to visit him; today he is the president of the court. He raised his gaze to me; mentally, I patted myself on the back for wearing a suit and putting on makeup. I didn't remember him faintly, not at all.

"You're a spitting image of your mother, Jade. Please have a seat, "he pointed to the chair across from his desk. I quickly glanced around the room. Everything was made of mahogany, emanating a strong, woody scent. There was a plush carpet in the other half of the room, where a couch and a bookshelf were placed. The wall opposite the door was entirely made of windows, offering a splendid view of the city. The wall facing the door was covered in a multitude of certificates. On the desk, there were pictures, documents, seals, and pens.

"Many people say, Your Honour," I say, "I apologise for disturbing you on a Sunday like this. I truly am sorry, but I couldn't come at any other time."

"You know, your father meant a lot to me. He was a great friend. But you tell me. What happened after you ran away? "He smiled.

"I went to pursue acting, but I didn't become famous, rather infamous, "I smiled.
"I've heard a thing or two. What can I do for you? "Asked, and I began explaining all my troubles and issues and he patiently listened, making some corrections here and there to ensure everything was within the bounds of the law, but he didn't oppose my plan as much as I thought he would. He said I would need two people to execute my plan, one being his son, who is a lawyer, and the other being a county police officer, whom he also knows. He would send both to me, but for the sake of secrecy, they might visit me in the city. I was extremely grateful for his help and thanked him humbly, and then I left. I only lost about forty minutes with this. It didn't matter. I didn't think Steve would follow me. It didn't hurt to be cautious. I hurried as much as I could. What if there's a tracker in the car? Flashed through my mind. After getting on the highway, I called him, just to be on the safe side.
"Hi "I greeted indifferently.
"I knew you'd miss me, "he said, and I couldn't detect anything special in his voice.
"Of course, handsome. Guess what, I went into town to get a coffee and visit my favourite clothing store, and as I stopped, I ran into an old co-star and could hardly get away. I told him I had to leave and headed back, going nowhere.
"Don't joke! "There was suspicion in his voice, but it could have been just my imagination.
"I was even more surprised. Anyway, it doesn't matter. I didn't really lose much."
"I don't know how you'll manage without caffeine."
"Don't forget about the clothes."
"Right. That's even worse."
"I think the same way, but anyway, I'll somehow survive without it. What are you up to?"
"I went out for a horse ride. Let me know when you arrive."
"I will. Bye, Steve "I ended the call.

It didn't reassure me. I kept an eye out. No one followed me for sure, but I didn't think about the possibility of something being in the car, or worse, on my phone. Maybe I'm just becoming too paranoid, but better safe than sorry. Then, when I reached the city, I had just enough time to replace my phone. I kept the same number, but switched to a very basic device. It wouldn't have been bad if Brandon were my ally. He knew many people, including some shady characters, who would have come in handy. Well, not that Brandon himself wasn't shady enough. I'll ask Richard for help. I galloped to the hotel. Someone had already booked the same room I stayed in last time. And it was paid for three weeks. I assumed it was because of the shoot. I went upstairs, and there were flowers everywhere and various accompanying cards. It looked like fans had sent them. The entire room seemed to wait for me to return. The receptionist was friendly and smiled a lot, but I attached little importance to it. As soon as I closed the door behind me, there was a knock. I opened it in a panic. Richard was standing there with his huge, genuine smile.

"Hey! What happened? "I asked as I stepped away from the door.

"Since you didn't give me your phone number, I couldn't brief you. They paid for our accommodation during the shoot, and everything else because the pictures turned out so great and the campaign was such a success that people were already going crazy for the movie. The premiere tickets sold out immediately everywhere."

"Oh, my god! You scared me with that! "I hesitantly sat at the end of my bed, and he took the armchair. And he kept smiling non-stop.

"You don't have to do anything different, just what you've been doing. Play your role amazingly."

"Well, it wouldn't hurt to stay out of any trouble."

"Perhaps that contributed to our brilliant success. You were seen online with your knight, making out on the highway. And of course, it was also there that we were sitting together at the bar."

"Holly?"

"She's handling it well, don't worry. I talked to Brandon. "My heart skipped a beat at the mention of his name.

"And?"

"I asked him to stay away from you. He went to see a doctor. He told them everything. You don't need a personal bodyguard anymore, but because of the film, wherever we go, there will be security personnel around."

"So now I've become the bad cop?"

"No, Jade, not at all. I just got a glimpse of his side a bit, and maybe it's more understandable, but still not acceptable."

"You know, I really loved him. And when I left, he didn't love me back. Maybe that's why I left. I went through hell during the time I was his mistress and shared with his friends. And I could forgive him, but I couldn't bear how he treated me afterward, love or not."

"I understand."

"However, this will surely come up, along with everything else related to me. Were these smart people prepared for that?"

"Yes. They were terrified, hesitated, but the writer said he wants you. So, nobody had a choice."

"So, they didn't want me. I suspected as much. I didn't know why I got the role."

"But don't take it the wrong way, Jade. They don't have a problem with you. Everyone thinks you're a talented actress. It's just..."

"The scandals. The farm.

"Don't worry about that, Jade. Just keep playing the way you have been and be yourself."

"I'll try."

"Don't you want to go to the upper floor? The rooms there are much bigger."

"No, it's perfect here."

"Alright. Good night. See you in the morning."

"Richard, I have a question. "I summarised to him what I wanted. He immediately knew who I should contact. He gave me the address and phone number. As soon as he left the room, I called the number. I didn't question how he knew about these things?! The person didn't live far away. I took the car to the guy. Now I'll wait to see what they say before I even call Steve with some silly excuse.

I drove for fifteen minutes. I parked in a garage as instructed. The gate closed behind me. A plain, white-painted garage greeted me with the usual things: a lawnmower, unused toys, dusty garden tools. A black guy with dreadlocks came forward through an inner door. One of his canine teeth was made of gold. He greeted me with a wide grin.
"Hey, little star. What's up? Jealous husband?"
"Yeah, you could say that. "I told him. He was wearing a tracksuit six sizes too big, with the bottom stylishly hanging out. He smiled as if nothing had ever ruined his mood. Skilfully, he pulled out a gadget from the closet and started inspecting the car.
"Quite a conspicuous vehicle, I must say. "He pulled and tugged on the device. It didn't give any signs. It lit up red and then green, but even if it had been illuminated in neon lights, I wouldn't have known what it meant.
"I like attention."
"I heard. "He positioned himself in the pit and examined the car from underneath, and then from the inside. He was thorough, as far as I could tell. "I found three, "he said after climbing out of the car. He dropped a bag into my hands containing three large metal discs.
"Great "I said. "How do I make it less conspicuous? How do I get rid of it?"
"You can't. The person will just install a new one. Experience."
"So, is that the big advice?"
"No, it's not. Find someone whose route is like yours. Another... talk to that person and force them to answer. You know who it is, right?"

"Yes. Thank you. How much do I owe you?"
"One autograph."
"Alright, I'll even sign your ass. Just don't tell anyone I was here."
"Obvious. "Finally, I had to give him to a note, which reassured me. I didn't know what to do. Felt the weight of the small package I hid deep in my bag. I didn't plan to tell him about it. One more reason. I drove back to the hotel, took a shower, and tucked myself in for tomorrow. I didn't call Steve because I might have slipped up. Once again, I had to acknowledge that my naivety knows no bounds. They fooled me again. I really can't figure out the men I get involved with, or maybe I don't want to figure them out? Am I afraid of loneliness? Am I afraid to take responsibility alone? Or why do I always cling to a man who turns out to be a liar or mentally unstable? I didn't think too much because I was exhausted from all the pondering, and I fell asleep.

The filming was still going well for everyone. Although there was extra pressure on us regarding the expectations and demands of the directors. So, we missed out on a lazy week. They wanted new pictures, more daring ones, and scheduled the next shoot for Wednesday. Last time, not everyone was present in the pictures, mainly just Richard and me. But on Wednesday, they wanted everyone, and the pictures were getting increasingly provocative. If the fans hadn't gone crazy enough by now, they would with these. Tuesday passed quickly. The lawyer and the police officer both checked in on Tuesday afternoon. I thought they came together to save taxpayers' money or to avoid getting bored. It didn't matter. I felt a little ashamed because of my plan, but that lasted only until that night came to mind. After that, I wanted to carry it out even stronger and sooner.

After the filming, without changing clothes, I rushed to the hotel. We were shooting a love scene, so I wasn't wearing much, but I didn't really care. They were already waiting for me at the front desk. Two men. One of them clearly looked like a lawyer: a three-piece suit, not just any brand or material. The other one clearly looked like a police officer. I had little to do with them, but I immediately knew who was. The doorman was already waving and pointing from afar. He was worried. He was adorable. His name was Josh, and he was always at the reception when I came and went. He was very young and very conscientious. Maybe he was my fan too. "Thank you, Josh. I know them, they came to visit me. Don't worry. "None of them reacted to my outfit. They introduced themselves. Brian Brosnan, the lawyer, and Tom Kelner, the police officer. We got into the elevator, and they didn't say a word even there. Tom looked around the hotel reception as if he feared a terrorist attack. It wasn't hard to figure out that he was the police officer. The lawyer boy didn't even pay attention to it; he was more concerned about how his clothes looked on him. He seemed quite dapper, but who was I to judge? When we entered the room, I had them sit in the armchairs. I grabbed a sweater for myself and sat on the bed for the conversation. I had to tell them everything that had happened and what I wanted. They asked questions, took notes, corrected me, and understood the situation better than I did, or better than the judge, who was already out of practice with these kinds of things. They didn't dissuade me, and they didn't want me to give up on my plan either. Finally, the lawyer left, taking the documents with him, and promised to contact me by email.

  Then only Tom and I remained. He asked a few more things, then requested I hand over the tracking device; not to worry because the perpetrator wouldn't put it back in this case. He told me not to mention it, to act as if nothing happened. He said I should take my first step next week. Until then, they will take care of the other steps and prepare the ground. They will write my statement. I thanked them for their help and told them to bill me for everything together. He said he had nothing to bill. He was doing what he swore to do, but he mentioned I should tighten my belt because the lawyer's fees wouldn't be small. I didn't care. We bid farewell, saying I would take the next step on Monday and we would meet there. He would work undercover for me on the scene. I couldn't wait.

I closed the door; a heavy weight was lifted off my shoulders when the tracking devices were taken away. I called Steve because the show had to go on. I told him about my day and the photoshoot for tomorrow. In that meowing, whining voice that usually made men faint. I will never understand why?! It still gave me chills.

I wasn't as tired during the shooting days anymore, although we usually finished in the daytime, so I went shopping, had coffee in the afternoons, enjoyed this city because it didn't matter how big the film would be, a washed-up or undiscovered actor didn't come up to talk about it. I was calm and balanced. When I first stumbled upon a giant billboard with my face on it, the feeling was incomparable. I just stood there and stared for a while. I was proud, bashful, and critical at the same time and didn't stare for long, and I wished I hadn't seen it at all. Well, it quickly left my mind after that.

On Wednesday, we were still shooting pictures until 10 o'clock in the evening. That was the price we paid for the more relaxed workflow in previous weeks. Everyone was exhausted and irritable by the end. Unfortunately, we didn't have the luck to be sent off on Thursday, so as soon as they announced the end of the photoshoot, I rushed back to the hotel. Since yesterday, I had received no messages from Steve, and I was worried that he somehow found out, but then I dismissed that thought. So, I didn't write to him either, as that would have given me away. Besides, I practically collapsed into bed; didn't have time to dwell on it much, woke up tired and grumpy in the morning. I didn't even bother packing since I somehow felt that Steve wouldn't come today and rushed to the shoot to avoid being late. I wasn't the one topping the list of latecomers, which I was quite proud of. The day's shooting didn't go as smoothly as before. Everyone was fed up. However, the producer showed no mercy. He argued with everyone; nothing pleased him. Throughout the day, I kept wondering if Steve would eventually show up and why he hadn't written. I tried to concentrate on the work. I didn't have too many scenes to redo.

Even if my thoughts wandered, my determination to perform was much stronger. This meant much more to me than fame. It was a job I loved. Besides, it was currently my only source of income, and it mattered whether I did things with full effort. There was no middle ground for me to just coast along. Either I was present, or I wasn't. I had been to a few shoots before, but I had never appeared in such a large-scale film. The crew itself was the size of a small village. Yet they were so professional. When I look back at all the films I remember, there was always someone getting together with someone else from the crew or some kind of conflict arising. I was the weakest link here.

Maybe the troublesome people disappear one level up, or they just know how to conceal themselves better. But I didn't see anyone sneaking away with someone else, nor did I witness any secret schemes. Fame didn't make me crazy. Men did. Somehow, this had to end, but I didn't know how yet.

Yesterday, while changing outfits, I chatted with Kim, one of the former girlfriend actors. She was older than me, but it didn't show on her. She already had a child and told me she had gone through what I was experiencing. Casting couch, rough rehab, but here she was. She didn't give up; didn't know any other way. She reassured me that everyone would eventually forget, and I could start anew, but I would have to work even harder and live a puritanical life so no one would remember what happened. No one could tell what she did and with whom ten years ago. The biggest news about her nowadays was what kind of dog she bought and what it eats. Of course, a proper companion is needed for that. That was the problem here. But she reassured me. A little. Thursday afternoon came as well. Steve didn't get in touch, but when I arrived back at the hotel, he was sitting in the lobby. I could see him from afar. He had a distant, vacant gaze, lost in his thoughts. He was oblivious to the outside world. Even from the entrance, it was clear how burdened he was. I approached him.

He slowly lifted his gaze from my feet to my face, as if he wanted to give himself time to compose his features. Finally, he looked at me. At first, a fake smile spread across his face, but then a genuine one appeared.
"Hi, Jade! How are you?" he greeted. He stood up and hugged me. Today, I changed clothes and remove my makeup earlier.
"Hi, Steve! Everything's fine. And you?" I ask. Meanwhile, we went upstairs. He didn't say a word, just stared ahead. I couldn't tell what was going on? In the room, he remained silent, just sat on the bed, and scrutinised me. I went to take a shower. After much hesitation, he joined me, and then we ended up in bed. But he was still silent. I could sense as much anger in his movements as despair.
"Shall we go somewhere for dinner? "He asked while buttoning up his shirt.
"Sure. Let's go, "I replied. I quickly got ready. While he wore black trousers and a blue shirt, I put on a tracksuit and a baseball cap. I wasn't in the mood for any fancy place.
"Are these flowers here because of me? "He gestured around the room. New ones arrived every day. Cards, flowers, chocolates. From all over the world.
"Of course. Your fans couldn't wait for you to arrive," I say.
"I'm liking this!" he smiles.
"Where would you like to go?"
"Doesn't matter. Just let's eat something because I'm starving," he says. "I led him to one of my favourite places. Jess and I used to eat here a lot back in the day and was quite far from downtown. It was a mid-range place, although it meant to convince everyone that it was higher than that. It

had a nice little terrace covered in vines. But I didn't want to sit outside. The outdoor area tried to give the impression of an Italian restaurant, and many tourists fell for it. Then, upon entering, they were greeted by an American-style diner. Red leather booths. Glass-topped tables with American football articles underneath. I went to my favourite booth, all the way to the back, next to the restrooms. My tracksuit and Steve's shirt were perfectly fine here. Three styles mixed in one restaurant. The terrace lured tourists in with its Italian vibe, the front part of the restaurant was designed in American style to entice hungry people, and at the very back, a dark, Western-themed bar section awaited, made entirely of wood, promising darkness, and the scent of beer to lovers or mourners. I had been there only once in my life. To mourn, of course. It was a long time ago. Maybe it wasn't even true.

    Steve also looked around with interest. We were given a menu and a drink list. I ordered orange juice, while Steve ordered whiskey, which caught my eye. I didn't know the bartender girl, but it didn't matter. She had a bored expression on her face and chewed gum with exaggerated grimaces. She mostly talked to Steve, but he didn't really react to it. I would have bet she was an aspiring actress off duty. The restaurant was sparsely populated. The usual muscular guys were showing off their strength at the arcade games next to the bar. When our drinks were brought out, we ordered our food. I didn't know what the problem was, but I thought if he wanted to, he would share it with me. He almost downed his drink in one go and signalled for another. I just couldn't control my mouth.

"What's wrong, baby? "I asked. He looked up from his drink, desperation hiding in his eyes. The waitress placed the drink in front of him, said nothing, just blew bubbles with her gum. Steve didn't notice any of this. He just stared at me as if I had just arrived and he couldn't understand how.

"My dad is coming out in about a month," he says. So, Tom and Brian are past the first step.

"I thought that's what you wanted, "I said.
"Yes, but I have a lot of preparations to make."
"I'm happy to help in any way I can," I say. I almost pitied him, but only for a moment. Reached across the table and squeezed his hand in encouragement. The food was served. We ate quietly. Both of us lost in our thoughts. The food was still great. Steve ordered a burger with fries, pickles, and a salad. I had my usual dish. Fries and garlic-flavoured meat with a wine-mushroom sauce. I enjoyed being on home turf. He had another whiskey after dinner. Well, it only served him in this case. He became more relaxed. Then, standing outside, we started kissing, and I let the city take care of one of my problems. And so it happened.

The next day we were on the local news, but it didn't matter. We were also on the internet. I took advantage of the popularity of the movie, and Tom would already know what to do. Steve didn't see either of them, as I looked at the pictures in the dressing room, and he wasn't familiar with this place. He didn't come with me. He said he'd rather go home, and we would meet there. I told him I wouldn't leave today, maybe only tomorrow morning. But it's as if he didn't even hear it. That's how I bought myself some time. Then, of course, I set off, but instead of going home, I went to Tom and Brian's. Before leaving, I had my gold-toothed friend check the car, but he signalled that there was nothing new with it. I could relax. I went to the courthouse first. It was already late, but Brian usually stayed there at this time, or at least that's what he wrote earlier. His office wasn't on the top floor, but it was just as prestigious as his father's, the judge, and he was proud of that. Although it was already seven o'clock by the time I arrived, his suit and appearance left nothing to be desired. We discussed the implementation of the plan and the next steps. He behaved reservedly but helpfully. After discussing what needed, we went to my car together.

"Do you have any reservations about the case?" I ask.

"I've heard things, Jade, and while I didn't swear to deceive the citizens, my father loved your father. He lost his best friend when he died."
"But you swore to protect people, and now it's me."
"I'll help, but I don't fully agree with it."
"Of course. It's enough for me you're helping. You wouldn't understand unless it happened to you."
"Good night, Jade. See you on Monday." He walked away and disappeared into an alley a couple of blocks away from the courthouse building.

I went to the police station using a GPS. It was also located downtown, near to the courthouse. An aged building that probably dated back to the 1970s. The city's budget couldn't afford to renovate it anymore. It had five floors, and the prison was within it. Although I didn't see it from the street, I just knew it. Ten steps led up to the entrance. As I entered, I was greeted by what I expected. Worn-out tiles, white walls. A busy reception desk. About ten people were queuing. It wasn't surprising for a Friday evening around eight. There were women who looked like streetwalkers and, of course, their boys. An older police officer managed the front desk. He was probably a retired officer supplementing his pension with this job. Behind the reception desk, many cameras monitored every floor of the building, the entrance, and the waiting area in front of the desk. The man patiently explained something to a mentally challenged individual who was standing in front of him. He didn't understand that he couldn't file complaints about police misconduct tonight, only on Monday when someone would be in the office. But he couldn't wrap his head around it. There were quite a few people sitting in the waiting area, but surely there were some who just didn't want to spend the night outside. I hadn't been to a police station very often in my life, and judging by the sight, I didn't regret it too much. A swinging door separated the stairs from other rooms. I couldn't see very well. I joined the queue so as not to stand out too much, but I had already

messaged Tom that I was here. He came down angrily but composed his features when he saw me.
"Jade, hi," he greeted me with a warm smile.
"Hi, Tom. Sorry, I only made it here now."
"No problem. I'm on the afternoon shift. I still have some time left." he glanced at his watch. Meanwhile, we passed through the swinging door and headed up the stairs. I was quite tired, but I didn't complain. We went up to the third floor, and I was glad I hadn't been smoking recently because I would have coughed up my lungs now. This floor housed several small cubicles instead of separate offices, allowing everyone to have their own space while still being able to see what the others were doing if they stood up. Perhaps they wanted to save costs with this layout, or there was some psychological significance to it I didn't know. Well, it wasn't conducive to privacy. I counted twenty-six of these small cubicles, interconnected by different corridors. We just passed through them, and Tom grabbed a notepad, presumably from his own desk, and we continued. Following the cubicles were meeting rooms and interrogation rooms. I hoped he would take me to one of the former.

 Inside the meeting room, a large table dominated the space. There was a small coffee corner near the entrance, and on the other side were props for presentations. The wall opposite the entrance was entirely covered in glass. Tom settled into a chair with his back to the window, and I took a seat across from him. He looked tired and very young. His hair and eyes were dark brown, contrasting with his fair skin. He had distinctive features. He wore black trousers and a blue polo shirt and still gave off a handsome and likable impression.

"I don't want to take up too much of your time. Just wanted to go over things again. I feel like we're making good progress, "I say.
"Yes, everything is going fine. But what prompted you to do this? Why didn't you just report it normally?

"It would be hard to explain. Well, not that much, but it's long, and I'm not sure if you have time for it.
"This is part of the case, so tell me. I usually deal with disappearances, and there isn't much I can do in the evenings anyway," he took out his notebook; it made me uncomfortable. I would share my innermost secrets, and he would make notes about it. I pushed aside my uneasy feelings because, after all, he was going to help me. I poured out my entire life to him. And it regained meaning for me as well, why I was doing all of this. I hated the perpetrator even more than before. He was an attentive listener. I didn't blush. I spilled everything. Brandon, Steve... everything. Fortunately, he didn't take notes the way it's usually done in university, just wrote words that wouldn't reveal anything to anyone. I was sure he wouldn't forget. Sometimes he raised his eyebrows, but he didn't interrupt unless he didn't understand something.
"There are things I can't give my blessing to, but let's just say I won't stand in your way."
"Thank you, Tom, that's enough for me."
"I once had a friend who wanted to be an actor, and he became one, but since then, he doesn't even recognise me. You're different."
"I suspected you would say that. It's very common for someone to forget where they came from, but I think thanks to my background, it doesn't affect me. It's just another job for me, like any other."
"I'm glad I encountered such an example. People can generalise, and although I try to consciously fight against it, sometimes it's difficult. When the judge first called me and explained what the case was about, I grumbled about it for a day. I read what was available online about you, but I knew I had to dig deeper, yet the material was dense, and it made me grumble even more. I kept complaining to Brian on the way there, wondering why we had to deal with a spoiled actress, "he pointed at me and smiled. "But when we met at

the hotel, and I saw you in your costume, which I thought was just regular clothes, I concluded you suffer from attention-seeking. But then we went upstairs, and you put on the sweater, and filming had ended, and you were trying not to relax because we were there, yet we didn't just meet a glamorous actress, but you. The heiress. You'd rather wash off your makeup and put on a tracksuit. You immediately became likable.
"Thank you, I guess. So, I'm not that good if you could see through me like that." we were still sitting there and talking.
"Brian noticed nothing about it, so yes, you're good," he replies.
"Well, you haven't convinced me. What do you see now?"
"A beautiful and ready-to-fight woman."
"Was hoping you would say that. I mean, ready to fight. I'll go now, so I won't keep you."
"But where are you going?"
"To some hotel. I'll rent a room until tomorrow. I'm tired, was filming."
"Aren't you hungry?" he asks as we got up and headed outside.
"Hungry? Well, I can only think of sleep at this point."
"Stay at my place," I didn't say a word, just waited to see where he was going with this, knowing that he knew my entire life. "I have a guest room. Why pay for a hotel?"
"That wouldn't be too ethical," I say.
"You're absolutely right, but this case isn't anyway, and why shouldn't I help a friend?"
"Friend?" I savoured the word. I liked it. I hadn't had a friend for a long time. Since Daniel Jacobs, I haven't had a friend. Back then, we were Dawson and Joey, but that was a long time ago. But it was so good! We were inseparable. We discovered and did everything together. Then, of course, it turned into love. And everything got messed up.
"Okay," I gave in. "But you're not finished yet."

"I also deserve a lunch break," he says. "They can reach me on my phone wherever I am." He waved to everyone we encountered on our way out. Everyone smiled and winked at him.
"Do you live far? Should I leave my car here?"
"This?" he shrugged. "Isn't it conspicuous enough?"
"I got it, "I raised my shoulder.
"Leave it here. I'll bring you back in the morning. "I took my bag out of the trunk. The bigger one.
"I'm not moving there," I reassure him with a smile. "Just since the fire, all my stuff is in one bag."
"I don't mind, "he smiled.
"Will I be bothering you? Do you live alone?"
"I don't live alone. My grandma and mom are there," he chuckles at my expression." I'm just messing with you, of course. I live alone, don't even have a girlfriend now. But is it okay if I grab some food before? Can you wait for that?"
"Of course, I'm just a guest. "We got into his patrol car, which I wouldn't have guessed from the outside. It was just a regular dark blue sedan. Nothing eye-catching. But inside, it was noticeable that it was a police car. Sirens. A CB radio that kept saying something. Mostly numbers, which I couldn't make any sense of. Gadgets. Soda bottles and food bags. He must have spent a lot of time in there. He just brushed aside the things he had piled on the seat, mostly papers. We stopped at a fried chicken place where he got out, and I stayed in the car; I almost fell asleep by the time he came back. Now the smell of fried chicken filled the car. My stomach growled warningly, demanding something, but I dismissed it because sleep was more important than eating for me. He drove for ten minutes to the west. I wasn't familiar with this city. Sometimes I went with my father to the judge, but that's it. We stopped at a small house. There was no parking lot, he just parked by the side of the road. This was still part of the downtown area, so I figured a small house

wouldn't come cheap here. He locked the car and brought my bag.

As we reached the entrance door, a motion sensor light turned on, allowing me to look around. I couldn't see much because of the many green bushes, trees, and plants. A few steps led to the house. He quickly and skilfully opened the door. We entered a small hallway where coats and shoes were placed. I quickly took off mine. There was another door leading to the dining room and kitchen. Although brown wasn't among my favourite colours, it still looked great. The elongated brown tiles on the floor gave the impression of wooden flooring rather than tiled, and they were even grooved. The walls had insets, all covered with tiles. Handcrafted wooden furniture. A false ceiling. Everything built-in and hidden. Glass dining table with black leather chairs. There was a corner, separated in the living room, with a TV and a sofa. The lamps were concealed or spotlights. I liked it. It was very cosy, with a mix of modern style and wood. It was masculine, yet pleasant at the same time. Order prevailed. There were no dirty dishes and scattered newspapers like in the car. There were two rooms branching off from the living room in both directions. A counter separated the kitchen and didn't seem to be used much. Not even a single glass was left on the drying rack. There was a door in the kitchen that led to the backyard, but I couldn't see anything from there.

"Does the police pay that well?" I ask when I looked around the house.

"I can't complain, "he said, but he left the topic at that. "This would be your room. Would you like to eat with me?"

"No, thank you."

"There's a bathroom in the room. If you need anything, just let me know. I'll be sleeping in the other room. Unless I fall asleep on the couch, then on the couch."

"When do you leave in the morning? Could you possibly give me a ride?"

"What time do you need to be home? So, it won't be too noticeable?"

"Around eleven. But you don't have to rearrange your day. When you wake up, we can go."

"Ten o'clock works for me. I have an afternoon shift. But I'll be up around eight. Goodnight, Jade." A smile spread across his face as he looked at me.

"Thank you. Goodnight to you, too."

As soon as I laid my head down, I was already asleep. I had looked around the room so much that I realised this might be the cluttered room. It was filled with labelled boxes. And there was construction dust on the tiles in the bathroom. Compared to the rest of the house, this room was quite austere. A bed, a small cabinet, and a wardrobe. In the bathroom, there was a towel, a sink, soap, shower gel, and nothing else. It didn't matter to me. The window of the room faced the side of another house, where there was nothing. It was almost perfect for me. I fell asleep quickly and deeply. It was already past eleven when I went to bed. In the morning, I wanted to jump out of bed quickly: my eyes popped open, but my initial level of adrenaline quickly plummeted, so I sluggishly went to find coffee. Since then, I had got a pyjama, so I could comfortably go out. Luckily, the homeowner was already up and brewing coffee.

"Good morning! "He said with a smile. He was already dressed. Today he wore a green shirt, which suited him even better.

"Thank you so much for letting me stay here and for the coffee," I say after taking a few sips. We were sitting outside in the garden, which was quite small but served its purpose. The back part was nicely landscaped with grass. On the terrace, there was a BBQ setup, chairs, benches, and tables. There was a patio umbrella, which wasn't raised now. The neighbours couldn't see through because dense and tall hedges on both sides bordered the garden. The entire house and garden were perfect. I envied his privacy. Even if I had a large area at home, I was never alone. I could only lock myself inside the house, but not indefinitely.

"It's nothing, Jade," he says. He was smoking, too.

"Well, if it's nothing to you, why doesn't everyone take someone in? "There's no such thing as someone doing something good without ulterior motives. Or maybe I've just met the wrong people so far.

"You're a beautiful woman and an actress in a shitty situation. Why shouldn't I help?" he asks suddenly, and his request surprised me.

"Sure, there's no problem, "I said, after recovering from the surprise. "On Monday, you're coming anyway, and then I'll go back with you."

"Perfect. I'll go take a shower."

"I'll bring some food until then."

"Ok."

He came back. I was ready. I wore jeans and a T-shirt, nothing fancy, left the room as I found it and put my stuff on a chair in the living room. He bought pastries. We sat at the dining table and talked about everything, but mostly I asked questions because he already knew my whole life. He told me he had a brother who was also a cop, but he was at a much higher level than he was, belonged to some special unit and he wanted to reach such a prominent position too. He loved the police. Or rather, investigating. He had always wanted to do that; and was goal oriented. Their father was too, but unfortunately, he was killed in a shootout, but he wouldn't give up making the world a better place. I listened with admiration. He excelled in sports too, back in the day. He could have gone to a prestigious university on a sports scholarship, but he wasn't interested in that, just this. His mother was very protective of them. Sunday dinners at her place were mandatory, where she always told them they shouldn't have chosen this career and why they couldn't find decent wives already. Because his brother didn't have one either. They only lived for their work. They usually had girlfriends, but nothing serious. And what are women like today, anyway?

"Don't even tell me. I know what women are like today, "I said gloomily. "They all want a career and independence. It's a nightmare. None of them want to do laundry, cook, clean, and smile in bed for their husband, who spends his days either at the pub or some brothel. Terrible."

"I don't have a problem with career-oriented women, "he said. "I'm not an antifeminist. Maybe fate just brought me together with the wrong women, or maybe I haven't been in love yet. I don't know."

"Don't joke. Although I've had my heart broken by great loves so far. But the feeling of love itself is wonderful. Even if my heart was shattered, I still say that. The continuous adrenaline and the hormones responsible for happiness, how they work during that time. You really feel you're walking three meters above the ground. It's an uplifting feeling."

"I envy you."

"I envy your personal life, so one for each."

"Are you going to keep the Farm?"

"That's not a question. The plan is for this to be my last film."

"It's going to be a box office hit, I heard. They say tickets have already sold out in every country for the premiere."

"Because of Richard. Women go crazy for him."

"And what about you?"

"Am I crazy about him? No. I already know his wife. But even aside from that, he's just not my type. Or how should I put it? Too handsome for me? I can't express it properly. He's a good guy. I adore him. But I just can't see him as a man. We went out for drinks on the first night and talked about our lives. It was nice. Maybe I haven't felt this way about someone since my high school friend. It didn't matter what I said, he would still like me."

"Interesting. I looked at the pictures, and I think you look great too. You're going to make a lot of men have wet dreams."

"Oh, come on. I think you're just teasing, but I don't mind. "I smiled.

"And what if you can't get out? If you want to continue because this is going so well?"

"I hope it goes well, too. I'm giving it my all. It matters a lot to restore the Farm."

"I really like you, Jade Donovan, "he said, looking into my eyes.

"Thank you, Tom, you're a really nice guy too."

"Thank you, although you said it as if I were your little brother."

"No, not at all. We must go. "I stood up. His gaze made me a little uncomfortable. I didn't want to see the same thing in him as in almost every man I had dealt with before.

"Let's go! "We didn't talk during the car ride. There too, I just got out of his car, put my bag in, thanked him again, and I was already on my way. He spoke as if he were much younger than me, but that could also be attributed to the fact that he had little experience with women yet because he was so focused on building his career. It was still strange to me how he talked about love and women as if they were very distant from him. But in other matters, he behaved maturely. I couldn't decide how old he could be and why he was like this. And why did he want to come to the shoot, and why did he accept me?

My first trip led me to the Farm. Everyone was there, even though it was Saturday. I got a few ideas, so I wanted to talk to the builder. I wrote to Steve that I was already at the Farm, but he didn't reply. Linda said everything was fine. There were some sales, so now that everything was slowly falling into place. The foundation and walls of my house were done, but that's it. I asked if I could make some adjustments. I created a little privacy for myself by moving a couple of walls. Then I planned the equestrian school with Linda. If we put up some obstacles in the course, maybe we could succeed. We weren't in an excellent location. I didn't really believe it would work. The nearest equestrian school was in the city, and it had quite high prices. If I did it for half the price, maybe it would be worth it for them to come here. From there, it's just one step to buying milk or meat, eggs, or apples. That's what I was hoping for.

It annoyed me. I couldn't do everything all at once. I hated waiting, but patience is the key, isn't it? Patience is everything. The workers were only focusing on the house, and supposed they were making good progress; I couldn't judge that myself. We needed advertising. Finally, Linda and I separated to work on our respective tasks. Told me about the week. She said that expenses still exceeded income, but she remained hopeful, but didn't have any experience in boosting the Farm's revenue. She hadn't studied marketing, only knew about animals. An idea was lingering in my mind, but it hadn't surfaced yet. So, I let it be. Finally, Steve replied, telling me to come over once I was done there. It was already five o'clock, so I went over to Steve's. I was thinking about Tom, Brian, and the case. For the hundredth time, I questioned whether I was doing the right thing. But when I went through the events in my mind, it reinforced my determination once again. The gate was open. Steve was already waiting at the door. He seemed nervous, looking around as if someone could see us, as if it mattered. But when he spotted me, he smiled.
"Hi, Jade! "He said, pulling me towards him as I climbed the stairs. I planted a long kiss on his lips. He enjoyed it because he didn't want to let go. Somehow, I couldn't see him the same way as before. It was just a game now. And I was quite good at it. "How are you? "He asked as he led me into the living room, still holding me in his arms.
"I'm doing great now, "I said. I kissed him again and felt my power over him. He was in love, and he resisted with all his might, but love is not something you can resist. Was he acting against it because of his father? That's what I suspected. Before, he resisted because of his masculinity, but now the resistance against his feelings had taken a much stronger

form. I felt it caused him almost physical pain. He couldn't regain control of his emotions. The fake fire in the fireplace was glowing in the living room, crackling and popping. It didn't radiate any warmth. A half-empty crystal glass of golden whisky shimmered on the coffee table; the fireplace reflected the lights. He couldn't restrain himself much; his hands moved up and down my body, tearing at my clothes. I didn't want to give in to him just yet. Wait, a little longer.
"Couldn't we eat first? "I asked.
"Oh, of course. I'm sorry! "He reluctantly let go. He sat down on the sofa and stared into his glass, and seemed troubled.
"What's wrong? "I asked, sitting beside him.
"It's my father."
"I don't understand. You said you wanted everything to be like it used to be and should be happy then, shouldn't you?"
"You don't understand, Jade. My mother is not here. Even if I could bring my brother and Linda back by then, what would happen? Linda would run away to the ends of the earth. My brother would only be clean for about ten minutes before he goes back. My mother can't be brought out, she's too ill. I was supposed to hold the family together and look at what happened."
"Don't be silly, Steve. If you want, I can talk to your brother. I've been an addict too. And I can talk to Linda, but you also must put something on the table, if you know what I mean…"
"I know you understand…"
"If your mother came back and saw that everything was fine, maybe she would recover."
"Why do you want to help? After what happened…"
"Because that's who I am… "Or rather, who I used to be, I thought to myself. The afternoon and evening passed rather quietly. He was withdrawn and said little, his movements filled with nervousness. Because it was Saturday, there wasn't much he could take care of. Morning came early enough. I went to the Farm, went horseback riding, chatted, little deeper into them, but everything seemed in order.

Tina Colt – Role/Play

## Chapter eighteen

There was no noticeably enormous expense or remarkably high revenue that couldn't be accounted for. Everything was fine, but I still had some doubts. Linda only asked me once why the police were here, but I cleverly avoided answering. Today, she asked if Steve and I were together. I didn't say yes or no to that. Steve sent a message asking if we could have lunch together. I accepted the invitation.

Next weekend, I didn't even want to go to him anymore. I exchanged a few messages with Kyra, but she still hadn't been working since the incident; she wrote she didn't really mind. I said goodbye to the others. I talked to Thomas and told him to let me know if there's anything, but I don't know if he took it seriously. It turned out that he and Katie got together, so he won't be living on the Farm either. And after the summer, he planned to continue university, so I won't have a permanent person on the Farm anymore. I went over to Steve's, although I didn't feel very enthusiastic about it anymore. I was too anxious and worried. Today wasn't much better in terms of mood. We didn't meet in the morning, and by the time I got up, he was nowhere to be found. He was in the dining room, where a table was set for one. I found the situation interesting. What did he want then? "Hi, Jade!" He didn't smile anymore. "Would you sit down for a moment? "He asked.

"Hi, Steve! "I said, placing my jacket on the arm of the chair, which was being recorded by the camera in the brooch I got from Tom and was standing behind the chair, trying to pull it out, but he pushed my hand away. I knew I did the right thing by taking this little device away from Tom and I didn't even regret bringing my denim jacket, even though it was almost summer, and a denim jacket wasn't really my style, but he didn't seem to notice any of it.

"Why are you doing this? "He shouted at me, and I got scared that I was caught, but then it crossed my mind it was impossible. Then I didn't understand what he could talk about.

"Why am I doing what, Steve? "I asked, standing defiantly with my hands on my hips. Women are fully convinced that hands-on-hips have power. Not a moment passed, and he was standing next to me. Pressed tightly against me." Why are you saying my name like that? Why are you getting me worked up? Intentionally, right? "He pressed against a marble pillar next to the dining table. The cold pierced through the thin fabric of my clothes.

"This is your name, isn't it? Steve, "I continued to push his buttons.

"Stop it, or I can't vouch for what I'll do."

"Come on, Steve! "He tightly pressed his hand against my mouth and forcefully pushed himself against me. He didn't care about anything. Tearing at my clothes. Meanwhile, he passionately kissed me. My head hit the pillar a few times. When the fabric couldn't handle it anymore, he grabbed the knife from the table and cut off my top and bra. But he didn't stop there. He tried to remove my pants as well. The dining room was big enough to accommodate a six-person table, with a swinging door leading to the kitchen, presumably where Cassey and Simon were on the other side. And there I stood, naked in the middle of the dining room. Just one last time. No man will ever do this to me again. But I had to endure it now. Without causing a scene. I turned my back and pressed naked against the pillar. He pulled down his pants and forcefully entered me and raging. He pulled my hair back by the roots and whispered unpleasant things in my ear while reaching his end with powerful thrusts. Then, as if nothing had happened, he pulled up his pants, went back to the table, and left me naked. If he thought I would run away crying now, he was mistaken. I took back my torn clothes. And the denim jacket, which was long enough. I didn't want to sit down anymore. "Is this why you called me over?"

"Not entirely. I just wanted to tell you that you can't come here anymore."

"Alright, Steve. Goodbye. Do you want the car back, by any chance?"

"No, keep it. I already told you it's in your name. The sex was worth that car, anyway."

"Goodbye, Steve!" With that, I walked out the door, but I hadn't even reached the car when I sent the recording to Brian and Tom. If I had waited, I wouldn't have dared to send it in the end because of the shame. I got in and drove off. I was angry, disappointed too. Now I knew I was doing the right thing. After all, I chose the lesser of two evils. That's what I thought back then. But at least Brandon loved me. He just didn't express it properly. But I didn't need either of them anymore. I knew that now, and that was the most important thing. Brian and Tom kept calling alternately, but I didn't want their pity. I didn't want to talk to them either. Let them use that damn recording for whatever they need. I reached the city in record time. I didn't even have to go to the reception at the hotel since had the same room. However, to my great surprise, a bunch of paparazzi were waiting there. Thankfully, I stopped to have coffee and change clothes. I wore a baseball cap, so they barely recognised me. By the time they realised, I was already at the entrance, practically running away from them. I was grateful for that and for changing my outfit because otherwise, tomorrow would have started with such a scolding I couldn't handle. They snapped about a hundred pictures before they lost sight of me.

Once I arrived, the elevator was already called for me by the time got there. I just had to hop in, and it took me upstairs. My room was almost impossible to enter because of the flowers and chocolates. This was not a state I wanted to be in. It was difficult to move around. I called the reception and asked them to send the flowers to the nearest hospital. I

would pay for the taxi. They said it was just two streets away, so someone who was on a break would gladly take them. Great, one problem solved. I didn't want to call either of them. Neither Brian nor Tom. We would meet tomorrow anyway. Instead, I washed away the taste of Steve. I wanted to throw away my torn clothes, but as a precaution, I didn't use the hotel trash bin; I've heard stories. Tomorrow, I'll take them with me and dispose of them in a shared bin on the set. I took a slow bath and took my time getting ready, ordered some food. I didn't plan to go out for them to take a thousand more pictures. Just like last week, Richard showed up. A continuous smile on his face. I made some space so that he could at least reach the armchair. He said nothing until I settled at the end of the bed. In my pyjamas, half a pizza in my mouth.
"What's the situation, little girl? "He asked.
"Everything's fine. I need one more favour, "I said and smiled while we indulged in the pizza.
"Tell me, "He said, humming in appreciation of the food, his way of expressing liking.
"A commercial. "I looked around in alarm among the flowers, chocolates, and balloons, as if questioning my sanity. "For the Farm," a light bulb went off in his mind. I didn't want to involve him in the other matter at all.
"What do you mean?"
"Not sure. I thought you might know better. A thirty-second commercial to be aired on TV. I know this is a show-off parade. I didn't mean it for here, but for the public television."
"With your face, taking advantage of the fact that we're shooting the film now. Clever girl."
"It would be better when the film is released, but I don't have time and need the money."
"I know someone."

"Don't know anyone and would appreciate it if you at least asked. I'll babysit for an evening while you and Holly go somewhere. How about that?"
"Perfect. Holly will love it. I'll take care of it then."

He practically dropped his food and was already on his way. I don't know if it was the commercial or the free evening with his wife got him so excited. Just joking. Within a few minutes, I received a message saying they would gladly accept, just call the TV company, and coordinate a date. I completely forgot that we had planned for him to come up, and we would go back together tomorrow. It only crossed my mind when I got a call from the front reception, saying the police were looking for me. I was sitting in my pyjamas with the leftover pizza. It was around eight in the evening. I didn't even ask Richard about this and quickly called him, but his mobile was busy and guess he was sharing the news of the free evening with Holly. I called his room. He answered.
"Richard, one more thing..."
"Just don't push it too far, Chica..."
"Someone I know, a detective, would like to watch the filming tomorrow. A decent guy. "
"Well, who cares? Goodnight."
"Tomorrow."

I called back to the reception to let him up. They said it's not that simple; either I go down to get him, but they understand if I don't want to, or they can send a security guard. Well, I didn't want that, but nothing else left. They brought up the package. There was a knock on the door. I waved to the security guard, who left immediately. Tom smiled widely at me, though a hint of concern lingered in his eyes.
"Hi, Jade!"
"Hi, Tom. I'll be honest: I forgot you were coming today."
"Because that wasn't the plan. The plan was for me to come tomorrow, and we'd go back together. Or rather, to the city.

But you sent that video, and I thought you wanted to cry. Or rather, it deeply moved me."
"But I don't want to. I'm fine, Tom. Everything is okay, really. Come, have a seat. We just finished eating. Join me."
"You and the flowers?"
"No, me and Richard, but he already gone. "Stupid ambiguous words. I just caught my breath for a moment. "I mean, he already went upstairs. It doesn't matter."
"That Richard? The actor? "He asked, completely perked up. "Thank you. I accept. How are you? Nervous about the filming?" He rambled everything at once.
"No, I'm more nervous about tomorrow afternoon."
"I think everything will go smoothly. I spoke to the judge. He would be happy to help you with anything. Fortunately. Our advantage might be even greater if we had the queen on our side, but we already have a winning case. Did you know he bought your dad's cars?"
"I didn't know. I'll take them back, eventually. It's true that the garage burned down, but once everything was rebuilt, there won't be room for them anymore. But I'll take care of it. Let's just get through this and the filming." He was wearing a black shirt today, and it suited him well. He looked ridiculously young, but it could be a sensual illusion. I didn't dare ask, didn't want to hurt him.
"I saw the paparazzi downstairs. Did they catch you?"
"Just a little. But tomorrow, you'll be in the picture too."
"I won't get any closer to stardom than this."
"Why? Do you want to?"
"No. I just want connections that can move me forward."
"That's not me, it's Richard. Although I don't know how that would contribute to your career advancement in the police department, but we're happy to help."
"They'll be more willing to push you up if you have many good connections."
"But actors? Is that why you came?"

"Actors too. Not just for that, I'm curious about how film shoots go. I love movies. All of them. And I'm very interested. I have quite a collection. And because of the video. Or rather, because of you."
"Do you have my previous films?"
"Of course, Jade."
"But why? "Things like this still surprised me.
"Because Brian and I grew up together, we're great pals. I used to hang out at their place a lot, and the judge often mentioned your family. You came up in conversation too, and that you act. So, naturally, we got hold of them. Well, that was ten years ago. The first one. We were practically kids. We still have all of them."
"I'm glad to hear that. Well, this really surprised me."
"You're funny, Jade, "he said, grinning sincerely at me, and I didn't understand what he found so amusing.
"Why?"
"Because you're an actor, making movies, and you're surprised when someone has seen your films; you handle it all as if it were just an ordinary office job."
"It's far from that. Yes, because they were crappy films, and I didn't even achieve much, and how could I? Anyway, I couldn't talk like this with a fan, but an honesty outburst caught me. I'm sorry."
"It's okay. You're funny."
"No one has accused me of that before, "I smiled. It was impossible not to like him; he always had such genuine curiosity in his eyes. And he had good intentions. So much so that maybe even I couldn't turn him into a beast, as I had done with the others.
"I should start getting some sleep soon, "I said. It was already close to eleven, and it was good that I had done everything I wanted. Time flew when we started talking; I noticed hours felt like minutes, or rather, I didn't notice until it was time to go.
"I'll sleep on the floor. If there was room, that is."

"No, the bed is big enough. Or I can book a separate room for you if you have any objections."
"It's perfect for me if it doesn't bother you."
"No "I lied. I felt like I was giving myself away again. But I had nothing to fear from him, and I shouldn't have felt this way in front of him, but perhaps this afternoon had left its mark on this feeling. "I must leave at nine. I wake up at eight. You can still sleep; you don't have to come with me in the morning.
"Don't joke, I can't wait..."

In the morning, when I woke up, he was no longer there. I heard nothing. Well, I've always been able to sleep. Not a lot, but deeply. I quickly got dressed and put on a baseball cap. By the time I was ready, the key turned in the lock. I tried to push away the similar memory I had with Steve. He balanced coffee and pastries in his hand. He brought a small bag with him yesterday, but today he had a fresh shirt on again, and it wasn't wrinkled. There must be a secret. This shirt was blue. As if he only wore shirts.
"Good morning, Jade! Sorry if I woke you up early, but I thought I'd take advantage of it before they see me with you and start sticking to me, and I brought coffee. Suspect the coffee here is lousy."
"Good morning. Yes, it's lousy. Thank you very much. Did you see anything interesting?"
"Are you kidding? Actors everywhere. I didn't know where to look. It really is like in the movies. I like it a lot. Although the prices are also like if famous actors were shopping everywhere."
"True. I'm glad you're enjoying it. It's nice to hear you talk about it. You didn't wake me up."
"How far is it to the set?"
"Five minutes if I'm driving."
"Why, what if I drive?"
"Then it's ten. "He looked at me with feigned offense.
"Don't joke. Then I'll challenge you at home, and we'll see."

"I'm up for it, but you should check out how I drive first. It would be embarrassing if you lost to a girl."
"I proudly accept defeat, even from a woman, but that will not happen."
"Alright. High five! "I laughed. "But shouldn't you, as a law enforcer, be against illegal races?"
"I deserve a little fun, too."
"Count me in! "We smiled as we got into the car, and indeed, we arrived in five minutes. The crew parking lot was filling up, but the latecomers were just getting out of bed. I lost sight of Tom as soon as we crossed the gate. He was in a state of shock from that moment on, just staring around in awe. His mouth was even agape. I told him I had to change, but I don't think he heard a word. An hour later, I was done with makeup, hair, and wardrobe. I went to my filming location, but Tom wasn't there and figured he was old enough to find his way around. I tried hard to focus on my role and give it my all, but mentally, I wasn't fully there because I kept thinking about the afternoon. However, we didn't have to redo anything. It was just me who didn't feel like I was doing well. Anyway, if it was good enough for them, it didn't matter what I thought. During the lunch break, the producer pulled me aside. I was hungry. I needed to make a phone call, and I wanted to go to the restroom, but I didn't show any signs of that.
"What's wrong? "Nick asked. He was a tall, slim guy, wearing glasses. Unremarkable appearance. Freckled face, but with expertise and an awful demeanour.
"Nothing's wrong. Maybe my mind is just somewhere else. "I was ashamed that he noticed, after all.
"Is it because of the guy who's wandering around here today?"
"No, not at all. He's just a friend of mine. I'm sorry, will give it my all in the second half."
"I didn't say you were bad, just noticed that something's different."

"I'm sorry. I'll focus. "With that, he left and said nothing else. I quickly took care of what I needed to do, then found Tom and took pictures with everyone. He was quite shy among the actors, but they knew their job well and quickly eased his tension. After that, they started joking around.

Everyone rushed back after the break. Today, it seemed like everyone wanted to finish on time. Especially me. I hoped four o'clock would do us and focused intensely on shooting my scene scheduled for today. My head ached from the intense concentration, but at least we could leave at four, unlike those who had to redo their scenes. I didn't mention that I might be late tomorrow, planned not to be. At four-fifteen, we were already in the car, speeding home. Well, not exactly home. In the meantime, Tom and Brian were on the phone, taking care of things. We discussed and rehearsed everything in advance. We estimated it would take about ten minutes, but it required much more organisation. Tom didn't seem terrified when he hung up the phone. He didn't even raise an eyebrow about my driving because that five minutes in L.A. was not the same as here in the open field. After that, we started talking about various topics. I couldn't tell if he wanted to distract my attention or if he genuinely wanted to have a conversation. We discussed everything he had seen today, as well as favourite foods, colours, loves, classmates. The topic of ownership came up, and eventually, my family. Then we fell into silence for a while, and out of nowhere, he asked why I didn't attend my parents' funeral.
"I was ashamed. Ashamed of what I did with Brandon. I couldn't look them in the eye for leaving, and how I left. I ran away... in the end."
"That's true, but they didn't support you. Maybe it's not your fault."
"They did the right thing, Tom. I mean, to get those roles, I did things I wouldn't have done if I stayed still and married the first person who came along.

"Jade, you love to act. It's clear in every fibre of your being when you do it. There were many talented actors there today. But I didn't see that fire in their eyes like I saw in yours. Once your scene started, there was no one around you, just your character. You saw nothing else."
"Thank you for saying that. Regardless, that's the reason. I'm trying to fix what I messed up."
"With the ownership? The new film?"
"Both, but I owe it to my parents for the ownership. In the film, I just want to prove it to myself that I can do it without relying on a casting couch. After that, I'm out."
"We'll see, Jade."
"Why are you saying that now? "I asked, but by then we had arrived. The prison was in the police yard, which wasn't a bad idea. It was a massive building, and I counted seven floors in the extensive structure. I hoped it wasn't completely full. This is where medium-weight criminals were held. Highly dangerous ones were strictly guarded in a prison outside the city; compared to that, this was like a hotel, and these inmates didn't require excessive supervision. The level of strictness here was moderate. Tom changed clothes. Brian came down to me, looking impeccable in his three-piece deep blue suit. His hair was stylishly cut and groomed. I deliberately didn't change my clothes since I needed them for the role. There was a spare outfit in the car. Brian and Tom looked like night and day, and I couldn't fathom how they became the best of friends. We went through the plan with Brian once more. It was almost half-past six, so it was dinner time for the inmates. It was challenging for the guys to organise everything, but they did it. When Tom informed Brian that he was ready and in position, then it was my turn.

Another role. I tried to look at it that way. The inmates wanted to tear me apart in this skimpy outfit. It barely covered anything. I wasn't affected by such things anymore. They stretched out their hands beyond the bars. I tried my best not to get caught. I saw Tom, and I had to reach him. He was standing in front of a cell at the end of the corridor. I had to get there. Obscene remarks came from both sides, and hands reached out towards me. Disgusting things were said. The stench was unbearable. I thought about the red carpet and tried to give my best performance. The bait was on the hook, and as soon as I got there, it just had to bite. We had little time before dinner. We had to get to the point immediately, and I hoped he would buy it. And it did. It successfully took the bait. The conversation went as I had imagined. And the response was to my liking. Ten days, and it will all be over. When the acting was done, Tom left to change back, and Brian escorted me to the car. He showed no emotion. I couldn't tell if we did well or not. He said nothing. Tom appeared quickly. Brian wasn't surprised that I waited for him. They must have discussed something beyond what I heard. Tom got into my car, and Brian walked back towards the building.

"Is he not going home? "I asked Tom.

"He is, but later. He said he has some things to take care of here."

"Should I take you home or somewhere else?"

"Yes. You can sleep at my place. In the guest room."

"Is this some kind of payback because I didn't have one yesterday?"

"I slept with an actress, so no, any guest room wouldn't have been better than this."

"I think you're just trying to embarrass me."

"No, I'm not. Can we stop by the chicken place again? Will you eat too?"

"Yes, I'm starving. And I'll sleep at your place if you don't mind. I promise I'll be silent in the morning."

"Sure. That's why I suggested it. We're still good enough. We can eat and shower comfortably."

"Do you also wake up early?"

"Oh, not at all. "He grinned at me.

Arriving home, we devoured the chicken at the table. I've had better, but I was so hungry that it didn't matter. A weight was lifted off my heart. We discussed the day's events and many other things. He showed me his film collection, which was truly extensive. I didn't think anyone still invested in DVDs currently. It seemed like a good portion of his paycheck went into it. With this house and this collection, I really had to ponder whether I had chosen the right career. We looked at the pictures we took today, and they all turned out well. Richard and I were mostly featured in them. He was ecstatic about them, like a child on Christmas.

## Chapter nineteen

He seemed so childlike and innocent. Then it just slipped out of me, and I asked how old he was. He didn't say what I expected.

"Why? What did you expect?" He asks when he saw my wide eyes.

"Twenty-five, maximum. "I said truthfully. He laughed out loud. He could hardly stop, and I was still afraid that he would be offended and could hardly speak from laughter. "Well, I would say Brian, with his Peter Pan style, appears to be older. Maybe around thirty. "At that point, he laughed even harder. But tears started streaming down his face. I must say, it was nice to see something like that. I have experienced little of it since my high school years. In that carefree state. When he finally stopped laughing, he spoke up. Well, he wouldn't have been able to until now.

"If we had more time, and if it weren't about Brian, I would call him right away and tell him."

"Ha-ha. You should be happy instead."

"People always think I look younger, but not by that much. It's a shame you must wake up early. We could watch a movie."

"Maybe next time."

"When will you come home next time?"

"I think only next Friday for the big show."

"But if you're not coming because you have nowhere to stay, you can come here without worries."

"I could go to a hotel as well, but don't want to. It's better to have silence before the storm. Besides, we're shooting a commercial for the Farm over the weekend."

"Really? That's a good idea."

"I hope it will be successful. I'm going to sleep, Tom, because I don't know how I'll wake up in the morning. Thank you for everything."

"Good night, Jade, and thank you, too."

"It's nothing."

I turned twice, and it was already morning. The house was still quiet. I tiptoed out and grabbed a coffee, filled up the gas, and hit the road. I could be there on time if there was no traffic along the way and reconsidered the plan once again and couldn't find any flaws and felt like I had already overcome the hardest part and needed to hire someone for the farm, someone who knew what they were doing, instead of doing it myself. And beyond that, I would need more people if everything really started soon. From the car, I called the builder and asked for specific dates for the handover. It was already the third week. My filming also needed to be completed by next Friday. It seemed like everything was wrapping up on Fridays. I also called Brandon, but I couldn't tell why. His picture appeared on the screen, and my heart skipped a beat. It was still early, but his voice sounded alert.

"Hi, Jade!"

"Brandon?! How are you?"

"I'm doing well, thank you, just want to apologise for the past period. "I said nothing. If I had said there was no problem, I would have been lying, and if I had sent him to a warmer climate, that wouldn't have been genuine either. I was also at fault. "I'm seeing a psychologist and going through a divorce."

"I'm glad to hear that. I mean, about the therapist. What will happen to Lilly?"

"We're going through a legal battle. That's how it looks so far. Must heal for her sake. I'm sorry, I know it doesn't matter, but I haven't been completely honest about my parents and my childhood. I don't say this as a defence, just wanted to be honest this time."

"It's commendable. We can't meet, can we?"

"No. Not for a while, at least. I don't want to lose my sanity and hurt you."

"Ok. I hope you recover quickly. I'll be here if you need me."

"Jade, you need an agent."

"For a week? No way, Brandon."

"As you wish. "There was a hint of a smile in his voice. "Take care, Jade."

"You too, Brandon. Goodbye. "I was both happy and sad. It was because of how Brandon behaved. Maybe he'll become a better person, but he won't be the same anymore. It might have been foolish, but somehow, I felt like was saying goodbye to my Brandon, who had filled my past years, who taught me. Of course, I couldn't be selfish; it will be better for him not to be the raging, jealous monster he used to be. And maybe it's also better that this chapter has ended. I could bring up my memories out of nostalgia or as a continuous lesson, but somehow it didn't comfort me. It was over and was deeply in love with him back then and thought it would never fade away. I begged many times for it to end, for it not to hurt anymore. Sometimes I begged for someone else to be in my life whom I could love with such passion. It wouldn't hurt if that person wasn't a jerk. After a long time, my intense love for Brandon finally ended. But I couldn't pinpoint a specific moment when it ended and was cut off. It took a long time; it was a process...

 I arrived at the filming location slowly, and I already felt worn-out. Despite that, the day went by smoothly. Indeed, the designated Friday was the last day of shooting. They planned a gala for us, and the wealthy individuals involved or were just influential enough to be invited. I didn't promise to attend, but I had to come. How much would I have to spend on that one evening: dress, makeup, hair? I should also mention the Farm. And I can't show up in some cheap dress. It's crucial what I wear. I haven't become famous enough for V.W. to call me and ask me to wear her dress. Well, I'll look around and see where I can sell it afterward. Before going to the studio on Friday, where I was called for the commercial video, I prepared thoroughly. I brought Kyra's video and asked Linda for pictures of the progress on the new farm, the new animals, the apple trees, the poultry, the new enclosures, and the area. They were very pleased with how organised I was.

All I had to do was recite a script written by someone else, wearing equestrian attire, with my hair tied back, a hat on, but they left the makeup on me for the shoot to make the Farm "even more attractive." I didn't mind if it really worked. We watched it. They edited it together and said they were delighted that I'm an actress and the camera love me, so they were glad we didn't have to reshoot, and indeed, it turned out well and promised to send the final version on Monday for my approval. I had to pay after each submission. We agreed on one month, with the video playing ten times a day, and then we'll see. I didn't have any plans for Saturday and Sunday, so I asked Richard if they wanted to go for a romantic dinner on Saturday since I would be in town. He was thrilled and answered with a resounding yes. I got a book for Saturday night in case the little one allows me to read. In the morning, I slept for a long time to endure the fuss.

I had to be there by four. Holly wrote everything and explained it all. I told her we would manage. And off they went. They looked like they were going on their first date in high school. Both were all dressed up and smelled of cologne. Although I didn't think I would get bored as I looked around the apartment. I don't think there was a single cup, glass, or clean plate left in the cupboard. The baby quietly snored after the parents left. It had been so quiet that sometimes I had to go check if it was even breathing. It was such a cute, chubby baby, could barely close its chubby cheeks, so drool poured out of its mouth. Sometimes it made those cute smacking sounds as it searched for the pacifier. But that's it. It must be exhausting to entertain parents all the time. I'm sure she is tired of it.

She didn't wake up for anything. I washed the dishes and tidied up, put the newspapers and books back in their place. I collected the trash, and the apartment immediately felt more human. Holly only messaged me twice in an hour, but I reassured her that everything was fine. Then, about two hours later, when I was done with what I could do, the baby started crying, but I fed her, and went back to sleep. Although the last time was the first occasion, it really felt as if it came instinctively. It was as if it was encoded in me what to do and how. I didn't believe in this instinct that everyone talked about before, but now it occurred to me that there might be something to it. I still haven't been caught up in the urge that I need one quickly too, but if it were to happen, I wouldn't be terrified after this experience.

Of course, I knew that being a mother is not just a two-hour Saturday afternoon thing but observing my feelings and how I reacted to the crying, feeding, and everything else, I thought I could do it with love and dedication if it came to that. The cot-bed was in the middle of the living room, next to the sofa. When I finished with everything I intended to do, I settled down next to it and watched the baby sleep. It was cute. The entire house was comfortable, though it might be because of the new resident. There were baby toys and seating arrangements everywhere in the living room with soft pillows. Across from the sofa, there was a window and a glass door facing the garden. On the other wall, there were pictures and a fireplace. The kitchen was connected to the living room, and they mostly heated food and only brewed coffee there. I assumed this because the stove seemed almost untouched, and the trash was filled with takeaway boxes. Upstairs, I thought, there must be the bedrooms. I didn't go up there, and I don't think they did either.

It seemed like their whole life revolved around the living room, the downstairs bathroom, the kitchen, and the garden. I didn't see any evidence of them going outside in the garden, either. So that's out of the question as well. But I've heard a lot. This is how it goes when you have a child. The child will grow up on a lying/sitting contraption, and you will become a parent in the best-case scenario. In their case, it was the living room. I fed the baby once more, and she continued sleeping. I kept sending messages to Holly, letting her know everything was fine. Then, around eleven, both came into the house with grins on their faces. It was a joy to see them. Like two teenagers who had just been caught by their parents, who knew what had happened. They were grinning like Cheshire cats. And I wished them good night. They stood by the cot-bed like two crazy people, grinning at each other and the baby. With that very loving look. I don't think they even noticed that I had left.

I reached the hotel quickly. I parked and as I approached the entrance; I was pleased to realise that there wasn't a single paparazzo at midnight. Maybe I should always come home by this time. I ordered food from the hotel kitchen; they were probably happy about that. But at least I didn't order shark fin soup or mushrooms that are found only in a very rare corner of the world. I ordered a burger and fries. I received it and then retreated to bed. Sunday passed by slowly and quietly. I couldn't wait for Friday, of course. I was also very anxious about it. But it wasn't the paralysing kind of anxiety. It was more of a feeling of "let's just get it over with and be done." Neither Steve nor Brandon bothered me anymore, which didn't mean I forgave what had happened. I went over it a thousand times sober, angry, and in every way, and I came to the same conclusion. I knew I shouldn't have sleepless nights, but they were there precisely because I was who I was. And then Monday finally arrived.

Tom often wrote, and I happily replied to him. I watched myself: I wrote to him as if he were a good friend, which he was. We talked about everything. We laughed a lot together. There was no forced politeness or lying that characterises a relationship where you try to sell yourself to your partner. Nothing like that. We spoke honestly about everything. I liked his mindset, his sense of humour, and his childlike openness. I knew almost everything about his family, ex-girlfriends, schools, goals. No pretence. Brian was a different story. He didn't resemble his father, the judge. The judge was a simple man, a child of the old era, who didn't complicate things. But his son, Brian, was a bit too much, with his fashion sense, trendy hairstyle, and snobbish style. Brian seemed like a decent person, but it felt like he always spoke down to people. Tom mentioned he had big plans, possibly even in the political area, which might explain his flashy style. His appearance was annoying, but still within bearable limits. Sometimes he made remarks that made him seem completely human and kind-hearted. So, he was still in the likable category, at least in the short term.

I never thought I would go on a camping trip with him, for example. Brian only wrote about the case. His involvement ended there. For now. He sent over the document that I needed to sign. The days passed quickly. We bonded well with the team by the end. Everyone exchanged phone numbers, and we talked a lot during breaks with everyone, regardless of their role, whether they were a janitor or a costume designer. Everyone was very nervous about the premiere. The tickets were sold out, but what mattered was how the film would perform afterwards. Richard was already an established actor, so he had already achieved partial success. I was the odd one out, but I hoped they were satisfied with me and the current progress of my life. There had been no scandals recently. And from the paparazzi and flowers, I figured I couldn't be that bad. Of course, the gossip magazines had been focusing on the life of the cast, but I simply didn't read them. If there was something significant in there, someone would have brought it up. Everyone already knows about Brandon. That was old news. Everyone knows about the Farm and Steve, I think. Tom gave me a scare with the photo he showed me of Steve and me last time, but it was necessary for our Monday prison visit. But things will calm down, eventually.

They sent the commercial. I approved it because I thought it was good. It conveyed the essence, and for those who were looking for what we offered, it was enticing. The equestrian school was also a significant move. But of course, time will tell. Currently, I was very satisfied with how things were progressing. In return, although not V.W., a fashion designer of similar calibre reached out to me to wear their dress. I glanced at the dress and said yes. I would have said not only if it was extremely obscene, in no other case. It was a truly unique dress. They believed that because of my personality and the Farm, I would support the idea. They showed me the proposed hairstyle and makeup, and I agreed with them.

The dress expressed the importance of recycling, and they believed it would have a greater impact if an actor wore it at a gala where a million plus two pictures would be taken of me. I said to them I will wear if the producer and Richard were okay with it because it was important to me. I didn't want to get into a conflict with anyone, but I strongly supported the cause itself. The entire outfit was made of crushed aluminium cans, held together with wire. They were threaded onto a flesh-coloured fabric to prevent them from falling apart. Well, I wouldn't be able to sit, but it wasn't such a big problem. The shoes were a strange-shaped high heel, mostly made of cardboard. My makeup was also made of fantastic metal pieces, and my hair would be a huge bun, almost alien-like, adorned with pierced glass. It was a bit "Gaga style," but I really liked it, and I also strongly supported recycling. This concern also fell off my shoulders, which made me thrilled.

They came for the shooting to copy the shade of my skin if I agreed, so I was only wearing the aluminium cans. I was already prepared in advance that the evening wouldn't be about having fun for me, but focusing on not screaming because of the uncomfortable outfit, makeup, hair, and shoes. After they left, I also asked the producer and Richard, and they both said that I was born for this, to be a provocateur, so they didn't mind it for the sake of the good cause. I was glad to hear that. Although I didn't know how they came to this conclusion... Anyway, I was happy. There was a little fear inside me that something bad had to come after all the good things.

True, I was still very nervous about Friday, but I tried to dismiss it. I tried and rehearsed. I even knew the order of things when I woke up from my dream. On Friday, I had to leave here at two o'clock, which bothered me a little because the last day would have differed from the previous ones, but there must be a reason for it.

Linda wrote a day before, the paparazzi also found the Farm, but she didn't let them in until I'm back home. She said everything was fine and that my house would be ready soon. When I looked back, the fire seemed so far away already! Brandon, and soon Steve, too. Everything had changed so much since the day Brandon threw me out of his apartment. I had changed a lot too, at least in my own eyes. I think it's for the better, and the rest didn't matter.

It was Thursday evening. The shooting was done. The next day, we watched the film, which was a kind of last check because we can still make corrections at that point, but I didn't think we would find anything. It had been watched a thousand times, if not ten thousand. On Thursday, I packed my stuff, filled up the car. Nowadays, I couldn't go anywhere without a bodyguard and a baseball cap. I would really miss having someone follow me around on the Farm. Somewhere deep down, I felt that although and was fed up with everything now, I would also miss the shooting. The whole charade. The acting. Now I was much more anxious about tomorrow, but I tried not to show it. I could hardly sleep, exchanged text messages with Tom for about two hours and invited him on Saturday. A sudden idea came to me, and he gladly accepted. I told him to ask his friend for a fancy outfit. He asked what I would wear, but I didn't want to reveal it to him.

On Friday, I packed everything into the car in the morning. I thanked the hotel staff nicely for being so kind to me. I gave them flowers and gave away all the chocolates. They mentioned that it's very rare to find such a kind actor; they were thrilled with me and hoped I would come back. I said nothing. I just smiled. Then, upon arriving at the shooting location, the producer called for me. I was surprised to see him already there; he usually belonged to the chronically late group. Maybe this time he didn't even go home. I entered one booth he designated as his office. It looked like any of our dressing rooms, except there were no mirrors or hanging clothes, only a desk and a hundred monitors. He was sitting at the desk and didn't even look up when I entered. I sat down in the chair next to his desk, waiting for him to glance at me; he was reviewing a scene.

"Well, the last day has come, "he said, raising his bespectacled gaze to me.

"Yes. What should I say?! I will miss it."

"Me or the shooting? "He asked, not seriously meaning it.

"That's what I wanted to talk to you about. "He always tried to use the formal "you" with everyone, if possible. "It was a positive experience working with you. I must admit, everyone was scared and worried... but you gave a brilliant performance. I wish my daughters were half as talented as you. "By his daughters, he meant his students.

"Sorry to interrupt, but you're a producer, so could you tell me what you see in me? How do you perceive talent?"

"Could bring up many things because your performance is excellent. You play everything with such immersion, even I believe it. But it's not just that. The many scenes, the many rehearsals, the many costume changes, the makeup, and Brandon. You behaved admirably. Never a complaint, never a bad word, even when Brandon fell apart, you carried on as if nothing had happened. I don't know what led you to all those foolishness back then, but the way you behaved during the shooting, you are the real woman." Upon hearing that, tears welled up in my eyes. I let a few tears fall, worked hard for these words. Only I truly knew how much, but now it was all worth it.

"Thank you."

"I haven't finished yet, "he raised his finger and gaze. "A studio approached me for a film... and they want you. No matter the cost. "He looked at me, and I was speechless.

"But they haven't even seen the film yet!"

"But they saw the trailer."

"I've finished."

"If that's what you want, Jade, I'll tell them. But since they said, 'at any cost,' you can set whatever conditions you want. "If you want to shoot from Monday to Friday, then do it, and you can go home to the Farm on the weekend. This is double your payment," he brought up my payment.

"This is more than we agreed upon."

"Yes, because the success exceeded our expectations. If you don't need it, distribute it among the poor."

"Thank you, Nick."

"Tomorrow, you'll have to decide at the gala."

"Tomorrow, huh... I'll bring a guest."

"I don't mind. It's your premiere, not mine. You're one host. Invite whoever you want."

"Goodbye for now, Nick!" But he didn't say another word. He was back to watching the cameras. Despite his initial annoyance and constant jumping around, I eventually recognised his unmatched expertise, even if it occasionally bothered us. Sometimes he spoke harshly, but he did everything for the sake of bringing out the best in us and achieving even more. Slowly, I understood that my initial aversion prevented me from noticing that everything he did was for the success of the movie and indirectly for us. Then I started looking at him differently, and he no longer annoyed me; instead, I respected him.

As for the rest of us, we went to the cinema and watched our own film. With popcorn, of course. It was microwaved, but it felt just as good as homemade. I found some flaws in my performance, but if it was satisfactory to them, I wouldn't complain. At the end of the film, everyone sighed, saying it turned out well, and we could leave. We didn't indulge in long goodbyes, because we would see everyone at the gala. However, Richard followed me to the car.

"Jade! "He smiled at me. "Did you want to run off without saying goodbye?"

"We'll see each other tomorrow, anyway."

"True, but tomorrow will be chaotic. I wanted to take this opportunity to thank you for the playing. It was a tremendous experience."

"Don't joke, it's an honour for me, Richard! "If I hadn't been so nervous about what was yet to come, I would have burst into tears. I was grateful to have met him. I learned a lot from him, and as much as he could have made the shooting difficult, he made it easier with his fantastic nature. "Of course. Anyway, thank you for taking care of Maya. And for cleaning the house."

"You're welcome, Richard."

"Jade, if you need anything or want to talk, call me. And I'm not just saying that, Chica."

"Ok."

"I'll come after you if I don't hear from you."

"Understood. "It's like he could see into my soul. "Goodbye for now!"

"Bye, babe."

    I quickly rushed home. Tom asked if he should come over and if I needed a place to stay. I signalled that theoretically I could already sleep in my house. Just that there's nothing in it, I added to myself. I wrote I would handle it. He didn't need to come over. I stopped by the bank as well because I didn't want to run around with the check. I could fully repay the loan now, and there was still plenty left. I deposited it all into my account. Somehow, I felt like I couldn't trust anyone. I dressed elegantly for this occasion. It was almost three o'clock when I got home. Brian messaged at two o'clock that they were leaving the station. I went home. My heart was pounding in my throat, but I tried to hide my emotions well. After all, that's what was expected, even from me.

Everything was as usual. Workers were working on the house, and the guys were with the animals. I quickly entered the house; they were doing the final touches. In theory, the electricity, gas, and water were already connected. The new layout and tiling looked stunning. The main entrance was moved to the side facing the road, with a small front garden. When entering the house, the guest would find themselves in the living room. There were no visible wires, only spotlights everywhere. Everything that could be hidden was hidden. The boiler, wires, thermostat, alarm system, cameras. I won't make the same mistake again; I needed security. Air conditioning provided both heating and cooling, but the air only flowed through grilles. There wasn't a massive unit in every room. In the living room, one wall was covered with a graffiti painting, and I planned to hang photographs on the other side. The dominant colours in the living room were grey and black. Except for the graffiti, the entire wall was black, with silver borders, and according to my plans, silver modern furniture, a sofa, and a large sunken grey carpet. After the living room, the space split in two. One side was the kitchen-dining area, and the other side led to my room and the bathroom accessible from both directions. The bathroom was planned to have silver walls with black borders, and the furnishings would also be in those colours. My room was gorgeous, pink and white. While I used to paint everything black in my younger years, now I wanted the opposite: to feel feminine. I had to share the house with myself, and I liked it that way. The kitchen, like everywhere else, was the heart of the house. So, I planned it to be cosy. All the furniture would be carved wood, with traditional white paint and light brown cabinets. But that could wait a bit. A small guest room was separated from the kitchen, which was relatively simple. However, it wasn't furnished yet, but I could worry about that later. I thanked them for their work and had to leave.

Linda was busy with the horses, as always. I greeted everyone and then pulled her aside.

"How are things? "I asked. "Thank you for the pictures you sent."

"You're welcome. Everything is fine."

"Could you give me the bookkeeping and the letters? Do you have them?"

"Of course. "She went into the building reserved for the workers and returned with her bag, which surprised me a little."

"Do you carry it with you? "I asked.

"If I can't finish it here, then I'll do it at home. "She shrugged.

"Is everything in there? The past three weeks?"

"Yes. "She didn't understand why I was asking. I could see the doubt in her eyes.

"Okay. Thank you. Now I want to ask you for something. Go to Steve, we have a big announcement. I know you're not on good terms, but please, just do it."

"I'm happy to go home. "She said it with such a strange tone, as if it were her home and not mine. Or like I was intruding, but I didn't attach any significance to it. I had more important issues.

"Thank you. You can go now; I'll go over in a moment. "Meanwhile, I looked at my phone: the distinguished company would surely arrive soon. Linda left. I gathered some courage, along with the documents, and headed over. The gate was still open when I arrived. I didn't hesitate and drove through. Just as a black limousine arrived, as well. And who stepped out of it was the judge himself and Tom, which felt really comforting in that moment. It reassured me. I don't even know why I wanted to face them alone. They nodded, showing their support. Steve, his father, Linda, and Ben, his brother, were still standing in the yard, engaged in a heated

conversation, but it didn't seem too friendly. When Steve saw the cars, especially mine, he almost fainted. I quickly parked and got out with my enormous bag.
"I told you not to come here anymore."
"I'm glad too, Steve. "The others just stood there, and Linda's jaw dropped when she realised that there wouldn't be any good news.
"Son! "His father scolded him, which surprised him. "Jade, come in. Everyone, come in, "he corrected himself.
"Let's all go in. Is that okay? "I said. Ben didn't know whether he was coming or going. Rehab isn't much better than the addiction itself. At least I don't have to acknowledge him. We went inside. Steve and Linda seemed quite angry. Their father, Frank, looked exactly like his children, just older. Ben also resembled his siblings, but he was bone thin. The drug was more important than eating. In fact, it was more important than anything else. We gathered in the living room of the house, and everyone took their seats, except for me. Linda and Ben were on the couch. Across from them were the father and the other son. I positioned myself by the window like a teacher. The judge and Tom stood behind me, but words were few, they didn't say a thing. Everyone stared at me, waiting to hear what I had to say.
"Well, I don't want to drag this out any longer. I hope everyone is thrilled that their beloved family members have been bypassed. I'll ask for the flowers to be sent to my dressing room. The only price for this is to transfer the area at the end of the farm to me today."
"Don't make a fool of yourself, you stupid whore! "Steve said. He laughed. Tom stepped closer threateningly. He looked at his father, who wasn't laughing. Disbelief crossed his face.
"Why the hell would we do that?
"First, they released Frank, thanks to the judge, although I requested it. Of course, this could be reversed, but I don't want to tear apart loving family members. I haven't finished yet. "I waved off Steve when he tried to interrupt. "Let's

continue, okay? The fire on the Farm wasn't a coincidence, and it wasn't committed by who I thought. They found the homemade ignition device. But they could only determine that it was someone from this family. They didn't know exactly who. Well, what good would it do if I slept with one of them? With the samples taken, it turned out that the other one set the fire. So, I would like to present you with your resignation letter, Linda. Thank you for your help. I won't report you because the property means more to me. "I still wasn't done. "I'll continue, Steve. So, you were an accessory to the fact that you knew Samantha beat Kyra, vandalised and everything else. "I looked at him now. "But you bribed and kept the money for yourself, which is quite a few charges, and if it's true, Samantha will testify against you. "Of course, this was a bluff, but I was an actor, or so I thought. "This little video you made with me the other day. "I placed the phone between them and started playing the video. "It was already with the judge when I left this house. Frank, you shouldn't be left out either. "I turned to him now. "As you know, my father used to enjoy birdwatching, and he often set up bird hides, which meant he would leave the house very early and return very late to observe rare birds. And what do you need for birdwatching? A telescope and a camera. I think you've figured out what I'm getting at. He knew all along that it was you cutting through our fence, but he said nothing. Perhaps because he was a very kind-hearted person, or perhaps so that I would have something to use against you today. The fire helped in finding you. My father knew that if there was a fire, that damn brick pile wouldn't become a victim of the flames, and that's exactly what happened. The bricks were neatly lined up, and during the construction, we found a box full of photographs. I even attached a one-to-one document. "Everyone looked at me in shock. Perhaps only Ben didn't grasp any of it because he was absent-minded. "Before anyone ponders any foolishness, this material is with the judge, as well as with this detective here, "I pointed to either

side of me, "the latter being an investigator, and of course, my lawyer has it too. If a hair on my head bends or if anyone looks at me the wrong way on the street, I'll make a case out of it. If I get what I want, it can all go down the drain. Deal?
"None of them said a word. They just looked at me in dismay.
"Well done, Jade. Your father would be proud. Unlike me with my own children. Of course, I choose the deal. "I didn't need to be told twice. I already pulled out the contract. Steve signed it immediately, as he was the current owner.
"I hope you have a good time together. Don't forget to redo the fence today. Also, I hope it won't bother you if there's a car exhibition in that area. I'll repurchase my father's race cars, and they'll be displayed there because there's no room anywhere else. Thank you. Goodbye!"

## Chapter twenty

Outside, the judge silently got back into the limousine and drove away, only squeezing my arm as encouragement as we exited. Tom stayed behind and got into my car. I was happy about that at that moment. As I got into my car and drove out of the gate, I took a deep breath and exhaled slowly. All the stress suddenly left me. My hands were trembling, and I quickly took in the air. I did it; it was over. Never again.

They really came through and redesigned the area. Nobody said anything, they just worked in silence. I only knew because I rode out and saw it. I sent everyone home. Tom went to get some food. I ordered most of the furniture. I didn't mind that the house was empty. I wanted to enjoy my freedom; I didn't need any constraints. Then Tom returned. He brought some wine to celebrate. And a sleeping bag and food. I was grateful for it. And for his company. Only his...

## Epilogue

I stand by the side of the road, shivering in the cold. Winter is slowly but surely approaching. The driver is running late. Why didn't I dress warmer? I scold myself. And why isn't he here yet? Everyone has already left, and I'm the only one standing here in the cold. The wind blows snow in my face, but only in small flakes. It would be more enjoyable if I had a coat that provided more warmth. I glimpse car headlights in the distance. I'll give him a piece of my mind when he arrives, that's for sure. But the car speeds past me. I wait for another five minutes and call a taxi. True, I'm at the end of the world, but a taxi will come. The snowfall wasn't so heavy that they wouldn't dare to come. At least, that's what I hoped. This can't be true. Where is he? I'm freezing.

Life has become rather boring lately, or maybe just routine. Drama-free, I pondered. I took on the film Nick talked about on the last day of shooting. The party afterward was a great success. I went with Tom, and he enjoyed being surrounded by so many famous people. I enjoyed more being able to wear that dress, although towards the end, I really wanted to take it off. It turned out well. We were still shooting that film, and they were paying a lot. I would have enjoyed it even without the money because the team was great again, and I'm slowly entering the professional league. I really liked the story too. Finally, a crime film and not a romantic one. I would have been foolish to say no.

Since the commercial, the equestrian school, and the car exhibition took off, the farm has been doing well. More than that, fantastically well. If it weren't for me, it would have been an excellent source of income, but I would have got bored quickly. Of course, I enjoy acting, and the money is good too. I'm toying with opening an acting school. A completely different perspective. A new concept. Right next to the Farm. Directly next to it. Hard work and intense learning, just like in the old days. Without casting couches. Searching for talent and nurturing knowledge. But, of course, it requires a lot of capital. I'm just playing with the idea for now. Since then, I haven't met Steve or anyone else from his family. They say they've moved away for good, each going in a different direction. I didn't feel the slightest bit guilty about them. I could realise the car exhibition on the land they gave me, using the cars I took back from the judge. Many people came. It was only open on weekends, just like the equestrian school. During the weekdays, I was always busy with filming. I developed a great relationship with Tom. It's been several months now. I could even say we're best friends.

Today's plan is the same as always. "He'll pick me up, we'll go to the cinema, grab a bite somewhere, and then either he'll stay at my place, or I'll stay at his. Of course, in separate beds and rooms. Neither of us thought about love. He had his promotion, finally achieving what he wanted. He became the head of the investigators, but he didn't plan to stop there. We were both too busy to start any romantic drama, and it worked out well that way. Richard and Holly occasionally invite me to get together or ask me to take care of Maya while they go out for a bit. Richard is currently filming somewhere abroad, so on weekdays, I sometimes go chatting to Holly's. I haven't talked to Jess since then, and I haven't been near the castle either. I hope everything is fine with Brandon.

The number of employees on the Farm has increased significantly. During the weekends, there was one person at the car exhibition who knew about cars. He guided the visitors and answered all their questions willingly. Of course, it was Tony. He was crazy about cars. And on weekdays, he helped on the farm as he did before. He enjoyed it. And I was glad I didn't have to deal with a stranger. After the incident, they admitted Linda was odd to them and never really became a team member. I hired another girl named Karen to take her place. She was fantastic. She excelled in agriculture and had a wonderful personality. Everyone grew fond of her quickly. Suzy came back as soon as the house was ready. She had enough work to do. She cooked for the entire staff every single day. And when she had time, she took care of the flower garden in front of the entrance, for which I was very grateful. There was a gardener who mowed the lawn and tended to the apple orchard. Even in winter, I could give him work because there was plenty to do. Thomas went to university, but he often came to visit us, especially because of Katie, with whom he has been living since the fire on the farm. There were more new members, but it became a fantastic team. They stuck together and liked each other. We had to expand the dining area.

The current staff, if I counted everyone, were twenty people. The place underwent a complete transformation. I was selfish and completely separated the house from the backyard. There was a gate that separated the front courtyard from the Farm. I couldn't see behind, and they couldn't see ahead. Not because I was hiding something or didn't want to take part in the work, but I needed privacy sometimes. But they knew they could call or come to me anytime with any problem. They knew me, and I knew them. Our relationship was good. I didn't have to act like a boss, and I was grateful for that. Since someone was there at night as well, it was better for me to occasionally detach myself. They had a separate entrance. Their dining area also had accommodations if someone didn't want or couldn't go home. It had a recreational room with a TV, game console, internet, and musical instruments. Suzy cooked there too because my kitchen wouldn't be enough to cook for twenty people. When I was home, I was usually out on the Farm since I taught horseback riding, but in the evenings, I enjoyed being able to lock the door behind me. I think slowly the town accepted me as a full-fledged member, and no one scowled at me anymore.

The mayor himself asked if I would like to have a store near the Farm because if many people come on weekends for the exhibition or horse riding, it might be practical. Since Steve's plot was for sale, I seized the opportunity and bought it as well. In cooperation with the town, we had a small shopping centre there. It would provide jobs for many people, and it would also create good traffic. When I went into town, many people even smiled at me. Of course, there were those who constantly hated the changes, but it didn't bother me anymore. Where was the day when Brandon sent me away? So much has changed. But I liked this new routine. Filming on weekdays, the Farm on weekends. I felt a balance in my life. No drama. And I had fun with Tom.

I noticed a speeding car, and as it approached, I recognised Tom's car. It was too foggy to see inside, and it had tinted windows, anyway. It was his official vehicle. He doesn't spend money on his own car. He uses this one everywhere. True, it was so beat-up that I was surprised it started, but he said if it gets him from point A to point B, he's not willing to spend on a car, and the police department maintains it, anyway. It was convenient and cheap for him. With screeching brakes, he stopped next to me. The door swung open, and before I could even come up with a sarcastic comment about his lateness, the word got stuck in my throat. Steve stepped out of the car, holding a gun in his hand. Thanks to my current filming project, I immediately recognised it as a Glock 17, with 9mm Parabellum bullets not the best, but not the worst either, or at this distance, it could be deadly.

"Hi, Jade! Did you miss me? "A crazed grin spread across his face. He circled around the car and opened the back door, where Tom lay tied up, bleeding from his head, unconscious. I was horrified. He approached me, and I completely froze. No scream or any other sound came out of my throat. But he silenced me and tied my hands together. I couldn't resist. I was so shocked. "Get in, Jade! Or I'll shoot your friend in the head..."

To be continued...

## Introduction

I first saw the world on October 18, 1985—or so they say. I strongly doubt it, considering it was a harsh winter, and besides, a newborn can't see a thing. By then, I already had a sister, and my younger sister came along to bring even more joy later.

Since my early childhood, I've been wearing out paper, though these days it's more likely a keyboard. Whether it's fortunate or not, I can't seem to stop. Writing wasn't a choice for me; it chose me. Ever since I learned to write, I've been entertaining myself and now the dear audience with various stories.

In my tender green pea age, I edited different school and dormitory magazines. There were times when I even took part in recitations. In any life situation, I can recite Zoltán Zelk's poem "Ez aztán a vásárfia" (This is the Market Boy) with ease.

"If I were to record every thought of mine, I would be writing this from a prison cell," (author).

"I took one of my dreams off a shelf, dusted it off, and now I'm starting anew," (author).

"I read to broaden my horizons, and I write because the voices say so" (author).

@tinacoltauthor
tinacolt.wordpress.com

## Acknowledgement

If I want to be honest, I never read them in books. In this section, they thank the agents and family members who supported the writer or something like that.

Well, thank you for the hard work for myself, for believing in me and for not giving up on my books, without a day off, tiredly, every night. Thanks.

And now I thank you, dear reader, for getting here. Thank you too. Jade's story was the first to publish in Hungary in 2020; what I shared with the public, so it will always be in a special place in my heart. And it is not over yet...

# Contents

Prologue .................................................................. 1
Chapter one ............................................................. 4
Chapter two ............................................................. 7
Chapter three ......................................................... 11
Chapter four .......................................................... 22
Chapter five ........................................................... 30
Chapter six ............................................................. 46
Chapter seven ........................................................ 50
Chapter eight ......................................................... 73
Chapter nine .......................................................... 82
In a city a few miles away ..................................... 89
Chapter ten ............................................................ 92
Chapter eleven ..................................................... 101
Chapter twelve ..................................................... 122
Chapter thirteen ................................................... 139
Chapter fourteen .................................................. 140
Chapter fifteen ..................................................... 159
Chapter sixteen .................................................... 168
Chapter seventeen ............................................... 182
Chapter eighteen .................................................. 216
Chapter nineteen .................................................. 228
Chapter twenty .................................................... 245
Epilogue ............................................................... 246
To be continued… ................................................ 249
Introduction ......................................................... 250
Acknowledgement ................................................ 251

Printed in Great Britain
by Amazon